SANJIDA O'CONNELL

Theory of Mind

A thriller, a love story, an exploration of the human heart

SANJIDA O'CONNELL

Theory of Mind

A thriller, a love story, an exploration of the human heart

ROMAUNCE

Cirencester

Sanjida O'Connell was born in 1970 of Bangladeshi/Irish parents. She has lived in Pakistan, Nigeria, Northern Ireland, Wales and various parts of Britain and has attended ten schools. She studied zoology at Bristol University before becoming an Assistant Producer on Tomorrow's World. Now a TV Producer and science writer, she also contributes to the Guardian, the Independent and the Observer.

Theory of Mind is her first novel. She lives in London.

Romaunce Books

1A The Wool Market Dyer Street Cirencester Gloucestershire GL7 2PR
An imprint of Memoirs Publishing www.mereobooks.com

Theory of Mind: 978-1-86151-548-3

Published in Great Britain by Romaunce Books,
an imprint of Memoirs Publishing Ltd.

First published in Great Britain by Black Swan, an imprint of
Transworld Publishers Ltd in 1996

Copyright © Sanjida O'Connell 1996

The moral of the author is asserted in accordance with the Copyright,
Designs and Patents Act 1988

This book is a work of fiction and except in the case of historical fact any
resemblance to actual persons living or dead is purely coincidental.

A CIP catalogue record for this book is available from the British Library.

This book is sold subject to the condition that it shall not by way of trade or
otherwise be lent, resold, hired out or otherwise circulated without the publisher's
prior consent in any form of binding or cover, other than that in which it is
published and without a similar condition, including this condition being imposed
on the subsequent purchaser.

The address for Memoirs Publishing Group Limited can be found at
www.memoirspublishing.com

The Memoirs Publishing Group Ltd Reg. No. 7834348

The Memoirs Publishing Group supports both The Forest Stewardship Council®
(FSC®) and the PEFC® leading international forest-certification organisations. Our
books carrying both the FSC label and the PEFC® and are printed on FSC®-certified
paper. FSC® is the only forest-certification scheme supported by the leading
environmental organisations including Greenpeace. Our paper procurement policy
can be found at www.memoirspublishing.com/environment

Typeset in 11/15pt Plantin
by Wiltshire Associates Publisher Services Ltd. Printed and bound in Great Britain
by Printondemand-Worldwide, Peterborough PE2 6XD

To my family

With thanks to Richard Dale, Joanna Goldsworthy
and Patrick Walsh

Chapter One

She felt like Jesus. All around her the field of flowers shimmered, slick with dew, the hallucinatory blue of an ethereal lake. She felt that if she trusted in faith the path would appear, summoned by her feet. As she walked, the linseed petals tipped their tiny offerings onto her legs; her trousers were heavy and black with water by the time she reached the zoo.

She shivered slightly. It was early and a heavy mist hung thickly around her, obliterating the sun. But already the gibbons were singing; the humid air reminded them of the rainforest, and as they sang she thought of their calls echoing over mountains, of huge leaves angled to catch what little sun there was, dripping water softly from veins like creases in palms down to the dark and silent cathedral beneath where nothing grew. The gibbons were duetting now. First the female would start singing to the male, then the male would respond, the two songs gradually interleaving until it was difficult to say where one began and the other ended.

It was beautiful, but so loud that it was impossible to hold a normal conversation. Later they would quieten and sit dully in their cages, staring mournfully at the visitors and hanging from the chains of their long arms, their bodies the seats of swings.

At this time there was no-one about. The keepers were inside the animal houses and it was too early for the maintenance men to start work. There was the sound of banging, a tribal drum that added a beat to the gibbon song. Ferguson had seen her coming and was pounding on a barrel. As she approached he rushed towards her, pushing the barrel in front of him until it crashed into the end of the cage. Then he turned and ran back the other way, this time lifting the barrel and smashing it against the wall of his indoor house. His flesh puckered as if someone had pulled a drawstring too tight, and every hair on his body stood bolt upright.

She was almost level with him now. He pursed his long black lips and regarded her with a malevolent expression, then hurtled towards her, his arms trailing on the ground. A metre away from the wire his fists closed and he leapt onto the mesh, flinging a double handful of wood chips at her in a surly imitation of confetti. She continued walking and out of the corner of her eye she could see him still clinging to the wire, his biceps, larger than those of any men she knew, resolutely clenched. Slowly his hair wilted and became flat and smooth and he ambled back inside as if nothing had happened.

She was never quite sure how to take this performance of his. Ferguson was merely asserting his dominance over a female. But the compliment, if it could be called one, she thought wryly, brushing some of the wood chips off, was that he only did this to people he liked or was, at least, familiar with. She wasn't sure whether she had the dubious honour of being classed as a friend of Ferguson's yet.

Today, anyway, she wouldn't be watching him. She pushed open the door of the chimp house and sat down in front of the glass window that looked into their indoor cage. Immediately Ted, the most dominant male, came over to her. He touched the glass with his lips in a delicate kiss and tapped the window gently with one thick, black fingernail. She tapped back and then took out her notebook, pen and stopwatch. Fascinated, he tapped at each one, glancing from the objects to her as if she might explain what they were. He watched her watching him as she wrote down every two minutes what the chimps were doing and where they were looking. Did he ever wonder what it was they were revealing about themselves?

Eventually he got bored and wandered over to the others. This was the largest chimp group in the zoo: two males, three females and an infant, although this was nothing compared to the size of a wild group. The door to the outside enclosure was still shut. The chimps used one finger from each hand - as if they were chopsticks - to pick up sunflower seeds scattered on the concrete floor. This was the time when it was easiest to record data since they were all inside and were being quiet. As soon as the door was opened some of them would rush out. Ted and Sally were easy because he spent most of his time inside, and as long as it was a fine day she normally stayed outside. The others were not so tractable. If they saw her watching them, they would often run out of the indoor cage, wait until she had gone right round the building to get to their outside enclosure, and dart back in again just as she got there. But even when they were being awkward, they weren't performing for the visitors, and watching them whilst they were behaving normally, might allow her to find a chink in their armour, to peer into their minds.

Before she started studying at the zoo, she'd imagined things would be completely different. People always asked whether she handled them. They were far too dangerous to be touched, although a few of the infants were being hand-reared. She'd never gone near them. But it didn't stop her dreaming. She imagined sitting on the floor of the long corridor in the chimp house, wearing a gentian-blue dress, holding a baby chimpanzee in her arms. It was small with black hair and pale pink skin and eyes like melted carob. It clung to her and kissed her face. There would be a slight noise and she would look up and Corin would be standing in the open doorway at the end of the corridor, haloed by light. He would walk towards her and as he walked she would see him emerge from a black silhouette, his features moulding themselves before her eyes until she could see he was smiling. He had driven all the way up from London to surprise her. He would bend down and kiss her, one hand cradling the fragile head of the baby chimp as if it were a human child.

She always associated Corin with light: he was a magnet for it. Light swirled round his head and flashed in his eyes; she imagined his heart pumping blood and light in equal measures. The first time she'd met him had been at a party in Bristol. She'd been visiting her sister Lisa who was a television producer there. Everyone she'd talked to had been stimulating and polite, but she felt as if she held only a momentary interest for them. As soon as they realized that she had nothing to do with television and that her work, then only beginning, held no glimmers of a future programme, their attention paled. She was wandering around, wine glass in hand, feeling left out and half-heartedly trying to find Lisa when she saw him.

He was surrounded by a semi-circle of people, talking animatedly. Suddenly it seemed to her that the rest of the room had grown dark and he was standing in a shaft of light. For a few seconds the room was completely silent and she was watching him speak as if she were in front of a cinema screen where everything was etched larger than life but the sound had been turned down. His hair was the colour of ginger brandy and nearly shoulder length; as he moved it fell in sheaves like wheat in the wind and when he turned towards her she saw he had eyes as green brown as avocado skin. And then the light and sound came rushing back and she was standing so close she was practically touching him. She blushed furiously.

But he simply said, 'I'm sorry, I don't think I know you.'

She shook her head and said she was Sandra, Lisa Roberts's sister. He nodded and made room for her in his circle of friends and carried on talking. She watched him and some of his words filtered through to her as if they were being poured into a fine sieve where the occasional drop of water remained trapped like a drowning fish. He was making the others laugh and waving his arms about madly. She had never seen anyone who was so alive. Here was a man, she thought, who had the essence of existence, a thousand times as strong as vodka, and had mainlined it then and there. What she didn't realize was that he had just been filming and this was the adrenalin talking: the sudden release of tension, the elation as life was seized on strips of celluloid, the faint, yet still powerful echo of the gift of God to create and control.

As they were about to go, she looked for him. He was on his own, helping himself to some leftover food. He was eating frantically, as if he hadn't eaten all evening and was trying to make up for it. She walked towards him. She wanted to say, I'd like to see you again. She'd never said anything like that to anyone before. He turned towards her, still eating. He chewed and swallowed, watching her. Now that she was close to him, she saw that his eyes didn't quite match. One of them was a darker blue green. It gave him a strangely unfocused look as if he were staring at something on the periphery of his vision. She didn't know which eye to look at. The silence between them stretched and grew.

'I just wanted to say . . .' She blushed. The words twisted in her throat like butterflies trying to break free but their wings were too large.

'. . . goodbye.'

He wiped his hands and held one out to her. 'It was a pleasure,' he said smoothly, and as she turned away she felt a terrible emptiness.

It was summer and the room she was working in at the university was hot and stuffy. It had been a chemistry lab and still had small, conical basins of white porcelain and black taps that no longer leaked gas: they looked like slender-snouted dragons; she kept expecting them to turn their heads, sniff the air blindly and belch thin streams of blue flame. There was an old creaky fan that merely swirled the dust around and the distant but constant rumble of traffic outside.

She was killing time. It was almost a year since she'd started studying for her Ph.D. and now she was waiting to go to the zoo and start collecting data. She felt smothered by the London dust and dirt, arid as desert air and laced with fumes. She picked at the charred scars on the table tops, carved by some acidic chemical and bandaged by layers of varnish thick as amber resin. Her mind was full of images of Corin: he was like a photograph that had gradually faded and become sepia tinted, the edges curling and cracking.

One afternoon there was a phone call.

'It's for you,' one of the other postgraduates said.

'Hello,' she said listlessly.

'Hello. It's Corin.' There was a long pause and then he said, 'We met at the party in Bristol.'

'Yes, yes, I remember,' she said, embarrassed because her silence had been for another reason and now he thought she didn't. She wondered vaguely how he had got her phone number. Perhaps Lisa had given it to him.

'I've got two tickets to a preview of a film. It's about, I don't know how the hell you pronounce them, bon, bon . . .'

'Bonobos?'

'Yes, exactly. You must be telepathic. I thought it might interest you.'

'Yes, I'd love to see it,' she said carefully because her voice had started to tremble.

He told her the date, time and place without a trace of nervousness, and then rang off. She sat quite still until her heart stopped racing and then drank a glass of water from one of the basins labelled 'Not Drinking Water'.

* * *

He smiled at her as if she were a long-lost friend and swept her hand to his mouth to kiss it. She burst out laughing in surprise. The seats were thick and soft, the colour of damson jam, with armrests for the free glasses of wine that were liberally poured. The film followed one group of bonobos in their native habitat in Zaïre. She explained to him that their other name was pygmy chimpanzee although they were no smaller than common chimps, just lighter with longer legs.

It was eerie watching them on the big screen. Most of the time they walked around upright. The mothers cradled their infants in one arm, balancing them on their hips, and they regarded each other with wise brown eyes. The commentary explained that although they didn't use tools like common chimps they were thought to be more intelligent. They passed their days feeding, resting and having sex. All of them had sex with everyone else in the group: males with males, females with females, males with females, adults with youngsters; sometimes even whole orgies occurred.

Like humans, the females were constantly on heat. But unlike humans - fortunately - they advertised their receptivity with pink, swollen backsides. When they had lesbian sex, they pressed their pink parts together. It was called G-G rubbing, the narrator informed the audience in his heavy American accent that would, Corin said, definitely have to be changed. Most of the time males and females had sex in the missionary position, the two animals staring into each other's eyes and kissing from time to time; the narrator reminded everyone that humans were the only other animals to 'make love face to face with such deep intimacy'. Once the camera captured a male mating with a female from behind. Her two-year-old daughter caught them in the act and rushed over to insert herself between them. She lay on her back on her mother's back and made faces at her father.

Sandra expected Corin to be embarrassed, but when they went for a drink afterwards he said seriously, 'So why do they have sex so often?'

'They trade food for sex. If a male has found something nice to eat, a female or a youngster will come and have sex with him and then take the food.'

'Takes their mind off it, does it?' he grinned.

'They look really agile, don't they? Chimps are so clumsy in comparison.'

'You bet. You remember that position where there was a female hanging from the tree, and a female sitting behind her and the guy on the branch above? Beats the *Kama Sutra* any day.' He took a drink and said, 'We're closely related to them, right?'

'Yes, we share about ninety-eight per cent of the same

genes with chimps, and probably slightly more with bonobos.'

'So what happened? Looks like they're in a free love commune and we're the ones that've regressed.'

She drank far more than she intended. It had been a hot day and she had eaten almost nothing but it wasn't until she had to try to walk to the tube that she realized how bad it was. She clutched her ticket, waiting to feed it into the barrier and started to panic. She felt so bad, she wasn't sure she would be able to get off at the right stop, never mind negotiate the walk back to her flat. The machine had just swallowed her ticket when she felt a tug on her arm.

'Look, I don't think you're in a fit state to go home on your own,' said Corin, pulling her back. 'I'm sorry, I didn't realize I was letting you drink so much. Come on, let's get a cab back to my place.' He was already turning away, still holding her arm.

She resisted and he looked back and smiled. 'It's OK,' he said softly, 'I've got a spare bed. I'm not going to tamper with you. Much as I might like to,' he added, taking her hand.

She woke in a room full of filtered sun between crisp sheets that smelt of washing powder. She was still wearing her T-shirt and leggings, but her shoes and socks had been placed neatly by the wardrobe. She washed in a basin in one corner and climbed back into bed, trying to remember the cab drive to his flat.

There was a knock at the door and Corin came in carrying a glass of orange juice. He sat down on the edge of the bed.

'How are you?'

She didn't say anything, just stared at him.

'Good heavens, no,' he said in response to her silent question, his grin getting larger. 'You were too paralytic for anything.' He stroked her face. 'I don't make a habit of abducting drunk students, you know,' he said softly.

She leant over and kissed him. He looked startled and turned to put the orange juice down. She drew back, clutching her knees. She thought she'd made a dreadful mistake. But it was all right. He enfolded the whole of her curled-up body in his arms and his lips sought hers. They were like petals brushing against her skin and they became as hot and wet as a tropical fruit.

'You are dangerous, you know,' he said, his tongue tracing a line from the well of her throat up to her ear.

'Why?'

'Well, look at you,' he said. 'Here I am, over thirty, with someone barely out of nursery school who has hair so white it would put Leslie Nielsen to shame, shorter than an army crewcut and with more holes in her ear than an eight-hole golf course. And who knows all about the sexual behaviour of chimps. I can feel an inferiority complex coming on.'

As he spoke, he uncurled her; his hands traced spirals on her skin. She undid the buttons of his shirt, one by one, and slid it over his shoulders. His breath was hot on her neck, his chest burned. It had been a long time, she thought, such a long time, as his hair slid smoothly over her eyes and whispered across her face.

★ ★ ★

She looked down at her rain-soaked, muddy trousers and worn-out trainers. As if Corin would ever turn up at this hour. He was far too busy. And here she was, at the place she'd been so desperate to escape to: a zoo in the Midlands. She was living in a flat on the edge of a farm. It was little more than a bedsit situated somewhat oddly above a garage; the bathroom was at the back of the garage and smelt of damp. At night she could hear the cows lowing across the immense stillness of the fields and in the morning pigeons cooed in the eaves, murmuring like small children. The village was in the middle of nowhere and she knew no-one except Kim, and even Kim lived miles away, in Birmingham. She'd met Kim at a conference she'd gone to in the first term of her Ph.D. She hadn't known much about her subject or how she was going to work out what was going on in a chimpanzee's mind and she'd felt intimidated by the academics whose talks were so turgid she could understand little of them. Kim stood out of the crowd of drab lecturers in every possible way. For a start, everyone was speaking about animals or people but Kim gave a lecture on robots. Her first slide showed a cutesy Disney lion with its paw draped over a robot unicorn. Tall, thin, black, beautiful and wearing a tailored yellow suit, Kim was like an exotic flower. A carnivorous flower, Sandra decided later when she saw Kim move into operation at the conference party. Her prey, she thought with a grin, was the deputy head of Aston University's Psychology Department (title of talk: 'A Vygotskian view of Simulation, Explicitness and Self-Reference') who was now clinging to Kim on the dance floor, practically standing on tiptoe as he attempted to kiss her.

Sandra would never have dared speak to her, but it was Kim who approached her. She rushed onto the train just as it was about to leave, clutching a pile of bags to her chest, peered at Sandra and said, 'You were at the conference.' She immediately sat down next to her and by way of introduction extended one hand tipped with gold-painted nails. She was, she told Sandra, going to London for a dirty weekend with an old flame.

But much as Sandra liked Kim, she wasn't a close friend. They naturally saw more of each other now that she'd moved. Sometimes, when she was feeling sorry for herself, she thought of it as a forced friendship, a hothouse plant with a livid bloom and a sickly stem.

'It's as if you're living in a bubble,' Corin had said after he'd visited her a couple of times. He drove there, often at night, he stayed in her bedsit and then he went home; where she lived was not connected to anything else in his mind: it was a balloon tethered to him by a fine umbilical cord and for all he knew or cared it could exist in a complete vacuum.

She looked back at the chimps. They were all watching Joseph. He was hanging from the climbing frame, swinging backwards and forwards. His tiny hands didn't even reach fully round the bar. As he swung, the white tuft of hair at the base of his spine, characteristic of baby chimpanzees, bobbed like a cheerleader's pom-pom. Chrissie, his mother, was perched above him, anxiously watching his every move along with everyone else in the group. Even Ted had stopped eating. Babies were often the focus of attention, but she'd rarely seen a whole group look fixedly at one infant. Sally, one of the other adult females in the group, put out a hand and stroked his stomach. Sally was Chrissie's best friend so she was allowed to play with the baby. This was a real honour because Chrissie was a haughty female, fiercely loyal to the few chimps she liked and brutally callous to those she disdained. Joseph's face wrinkled up in an open-mouthed smile and he gurgled happily. Sally's calloused fingers were nearly as long as Joseph's whole body. She poked him in the stomach again. Like a child pushed by an adult, he used the momentum to swing faster. Sally turned away, bored.

One of Joseph's hands started to slip. His mother reached out, but she was too late. His hands slid right off the bar as if it had been greased. Kevin, the other male, stretched out lazily and caught the infant in one hand before he hit the ground. Chrissie immediately lowered herself to the floor, grabbed Joseph by the arm and hauled him back up to the top of the climbing frame. She placed him firmly in her lap like a mother confining a child to bed for being naughty. Poor Kevin, Sandra thought, never got any thanks. He was a real country bumpkin. Large and clumsy, he was much bigger than the agile Ted, but a lot less intelligent, with a permanent oafish expression. His brow was always wrinkled with worry and confusion and his skin was like an old man's, pale and blotched all over with large, ragged freckles. Kevin was also going bald, not through old age, but because he plucked his hair out, although whether this was due to boredom or frustration Sandra did not know. She thought he had the largest balls she had ever seen; he had become quite bowlegged as he attempted to avoid squashing them when he walked.

Kevin took great care of Joseph, playing with him more

than any of the others and certainly far more than Ted did, even though Ted was his father. She wondered whether he knew that Joseph wasn't his son. Certainly when Susie, Joseph's older sister, had been in the group, he had lavished just as much attention upon her.

Now, unfortunately, Susie was in the cage next door with another chimp called Jo-Lee. The two of them were allowed out for an hour every morning and the only way she could communicate with the big group of chimps was through the wire mesh that separated them. Susie and Joseph would spend horn's sticking their fingers through the wire, attempting to stroke one another and pressing their lips together in exaggerated duck-billed pouts. Then his sister would race to the other side of the cage, skittering on the sawdust, rush back, and collapse in front of him, only to run off again in this strange, one-sided game of chase.

Susie was a sweet, good-natured little chimp, playful but not obnoxious. She craved affection but was never clingy. Sandra hadn't been surprised to learn that when Susie was born, Chrissie hadn't looked after her properly: chimps, like humans, have to learn how to care for their babies.

Susie had been taken away from Chrissie and hand-reared by the director of the zoo. Now that she was two, it was hoped she could be returned to the group. It ought to have been easy since she was related to three of them and her mother lorded it over the other chimps like a queen. The sad thing was that Susie was being used as a pawn. The director hand-reared all the baby chimps. Joseph was the first one who had been allowed to stay with his mother.

The other keepers had told Sandra that the director, Belinda Williams, didn't give the chimp mothers a chance, she simply took the babies away from them. And of course that created problems. Chimps won't easily accept a stranger back into their group; as xenophobic as people, they normally kill them. A chimp that's been hand-reared by humans is demanding and cocksure whilst at the same time being terribly insecure. Putting a bolshy, over-confident chimp in with a group creates problems because she's not used to kowtowing and wants everything her own way. She doesn't understand that other members of the troop are senior to her, and so she has a hard time fitting in and is disliked by the other chimps, who want to put this upstart in her place.

But she is also insecure because she has no special friends with whom she's grown up, she has no mother, and she is wrenched from the richness of a house with lots of toys and constant human attention to the other chimps' brutal and boisterous world. Both Jo-Lee and Susie would often sit cross-legged clutching a huge bundle of straw or shredded paper to their chests, rocking backwards and forwards.

Jo-Lee had also been hand-reared. She'd been in Ferguson's cage, but now Miss Williams wanted to put her in with the rest of the group. And Susie was the go-between. The other chimps hated Jo-Lee but it was likely that they would accept Susie back into the fold. So Susie was to stay with Jo-Lee until Miss Williams wanted to risk moving them.

The outer door clanged open and Sally, wobbling rotundly, ran out, listing from side to side as her weight struggled with gravity. She was the middle- aged dowager of the group. She looked up to Ted and Chrissie, but occasionally would show an off-hand sort of affection for Kevin. Ted ambled disinterestedly after her. He was like a mob leader; slick, smart, self- assured, amiable to a point but he would flip into a tyrannical rage at the least provocation. Tracey skipped along behind Ted. She was the youngest and most junior-ranking of the females. She looked perpetually perplexed. Her face was black and pink- freckled and she had protruding ears. But their size was nothing compared to her backside. Every time a female chimp comes into season, her bottom swells up, and Tracey's seemed to be in a permanent state of tumescence. It was like a huge inflated beach ball, the skin stretched and shiny. Sandra winced every time Tracey tried to sit down. Once, when Tracey had been standing on her head in the corner, a visitor had asked why the chimp's face was so pink and distended.

She could hear a faint noise growing louder by the second, and sighed when doors crashed open. A crowd of school kids surged in and swarmed around her, pressing themselves and their greasy fingers and faces against the glass. Huddled in her chair, she tried to make herself as small as possible, but they still elbowed her, pushed in front of her and stood on her feet to see better, shrieking with laughter and screaming, Oh, look at the baby! Miss! Miss! There's a baby monkey!

Ignorant little twits, she thought, trying to peer over their heads. One of the teachers pulled ineffectually at a child who was practically sitting on her knee and mumbled something like, "Look out for the lady", but her voice was drowned by their high-pitched yells. They banged on the glass with their small fists and one of them elbowed her right in the stomach. They were acting as if she were a stuffed exhibit, she thought bitterly.

Ted had come back in to see what all the noise was about. He spat at them, and then carefully licked his spit off the window. The children screamed and pretended to be sick, mercifully backing away from the glass so that she had a slight breathing space. The keepers had told her it was always like this in summer: a constant stream of people from ten till four. The quiet hours were definitely over.

If the kids were bad enough, the adults were worse with their smart-alec, dumb skull remarks and invariably people would ask her what she was doing. Even when she was in the middle of collecting data, she would have to stop and talk to them politely.

It was always difficult to know what to say. Usually she just said she was studying their behaviour as part of her Ph.D. and left it at that. Once she told the truth and said to a young skinhead with blurred blue tattoos that she was watching their gaze. He drew back and looked as if he were about to punch her.

'What,' he said incredulously, 'you mean they've got 'omosexuals in there?'

But that, in fact, was what she was doing: recording what the chimps were looking at for, after all, aren't the eyes meant to be the windows of the soul?

She got up and squirmed her way past the children. Outside it was still chilly but touched with warmth. Five magpies flew overhead and alighted in a squawking gaggle on the small cherry trees by the path. They hesitated, looking far too large for the tiny trees, before flying down to the field, an area of grass behind the chimp house that doubled as a car park for a couple of days in summer when visitor pressure became too great. The grass was thick and lush and probably full of worms and leatherjackets; the magpies always went there. Five for silver.

She badly needed a cup of coffee but it was time for the keepers' break so she didn't want to go to their staffroom. They were a weird bunch, and they disliked students. She made a point of going there when they were working and she could sit on her own in the quiet dark and warmth that smelt of baked potatoes and hot milk on one of the hard plastic chairs, drawn up at hard plastic tables like a school canteen. She'd have to risk the education department.

Department was something of a misnomer. It was a dilapidated Portakabin, a squat satellite to the lecture hall, sandwiched between the giraffes and the elephants; from the window you looked out onto a red sea of mud. As she skirted the edge of the giraffe enclosure the baby followed her round, towering above her and swaying gracefully on legs like spun glass; she kept expecting them to snap under the weight of his body. His eyes scanned her every movement, the lashes fringing them as thick as reeds, and he poked out his cyanide-black tongue and drooled slightly.

And that was the length of their entire enclosure, she thought grimly and imagined them in the wild, the miles eaten by the stretch of their stride, running through air become viscous, running in slow motion as if in another dimension, grinding sand and stone and acacia thorn beneath their hooves.

There was no-one in the Portakabin. She sighed with relief and switched the kettle on. The heat was always on, even in summer, because of the animals. One side was taken up with warped metal bookshelves; the other housed tanks and cages. She sat quietly waiting for the kettle to boil and after a few moments the crickets began to sing and she could hear the faint and stealthy rustle of maggots rummaging through newspaper with their minute, voracious mouths. Then the door banged open and Pat staggered in.

Sandra groaned inwardly.

Pat breathed a foul dragon's breath of whisky and smoke at her and slumped into a chair.

'Get's a coffee, love,' she slurred.

Sandra piled three heaped teaspoons in the cup, poured in water and handed it to her. Pat frowned into the coffee and stared unfocusedly at the milk bottles. There was a collection of them in various states of decomposition. The oldest held a ship of mould complete with a delicate tracery of rigging and one would wonder with exactly the same awe how someone had managed to get a carving in the bottle, whilst the newest merely emitted a noxious smell and had thick clots of cheesy-coloured solids clogging up the neck. Pat declined to ask why Sandra had given her black coffee. Her head swayed back, she took a sip and promptly sprayed it everywhere.

'Christ, that's hot.'

'That's the idea,' Sandra said dryly. 'Haven't you got a talk today?'

'Probably.' She muttered under her breath, 'Shoot the little bastards. All of them.'

Pat had been there for fifteen years - ten years too many, Sandra thought - running the education department and giving talks to school kids. She went through karmic cycles of smashing cars and being given new ones by the director. When she had clocked her way up to three Isuzus and two Fords she had driven, paralytically as usual, straight into a police car, writing off both cars but leaving herself and the detective unscathed. Her licence had promptly been revoked and, as she lived at the zoo like most of the keepers and it was miles from anywhere, she had resorted to scrounging lifts and favours from more mobile persons. Sandra had reluctantly become a purveyor of liquor. She didn't think she was the only one blessed with this uncertain privilege, since she was quite sure that Pat could easily work her way through more than two bottles of whisky a week.

She looked at the list of talks pinned to the wall and said, 'You're supposed to be giving one now. In fact,' she glanced at her watch, 'you should have started three minutes ago.'

Indeed, the area outside the lecture hall and the Portakabin was brimming with milling school- children. But Pat seemed to have noticed already. She was crouched in sniper position at the window, aiming and firing a dustpan brush at them.

Chapter Two

It was nearly midnight before she heard the car, metallic blue green as a scarab beetle's wing, crunch across the gravel drive. She uncorked the bottle: Corin liked to have it sit and air to reach room temperature. She switched the gas on under the stew and put a loaf of partially warmed garlic bread in the oven.

'I'm sorry I'm a bit late, sweetheart,' he said as he bounded in, flinging his bag to the floor and his arms around her.

'A bit?' she asked, smothered by his embrace. He'd said he'd be there between half past eight and nine. At first his lateness used to upset her but she no longer let it worry her; it wasn't his fault his job was demanding and unpredictable and the drive from London to the Midlands was long. Now she cooked things that wouldn't burn and shrivel if left for an unspecified length of time.

'Couldn't we just go to bed?' He nuzzled her neck.

'No, sit down and drink this.' She poured out the wine. It tasted like tree sap.

'I'm tired,' he said, gulping his wine as if it were Ribena. He looked vibrant with energy though. He couldn't sit still. He pulled another sweater on, fiddled with his hair, leapt up to inspect what was in the pan and the oven, sat down again, jumped up to pour more wine, sat on her chair, and then started pacing up and down, his wine swinging in the glass. He made her feel exhausted just watching.

'What's this?' He stopped his prowling. 'Another card from Indiana Jones and the Serpent of Doom?' He snorted.

On the wall was a cork notice board where she kept all the postcards that Philippe sent her. He was living at a snake sanctuary in India, catching wild snakes and milking them for their venom. She'd gone out with him throughout her undergraduate years. They'd split up reasonably amicably and every month he sent her postcards of snakes, women in brilliantly coloured saris and tacky paintings of Ganesh, the elephant god. Corin plucked the latest card off the wall and started to read it. She said nothing about this intrusion into her privacy. To Philippe the cards were probably mundane; to her they were a glimpse into another world and she knew that Corin would quickly put the card back, bored by Philippe's talk of snake conservation, the genetics of isolated reptile populations and the latest baby croc that had hatched at the sanctuary. She also knew that Corin would immediately look round the flat: on the sofa was a tie-dye cotton sari she was using as a throw and by the window was a sandalwood Shiva. Philippe had sent them as moving-in presents. Corin did indeed look at the sofa and wrinkled his nose in displeasure, but this time he didn't say anything.

She ladled out the stew and tore the garlic bread into slices. The breaking of bread and the drinking of wine; it was like a holy communion. She leant over and kissed his lips, stained purple with the woodiness of wine, exuding the scent of oak. For one brief moment he rested his head against her cool forehead and was still but then he pulled back and started eating and talking, doing both fast and simultaneously. She wondered how he managed to eat so quickly without spilling anything.

He told her that at last he'd found a programme to make. At least, credit where credit was due, his senior, the editor of the series, had thought of it.

'Have you heard of the Parade of the Dwarfs?' She shook her head. 'Imagine if everyone's height, every adult in this country, were proportional to their income. Now, the average height is five foot five and that corresponds to the average wage. Imagine, also, that everyone marches past you in one hour. For the first fifteen minutes of the parade the people are dwarfs - they're only three feet tall. Halfway through the march, they're still dwarfs - slightly bigger dwarfs - about four foot six. It is not until thirty-seven minutes have gone by that the average person walks past. Twenty minutes later there are three minutes to go and these people are eleven feet tall. The last two people to walk past are nearly ten miles high!'

'So what's the programme actually going to be about?'

'Well, can't you see it?'

He sketched lines in the air and she half expected a trail of white heat to follow his finger like the plume left by a plane. 'It'll be Twin Peakesque - sinister red velvet drapes and grotesquely misshapen dwarfs - and then right at the end we see a shadow. We think it's of a man and then we realize that it's only the shadow of - of - his foot! And then it dawns on us that if that is his foot, he must be fucking tall. And somewhere we see the words, perhaps engraved in curling letters on the black and white floor tiles: The Giant.'

'Yes, but what's it going to be about?'

'Scientists! You're all so bloody literal. What it's going to be about, my dear, is the dwarfs of our society. The poor, the poverty-stricken, the dregs of Thatcher's Britain, and the ball and chain of Major's; how they might be poor but they're not all stereotypes. I'm going to say - and this may come as a shock to many - that poor people live in the south of England too. They're not all layabouts scabbing off the government; they too walked tall, but circumstances have cut them off in their prime. Mmm. That's a nice line, have to remember that. Prime or pride? Doesn't get the sense that they've been warped, deformed, though. It's as if they were shooting up like young healthy plants and then their, what is it, that hormone? I dunno, that growth hormone is leached out of their bodies, sucked out by a money-hungry government, and their growth is stunted. But the government gives all this lovely growth hormone to the already tall people and says, Here, have some of this, my darlings. Yes, nice, I like that analogy.' He took a swig of wine and added, 'Christ knows, I hope I don't have to meet any poor people.'

He lowered his eyelids and looked up from under his lashes. She couldn't tell, because of his wild mismatching eyes, whether he was watching her or gazing into the distance. But he suddenly pushed back his chair, spread his arms and legs, licked his lips and said, 'Fuck me, babe.' He laughed wildly at her embarrassment, swept her into his arms and staggered over to the other side of the room where he fell with her onto the bed.

She felt very strange. It was as if she were watching herself going through the motions of having sex. He kissed her. He moved inside her. His breath came in sharp gasps. Working at the zoo, she suddenly felt, had alienated her from ordinary human life. To begin with she'd spent time with the keepers learning how they filled their days, seeing what and when they fed the animals. She'd watched them chopping up apples and oranges, leeks, tomatoes, cucumber. She'd seen sleek green grapes disappear between thick dark lips; mouths opening pink and black like liquorice allsorts. And when she returned home in the evenings, her hands trembled ever so slightly as she made apple pie, sliced onions and cut florets from cauliflower.

Corin raised himself up on his arms and looked down at her. She thought of the bonobos in the missionary position. She thought of Tracey offering her shiny pink behind like a present. She imagined Ted's penis, purple-veined, almost triangular, thin and tapering, and she thought of how he held it in his fist as she had held Corin; she'd felt him twitch in her palm like a baby bird stirring. Her mind was filled with images of thick-skinned hands and ebony fingernails and she shivered beneath Corin's touch.

'Coffee,' he gasped, 'get me.'

She made real coffee, pouring the grounds into a filter that reminded her of the chromatography paper they used to pour distillations of grass and ethanol into in chemistry. They'd watch a flower fan from the centre in rings of blue and yellow, stiff as a carnation. Corin had bought the cafetière for her as well as bags of real coffee because he said he couldn't stand the junk instant that was all she could afford to give him.

She took the cafetière and two mugs over to the bed. She thought it was like pouring petrol into an expensive, cold and motionless car. After a few minutes the petrol would ignite, there would be a couple of revs and from then on smooth, perfect acceleration. She watched the spark kindle in his eyes and he was up and running, demanding to know what the day held. Within a couple more minutes he was on his third cup of coffee, both the radio and the TV were on and he was pacing up and down in front of the set, alternately interrogating the newsreader and asking what her opinion on Bosnia was and why the hell couldn't she make stronger coffee?

'Breakfast?' was about the only word she could get in edgeways.

'Mmm.' He waved his empty mug at her. 'More coffee.'

They walked round Bosworth battlefield, a couple of large fields with acres of wheat on either side. She felt as if they were in the south of France; the sun was hot on her back, the wheat, almost shoulder height, was the colour of boiled sugar at the tip, and where the individual seeds joined the rest of the ear was raw green and milky. The path was hard as baked clay and interspersed between the corn were ox-eye daisies and the florid, fragile blooms of poppies.

All the way around the battlefield were signposts with ghostly riders painted over the top of a line drawing of the horizon. Out of a whole platoon of horses and riders, the sign would unerringly pick out Richard III every time.

'So we've seen where he's drunk some water, we've seen where he spent the night, we've seen the village he marched from, no doubt we'll be treated to where he scratched his left buttock next,' said Corin.

'We're going to see where the final battle was, where he was killed.'

'In here?'

She nodded.

'There's hardly enough room to swing a lance, never mind troop in with several hundred men and have your final fling - you need square footage for death throes.'

The field was tiny, a small triangle of marshy, sandy soil where water gleamed with each footfall and forget-me-nots had knitted blue lace over the tips of the grass. He kicked the plaque fastened on to a large rock in the middle of the field.

'And it must have been all the more difficult trying to negotiate round this thing.' He glanced at his watch, the lengthening shadow of the sun falling on his face like a sundial. 'The pubs will be open. Let's drink.'

They walked across to Market Bosworth, the nearest

village, climbing over wooden stiles as hot as cats and passing beneath horse chestnuts, their five-fingered leaves splayed to shade a mist of dancing gnats.

'Christ! What are those plants?'

'Hemlock,' said Sandra dreamily, 'giant hemlock, and they're deadly poisonous, so don't touch.'

'It's a positive forest of triffids.'

Overgrown cow parsley, the hemlock stretched above them, their stems corrugated lime green and purple, the flowers, dense as plates of whipped cream, balanced on an army of stalks as thin as waiters' arms. She imagined how they would look in winter when all the other vegetation had died and they stood there, black against the whey-white winter sky, frost shining in their crevices and the empty seed-heads glimmering like an unknown constellation.

Market Bosworth was one of those quaint places ensnared by small-time consumerism. The central square no longer held horses and carts and butter churns, but Range Rovers, Volkswagens and Porsches, and it was surrounded by pubs with fake black and white beams and 'ye olde' written on the blackboards where groups of cyclists drank and locals watched satellite TV and played arcade games. The antique shops were filled with second-hand junk, pine furniture and horse brasses, and the flower shop sold passion vines and parsnips. There was a sign saying it had once won the Best Village in Bloom competition. Corin snorted when he saw that, and she thought that if he were not so well brought up, he would probably have mangled some of the ultraviolet petunias that were growing in the window boxes out of sheer wilfulness.

They sat outside even though it was starting to get chilly and ordered fizzy wine.

'You know, in the old days they used to write "the" like a y with a long tail and e on the end. So places like this write "ye" but it was in fact pronounced "the".'

'You're a mine of information,' Corin murmured. He dipped a finger in his glass and traced the outline of her lips in wine. He leant over and licked it off. His tongue was hot and sharp. Someone stopped and stared. She could feel the woman's eyes boring into her back but she was unable to look away from him.

That night she dreamt she was having a bath in champagne. Corin was pouring it in, bottle by bottle. They were stacked in rows, their mouths silver and broken, the glass as thick and green as old alchemy jars. The champagne foamed over her shoulders like the surge of a wave. When she lay down in the smooth golden depths her whole body was coated with bubbles and they pricked as sharp as ice; a hundred little needles piercing her skin.

It was always harder to get back to work after Corin had left. He sped round, whirl winding clothes and shoes and wash stuff into his bag, giving her a kiss that was a push and reversing out of the drive as if the car were being ejected. She was left with a flat littered with plates and cups and empty bottles, a pillow case that smelt of him and a room full of his absence.

He'd gone before she needed to get up but then she'd fallen asleep and now was late. Although there was no such thing as late. She could do as much or as little as she liked. Of course, if she did nothing, she would never get her Ph.D., but three years was a long time and it was composed of steps and stages, and those steps and stages fell into weeks and mornings where the long-term goal was like a white light whose rays touched her faintly in the place where she, at present, stumbling around in the dark, could only see the faint outline of her hands before her face.

She'd spent the first year cooped up in the old converted chemistry lab at the university reading papers and books and going to lectures and seminars. This was the beginning of her second year and the whole year was to be devoted almost entirely to studying the chimps at the zoo. But even a year was a long time. Better to deal with each day as it came. Normally she was fine: what was difficult was the transition from caring for Corin whilst letting him take over her life to the rude independence that was thrust upon her the moment he left.

* * *

There'd been a fight. Not too much of one because the chimps could really hurt each other if they chose, but still, Kevin was a little worse for wear. He was huddled in one corner tenderly cradling his balls, sneaking sideways glances from under his creased brow. Ted, nonchalant as ever, swaggered round, his hair rising sleek and black as he saw her. He swung his fist and pounded on the glass once.

'Did you do that? Did you?'

Ted looked smug.

'Well, it wasn't big and it wasn't clever. I hope you're proud of yourself.'

Kevin sat quite still, his head bowed. After a while Ted went and sat outside and Kevin got up carefully. He had a canine tooth mark on his left testicle. He walked painfully over to Sally and turned so he was facing away from her. For a couple of minutes, she continued to glance around and pick her teeth but then she bent down and peered at his balls. She touched the bite gently and, making her lips into a thin and narrow pout, caressed his wound. Every half minute or so she stopped and groomed his back for a while. Kevin started to look a little more relaxed: grooming releases chemicals in the brain that act a little like opium. Sandra reflected that might be why hairdressers were so busy.

'Did you see the fight?' asked Teresa, approaching her.

Sandra shook her head. 'That must hurt, though.'

Teresa shrugged. 'They've got a high tolerance to pain. They pick at their scabs and poke at cuts and things. It makes my stomach heave.'

She banged the door open at the far end of the corridor and disappeared into the back of Susie and Jo-Lee's night cages to clean them out. Teresa was tall and thin with long straight hair and eyes as grey as mackerel. She was invariably surly and bad-tempered. Most of the keepers here were a little strange, Sandra thought, but at least she didn't have to deal with very many of them apart from Teresa, the other chimp keeper Annie, and, of course, Belinda Williams, the director.

After Teresa had gone, Sandra thought about what she'd said. It was no surprise that chimps had a high pain threshold. You had to be tough living in the wild. But it certainly looked as if it hurt and Sally was not being her usual callous and off-hand self, but painstakingly grooming and licking the area around the wound. Surely, Sandra thought, that was a classic case of empathy. Scientists thought that humans were the only animals capable of showing empathy, the only creatures who could be compassionate to others. But it did look as if Sally understood that Kevin was hurt; she was being as tender as a mother with a child, and Sally wasn't renowned for her caring personality. She wasn't the only chimp who'd shown empathy, though.

Once Sandra had seen Jo-Lee fall. She'd been clinging to the wire mesh that separated the two chimp groups, calling to the others. All of a sudden both Chrissie and Sally had launched themselves against the wire screaming furiously, lips pulled back over their gums. Jo-Lee, in her fright, had fallen awkwardly to the ground, landing on her hand which had got twisted beneath her. She'd sat down and shaken her hand once but immediately Susie, Joseph's little sister, had rushed over and inspected it, turning it over between her two palms. She'd touched it to her lips and kissed it, then made Jo-Lee bow her head so the tiny chimp could reach up and groom her face.

Sandra had spent some time watching the spider monkeys so she'd be able to compare their behaviour with the chimps'. They were one of the most intelligent monkey species and they lived in groups that resembled wild chimps'. They had shaggy black, spiky fur, pale pink faces and bright blue eyes. When they were interested in a visitor they would press themselves flat and cruciform against the glass and peer intently out through their uncannily human eyes. But the best thing about them, as far as Sandra was concerned, was their tails. They were as dexterous as their arms and legs; in fact, the tips of their tails were bare of fur, the skin thick and patterned like a fingerprint. They would swing by them from branches and bars, grasp objects with them, and when they were resting they would curl them up into perfect spirals.

On one occasion Gof, the dominant male, had hurt his hand somehow. The first two of his thin black fingers were red and raw as if the nails had been peeled off. She could hardly bear to watch. He kept putting them in his mouth and sucking them, and every time he saw his favourite female he would stretch out his hand to her. She always ignored him. In desperation, he'd tried to stuff his fingers into her mouth a few times, but she turned her back on him and bounded away.

Monkeys, in Sandra's opinion, showed no compassion. They lacked empathy. When she was very young she had read a book called *Do Androids Dream of Electric Sheep?* by Philip K. Dick which was later made into the film *Bladerunner*. The central character 'retired' replicants: he killed escaped androids. What Hollywood hadn't shown and what to her was most fascinating was that the abiding norm in this future society was empathy. Even if you didn't have it, you had to be seen to show it. Nuclear radiation had killed almost all the animals, yet the only way you could prove to your neighbours that you had empathy was to care for one. The Bladerunner was killing the androids to raise enough money to buy a real animal so that he could show empathy in the proper way. All he could afford was an electric sheep.

Years later, just before her twenty-first birthday, it was Philip K. Dick's words that echoed in her mind: 'Mankind needs more empathy.' Those words gave her a kind of courage, so that when she found herself standing in Professor Dickinson's office the first thing she had blurted out was, 'I want to study empathy.' He had looked at her as if she were mad, and her heart immediately sank. She'd been hoping she could do a Ph.D. and that he would supervise it. But then his expression suddenly changed to one of predatory interest.

Professor Dickinson lived in a room full of skulls. One wall was completely filled with them. They stared out, hollow-eyed and creamy-cheeked, orbital bones stained nicotine yellow, cranials sewn together with a drunken ant's walk of stitches. He measured the smooth eggshells that had cradled brains: the rounded furrowed-browed skulls of Neanderthals, orangutans, baboons.

That first time she'd spoken to him, over a year ago now, he'd said empathy wasn't a proper subject for study. How would one measure it? At best you'd see it once: one type of empathic behaviour in one chimp. A one-off incident like that was an anecdote, a mere story. To prove to the rest of the scientific community that empathy existed in chimps you had to show that it could happen, had happened, would happen, over and over again. Hard data was what you needed, and empathy . . . well, it wasn't something you could calibrate, re-run in laboratory conditions, was it? Then he'd softened a little.

'Try approaching it from a different angle,' he'd said. 'If you show empathy, what do you need?'

'Well, that depends on your definition of empathy.'

He'd nodded appraisingly at her. 'And yours is?'

'There's empathy that's compassion, where you understand that another person is hurt. You can't know what it feels like for them, but you know that they're in pain. And there's empathy that's role reversal. Where you can understand things from their point of view. Where you imagine what it would be like if you were in that situation, where you put yourself in their shoes.'

'Exactly. And those capacities require Theory of Mind.'

She must have looked completely blank because he'd said, 'Put simply, that's the ability to understand that other people have thoughts: that they have certain beliefs about the world, and that they have desires - that they want food, or sex. And even humans aren't born with this capacity. When we're very young we don't know that other people have minds and can think. We don't even know that we can think! It takes us the first four years of our life to realize that.

'I'd say that makes it damn unlikely that any animal could have Theory of Mind and hence show empathy. But if that is what you would like to study, I would say it was an admirable topic for a Ph.D. But difficult. Remember that it will be difficult.'

After that meeting, she had gone to a pub on the corner of Chalk Farm Road filled with empty wine bottles oozing wax; the bones in people's faces were highlighted in brass-coloured flame. She imagined that she was an alien, sipping a Bloody Mary, wondering at its taste and the bits that clung to the side of the glass like a toxic scum of algae. She did not know anything but the bare essentials about these creatures who surrounded her with their smell of sweat and beer and talcum powder, dirty leather and scent vaporized from hot bodies.

She did not know if the sounds they made were a kind of communication, or what they meant if they were. All she could do was sit and watch and take notes. How, from the gesture of an arm, the swilling of liquor, the touch of a hand, a glance at the door, could she know what was going on inside their heads? How could she tell that they knew what was going on in the minds of their companions?

As she was walking back to her flat down the dark streets where passers-by avoided her eyes and the tarmac was silver with crushed glass, she concluded that if she were an alien, she would not think this species was particularly intelligent.

She left Sally still kissing Kevin and went for coffee. As she walked past the tiger cage, the male sidled up to the mesh and kept pace with her, matching her stride step for step, never letting her out of his sidelong and pale yellow gaze. She watched those soft paws pad along the path that he'd worn bare and thought of the claws sheathed beneath. How very wrong it was to think of them as large pussy cats and assume that just because they were fed hunks of horse meat from the knacker's yard the killer instinct had dried up. She felt uncomfortable knowing that he was half-heartedly stalking her.

Past the tigers were the tapirs. A new acquisition, they were huge, monstrous aberrations, a cross between a pig and an elephant. Their skin was black as silt, their snouts were enlarged flies' proboscies, a whip of a tail whistled against their thighs and their enormous bodies were balanced upon high-heeled hooves. They grunted at her, but didn't move from their rut in the straw.

Crouched in front of the sea otters was a boy. He was staring intently at them and she stopped beside him to see what he was looking at. The five otters were lying together on the grass bank, their wet fur twisted into locks like plaited rope, their bodies interwoven, murmuring to each other in a soft, high-pitched chorus. Occasionally one would nuzzle another's neck, or bat away an inquisitive nose. After a few moments they trotted off in single file round the side of their pen and up to the peak of an outcrop of rock. From the top a waterfall gushed; they lay on their bellies and slid down into the pool below, one after the other; like children taking it in turns on a slide.

She wondered who the boy was. It was too early for him to be a visitor. She looked closely at him. He was small and thin, probably about eight years old, with blue eyes and dark hair. Although it was difficult not to smile at the antics of the otters, he stared at them blankly and he still had not glanced at her, nor acknowledged her presence in any way. She shifted her feet on the gravel and sat down on the low wall practically in front of him. His gaze slid to one side and then he turned and ran awkwardly away.

Now she thought about it, she seemed to remember seeing him before, a thin figure skulking around in the shadows.

Across the grass she saw someone in dark green with a halo of blond hair. Annie. She waved and ran over to her. Annie was one of the few nice and almost normal keepers. She lived in the flat next door to Teresa and worked with the chimps on Teresa's days off. She was small with a mass of curly hair.

'Hi!' she called enthusiastically. 'Bit early for you to be going for coffee, isn't it?'

'Yes, but you know how it is, always takes me longer to get into my stride on Monday mornings.'

'Tell me about it. I've got the hangover from hell and I still had to get up at six thirty.' She rolled her eyes. 'Did Paul say anything to you, then?'

'Paul?'

'That little boy by the otters.'

'I wondered who he was.'

'He's Meg's - the gibbon keeper's kid.'

'No. He didn't even look at me and then he ran off.'
'He's weird. Really weird. He's never spoken to me either but he does seem to like Craven. The two of them sit next to each other for hours - don't think a word passes between them - they just sit there.'

'Who's Craven?'

'Oh, you must have seen him. He does all the odd jobs around the zoo. He's weird an' all. He and Paul are a fine couple.' She giggled and then stopped abruptly.

Meg had just appeared from behind one of the bird cages. She gave them a tired smile. She was only thirty but her face was lined and she had a white streak in her hair. She'd been working with the gibbons for over ten years. She bobbed her head at them by way of greeting and the three of them stood in silent embarrassment. Sandra wondered whether she'd heard them talking about Paul and if they'd upset her. She was intensely curious, but held back from asking a string of questions about Meg's strange son.

They were saved by Annie who broke the silence. 'Sandra's been watching your Paul watching the otters.' She was about to say something more when her face lit up and she waved. The others turned to see whom she was looking at.

'All right, you lot.' It was Lee.

Sandra smiled at him and said, 'Out drinking last night? Wearing sunglasses at ten in the morning with a keeper's uniform is a bit of a giveaway.'

He smirked amicably and leant over to pull one of Annie's curls. Lee was the golden boy of a zoo composed almost entirely of female keepers. He worked in a nightclub to supplement his meagre wage and had to wear shorts and a vest. He dyed his hair yellow and went on a sunbed twice a week. He was also sleeping with Annie and Teresa, seeing them on alternate nights. Since all the keepers' flats were together at the end of the zoo and Annie and Teresa were next to each other and he lived opposite, everyone knew what was going on. But what Sandra couldn't figure out was why he liked Teresa. Perhaps someone could like her, but not the kind of person who would love sunny, happy-go-lucky Annie. She wondered how the two girls felt about it. Certainly Annie didn't look as if she were treating this as a light romance. Sandra suddenly felt angry, Lee toying with her hair like that. But then, she reflected, it was none of her business, and how was she to know that he didn't love both of them equally?

'Heard about the new keeper?'

They shook their heads.

'A bloke. He'll be starting soon. I can't wait to see you lot fighting over him.' He grinned smugly.

'Get away,' said Annie, giving him a push.

Meg smiled politely.

'I suppose it'll make a change from them all fighting over you,' said Sandra lightly. She excused herself and set off for the keepers' staffroom. She wasn't sure she could take Pat's whisky fumes at this point.

Chapter Three

'Let's play mummies and daddies,' said Claire.

'How do you do that?' asked Paul.

'Well, I'll be the mummy and you be the daddy.'

'But you're not a mummy. You don't have any children. You're not old enough and I can't be a daddy because I'm not married to you and I don't have any children.'

'We're pretending,' said Claire in exasperation.

'Whose mummy and daddy are we pretending to be?'

'Teddy's. He's our baby.'

'How can he be our baby? He didn't come out of your tummy, did he? He's not a baby. He's a stuffed toy.'

Claire's eyes filled with tears. 'I don't like you. You never play nice games with me.'

'I think it's silly. Anyway, I don't know how you play at being a daddy. I haven't got one.'

They were in the zoo playground. The low evening sun,

falling through the slats of the wooden railings, cast elongated shadows over the still merry-go-round and the elephant-trunk slide. Paul was swinging, pushing himself higher and higher. He liked the feeling of leaning backwards as he was reaching with his toes for the sky, the sinking sun like a boiled sweet between his feet, and then he would lean forward and fall back to earth, the ground rushing up to meet him sickeningly fast, the blood rushing to his face. Claire was standing to one side, her leg wrapped round the support of the swing, her thumb in her mouth.

Jeff was watching, as usual. He lived in a caravan next to the playground and worked in the reptile house. Paul didn't like to be close to Jeff because he smelled. But he went to see him every week.

'I know,' said Claire, brightening, 'let's play doctors and nurses.'

'How do you play that?'

'I'll be the nurse and you be the doctor. I'll tell you exactly what you have to do.'

'All right.' Reluctantly he stopped swinging, falling like a broken-winged bird out of the sky, scuffing his shoes in the dirt to stop.

'I think Teddy is sick. We'll have to examine him.'

Paul stared blankly at her.

'Now you say "Yes, we must",' she said in a stage whisper, 'and you look in his ears and listen to his heart.'

'Yes we must,' said Paul woodenly. He picked up the bear and looked cursorily in his ears, but it was the heart that really floored him. He held the bear by one ear and said, 'He hasn't got a heart.'

Claire wailed. 'You're hurting him, holding him by his ear.'

'Am I?' he asked, genuinely perplexed. 'But he's not saying anything so that means he's not hurt.'

Claire snatched the toy from him and wrapped her arms fiercely round the bear. She stood swaying for a moment, on the brink of a tantrum, but then she said, 'I know, you can examine me. I've got a heart.'

'OK. Tell me what to do.'

Claire lay on one of the picnic tables. 'Come over here. Now lift up my T-shirt. Put your head against my chest and listen to my heartbeat.' She wriggled. 'Your hair is tickling me. Am I all right, doctor?'

Paul looked around as if looking for the doctor. Then he looked back at Claire's pale chest.

'You're supposed to tell me whether I'm sick or not.'

'You're perfectly well. And anyway, I wouldn't know if you were sick just from listening to your heartbeat. Lots of other things can show you whether you're sick.'

Paul noticed that Jeff was glued up against the window. He was looking right at Claire's knickers.

'I hate playing with you,' said Claire, getting up.

Jeff stepped back from the window and wiped his brow with a dirty hanky. The evening was still warm.

'You're no good.'

'No, I guess I'm not good. If you're good you go to school and you do as you're told, don't you?'

She looked at him as if he were stupid. 'I think you should go to school. But you do what I tell you to, don't you?'

'Sometimes.' He sat on the swing again and jiggled up and down.

'I can push you if you want.'

He looked suddenly shocked. 'If I want you to? Did I say I want you to?'

'No.'

'Well then, I guess I don't want you to.'

His manner was mild, but Claire started to cry. 'You're so rude. I'm going to tell my mummy on you.' She ran off.

Paul didn't watch her go. He stood on the tips of his toes and leaned back, launching himself into the air. Higher and higher. The wind singing in his ears, the chains cold in his palms.

He was still swinging an hour later when his mother came to look for him.

Chapter Four

Ferguson, as usual, greeted her with his wild display, swaying from side to side, hands on the window sill and lips pouted. When he'd worked himself up sufficiently, he let out loud panthoots and slammed the barrel round the cage. Jessica got out of the way and sat on a shelf eating crisps, occasionally lifting her feet up when he tore past. The two of them lived on their own, separate from the bigger group in the large chimp house.

Ferguson quietened down soon and went back to ignoring her and playing with his stack toy. It was a castle made of plastic, each part of it smaller than the preceding one so that they could all fit inside one another like Russian dolls, or be piled up to make a tower. Today was the first day Ferguson and Jessica had been given the toy, but as Sandra watched he successfully placed the cups inside each other and then emptied them out to build a miniature castle. In between stacking, he placed a cup to his lips and pretended to drink from it. Pretty soon he got bored and did what he did best: indulged in some wilful destruction. With a malicious expression on his face, he squeezed the largest cup between his huge hands, the muscles of his arms bulging, then put it in his mouth and tried to tear it apart with his teeth. That failed, so he stood on it, doing a ridiculous balancing act as he tried to get both feet and hands onto an area the size of a grapefruit. By the time he'd finished, the cups were pockmarked with white canine teeth marks and the ramparts and battlements were all bent.

Sandra watched him out of the corner of her eye. He was now swinging inside a barrel suspended from a climbing frame in his outdoor enclosure. He crouched right down inside it so that only the hair on the top of his head poked out and it looked as if the barrel contained a few rags. Suddenly he leapt out and the visitors screamed. Ferguson proceeded to entertain them to the best of his ability. He jumped onto the top of the barrel and swung manically, holding on to the chain with one hand and lolling his tongue out. From there he dived towards a bungee rope, dipped almost to the ground and bounced up again. Then he somersaulted neatly onto the bottom rung of the climbing frame, raced up to the top bar and ran upright along it with his eyes shut. The visitors were all pressed up against the barrier, laughing and shouting. Sandra smirked.

Ferguson leapt onto the wire mesh and thrust his pelvis a few times, spraying the onlookers with a copious amount of urine. They screamed and staggered back into a rose bed. Ferguson, pleased with his performance, swaggered indoors and curled up in a cardboard box. Jessica, who because she was female and younger and smaller never got to play with or do anything that Ferguson wanted to play with or do, had crept closer to the discarded castle. When Ferguson shut his eyes, she edged a bit further forward. Just as she was stretching out her hand, still watching him, his eyes snapped open. She immediately started to pick her eyebrow, as if that were what she'd always intended to do, and looked in the opposite direction.

Casually she got up and moved away a pace and then glanced over at the far window. Her gaze happened to drift over Ferguson in his box. As soon as his eyes closed she whipped back to the toy and picked up one of the cups. She put it in her mouth and grasped a second one in her hand. She half hobbled towards the outside enclosure, glancing from time to time at Ferguson. Ferguson opened one eye and shut it again.

As soon as Jessica reached the doorway, he hurled himself across the room at her.

She gave a little yelp of surprise and dropped both bits of the toy. But it was too late. Ferguson grabbed them, flung them as far away from Jessica as possible, then, holding her by her hair, half dragged, half pushed her into his bed. It was a small area, almost like a porch leading into their night pens. Sandra saw him bundling her in, yelling and screeching. He climbed in on top of her and she couldn't see anything more after that. Ferguson was quite capable of detaining her there for up to twenty minutes to be 'punished'.

She had no doubt that the little scene she had witnessed showed evidence of Theory of Mind. Jessica knew that Ferguson would take the toy from her if he saw her, so she tried to get it only when he wasn't looking and pretended to do something else when he was. But of course the scientific community could say that it was a classic case of Pavlovian conditioning: if Jessica had been beaten for taking the toy in the past she would have connected the beatings with the act of picking up the toy and rapidly learnt that it wasn't a good idea; she didn't need to have any understanding of someone else's mind at all.

'Did you bring it?'

'Bring what?' Sandra struck her forehead. 'Of course. No, I'm sorry, I forgot.'

Pat looked awful. Her hair was all over the place and her eyes resembled congealed egg white streaked with blood.

'Look, I'll go back and get it for you at lunchtime, OK?'

Pat nodded reluctantly. Sandra shivered. Things were getting pretty bad if she had to drink before work. They sat in silence for a few minutes, Pat uncharacteristically despondent, Sandra feeling sorry for her. A couple of crickets leapt out from under the bookcase and sunned themselves in a ray of light and a hissing cockroach scuttled across the floor, jerking like a wind-up toy. The radio fizzed and crackled; a lonely alien, spluttering through a mouthful of spit, trying to make contact. There was a volley of small explosions, cracking like a sawn-off shotgun. Sandra peered through the back window. The two baby elephants were blowing air through their trunks into each other's vaginas and flapping their ears in excitement at the ensuing wet farts. Visitors were looking shocked as they hastily pulled their children away.

'Jeeesus!' screeched Pat. She leapt up and almost did a full circle of the Portakabin, uncontrolled as a headless chicken, simultaneously trying to smooth down her hair and tuck her paunch into her jumper. She lifted up a few papers and dropped them again, then frantically started tearing up a head of lettuce.

'What are you doing?'

'For the Roman snails,' hissed Pat.

'But . . .'

The door opened and Belinda Williams stepped in. Pat continued to stuff lettuce into the snails' tank, obliterating them under a shower of greenery, then wiped her hands on her trousers and turned to face Miss Williams.

Miss Williams blocked out the sun. Once the director had been tall; now she stooped, her eyes were bleary and her skin was as wrinkled as an elephant's hide. She caked her face in thick white powder; she had blood-red lipstick and long, dyed black hair that looked as real as a mannequin's and stained her forehead purple. Her clothes were black and covered in white dog hairs and she wore a huge garnet on her index finger. At the grand age of eighty-three, she was still running the zoo like a cross between a corner shop and a slave fair.

'Patricia! What are you doing?' She exuded a smell of must and mothballs and stale dog.

'Feeding the animals, Miss Williams.' Pat had turned into a quivering wreck and lost thirty years.

'This place is absolutely filthy. I want it tidied up. Look at the milk bottles. And there are signs to be painted and talks to be given. I will not stand for it. You must pull yourself together, and stop lazing around like a - like a *bum*.'

She pulled herself to her full height and pointed one trembling finger at Sandra, raised veins like blue cables buried in her skin. 'What are you doing?'

'I'm studying the chimps,' said Sandra amicably. 'I'm just watching them at the moment. You remember, we've talked about it before.'

'Oh. Oh yes.' Miss Williams shrank back into herself. She was so close Sandra could see where the powder had settled between folds of her skin. 'And how often do you come in?'

'Every day during the week.'

'Very good, very good. Let me know how you progress. You!'

Pat jumped.

'You have a talk in ten minutes. Last week one of the teachers complained how indistinct your words were. Pronounce them properly and clearly. It's on the role of zoos in conservation and you must mention how advanced we are in this respect.'

She cast a withering glance around the Portakabin and left.

Pat shook her fist at her and blew a raspberry, still

unable to stop being ten. 'Conservation, my arse. We've just got a shipment of zebra. Are they endangered animals? Bollocks they are. San Diego wants rid of them and we think they're cute. And I leave the milk bottles out on purpose so she's got something to complain about. Heaven knows what she'd start on about if I didn't do that.'

She grimaced. "You must pronounce your words properly and clearly." She said, imitating the high- pitched rasp of the old woman. 'I hate her, I hate her.'

Sandra was looking mildly amused. She couldn't understand how the director reduced her staff to children who said nothing to her face but whined behind her back and repeated rude words as if they were a talisman.

'You'll see,' Pat threatened. 'One of these days you'll see and I'll be the first to say I told you so.'

She fed Topsy and Tiny two dead baby mice, the coral snakes slid bored and beautiful over to the pinkies and ate one each, swallowing them whole. The babies' unopened eyes were like bilberries wrapped in fragile, pale pink tissue paper; the eyes of the snakes glittered as they squeezed the mice down their thin tangerine and strawberry milkshake striped bodies.

A couple of weeks later, Sandra bumped into Paul again. It was the middle of the afternoon. She'd finished watching the big group of chimps for the day, and was taking the scenic route to Ferguson and Jessica's cage. It was amazing how close you could get to some of the animals, she thought. You could be inches away and they would carry on as if you weren't there. They ignored your presence by studiously avoiding your gaze; rather you were simply treated as part of the sky or the wall. Mind you, she thought, not many people would want to be within inches of king penguins' nests. They reeked of fish oil and were cemented with bird shit, stamped down by their emulsion-pink feet.

They had white eye-liner rimming their eyes and wisps of hair tufting from the tops of their heads as if they were mad conductors whose hair grease was not enough to contain their passion. But in the water they came into their own. She walked down what was in effect a subway and looked through a window into the penguin pool. They dived into the water, chlorine blue as a Hockney painting, and ricocheted through the net of sunlight trawling the bottom with the elegance of international synchronized swimmers wearing dinner suits.

Over to her right there was a commotion. She looked up. From where she stood her head was level with other people's feet. A party of school children were shouting and stumbling. At first she couldn't see why, and then she saw him. He was walking as if he were alone, seeing nothing and no-one, as though there were no obstacle but air between him and his destination, despite the fact that his slight frame bounced off the children he collided with. One girl fell and started to cry and for the first time he actually looked at one of them. As he stared into her tear-smeared face, an expression almost of awe came across his own. Without a word he straightened and continued. Sandra could see a teacher running towards him, her mouth creased with anger.

Sandra ran over and grabbed Paul's arm. 'It's OK,' she shouted. 'I'm sorry if he's been naughty.'

She pulled him back down the subway, picked up her bag and ran round the other side of the penguins' fake, smelly cliff. He stood there, not looking at her, his arm at an awkward angle, his elbow in her palm.

'Don't run away,' she said and let go of him. She rummaged in her rucksack, produced two oranges and gave one to him. She sat down on the ground and started to peel hers. After a moment's hesitation, he sat down too and placed his orange carefully in front of him as if he were afraid that it might escape. From his inner coat pocket he drew out a slender stem of metal and put it next to the orange. Sandra immediately recognized it and her heart started to beat a little faster.

From another pocket he drew out a small, worn cardboard box and tipped one of the packages it contained into his palm. He unwrapped the waxy butchers' paper and removed a razor-thin piece of metal. He fitted this into the scalpel handle and secured it with a tiny silver screw.

'Isn't it dangerous to have such a sharp knife?' she asked.

'If you get cut by a sharp knife, it's better than a blunt one,' he said. His voice was thin and reedy and somewhat high-pitched. 'A new blade like this doesn't have as much bacteria on it so the cut won't become infected and that means it'll heal quicker. If you should cut yourself deeply, then it's much better for the cut to be neat so the doctor can sew the edges together. If you cut yourself with a blunt knife, the edges are all ragged and it's hard to stitch it up.'

What a curious child, she thought. She revised his age upwards from her last estimation, but still, he was so little and thin ... he couldn't possibly be older than ten. And there was another strange thing about him: he had a very adult face, the bones finely sculpted.

He ran the knife down the orange with great precision: when he removed the cuneiform segments of peel, there was not a mark on the orange itself. He laid the peel out in a row like a line of canoes and started to shave the outer pith off the orange. This was put in a small pile by the boats; the white shavings and the thick inner core reminded her of a heap of tripe. He split the orange up into pieces and put these out in a line too, then started to work on each one individually, beginning with the first one on the left. Using only the tip of his scalpel, he slit the orange from end to end and peeled back the translucent membrane as if he were skinning an animal. The skins made another pile. It was beginning to look a bit like a whaling yard, she thought, the boats at the ready, the discarded blubber and outer flesh of the animals, the sad heap of naked carcasses, and at this next stage, for the first time, he spilt a little juice and it stained the concrete. From each naked orange segment he started to separate out the capsules that were the essence of the orange itself, and he made a collection of these offal-like organs. Only now, when he had finally dismembered the orange and dissected it into its constituent parts, did he eat the minute bags of juice.

When he'd finished, he wiped the blade on a piece of lens-cleaning tissue, took it out of the handle and wrapped it back up. He replaced it in his coat, but in a small plastic container in a different pocket. He put his knife handle back too, and then, without a word, he got up and ran off with his strange gait, one child amongst a crowd of visitors, lonely as a child, she suddenly realized, who has no concept that he is not alone. She watched him until he disappeared from sight and then she tidied up the bits of orange peel and went to resume her work.

Days like today, in the early evening, the sun angled low across a sky grown dark as a pigeon's breast. Every object looked as if its edges had been chiselled out of metal and the leaves of the poplars turned in the wind, flashing like fish scales. The zoo was on a flat piece of ground, but it was high up, and although the area surrounding it appeared flat too, the impression was deceptive. From the zoo the land fell away in a patchwork of fields, strung together by hedges and sewn in easy loops by narrow streams along whose length passed the slow fuse of the sun. Between the startling blue of linseed and the mind-numbing yellow of rape were small villages, each with a church, its tower like a needle, their names round-vowelled and double-barrelled. Up here she felt as if she were on a plateau, that bit nearer the sky, slightly closer to the sun which teetered on the brink of this plain, spilling molten rays of copper-coloured light. Six magpies flew across the iron sky like arrows and alighted sharp as razor blades, slicing into the trees. Six for gold.

She'd finished collecting data for the day and on her way home she usually walked past the ape nursery. Katy and Rex lived on one side and Gorky, the baby gorilla, had the other half. During the afternoon they were all allowed to play together but at night Gorky was taken into Miss Williams's house which was next to the zoo's entrance. In the mornings the two young chimps sat listlessly and nibbled on lettuce leaves, idly squashed tomatoes and half-heartedly played with one another. But in the afternoons they tore round their climbing frames, swung frenetically on the ropes and took it in turns to tussle with Gorky.

Everyone loved Gorky. His dense hair gleamed a lustrous black and he had huge, limpid eyes. He loved to fight fast and furiously, but only in play. He never hurt either of the chimps even though he was bigger than them. He was intensely affectionate but independent; at night, he left the cage without so much as a murmur of protest or a backward glance, riding piggy-back on the keeper, his thick arms wrapped around her neck. When the chimps played chase with him, they adopted his language. They stood upright and stamped first one foot then the other and beat their chests to get him to play. They screeched with laughter and tickled one another, jealously trying to keep Gorky for themselves. Now they were exhausted. Rex, looking left out, hung quietly in a tyre and gazed at Sandra mournfully. Katy and Gorky sat on the window ledge. Katy was sucking a smooth pebble. She took it out of her mouth and offered it to Gorky who also sucked it and then gave it genteelly back. Katy lent forward and the two of them wrapped their arms around each other in a tight embrace. Their lips met and they French kissed, dipping their tongues into one another's mouths, eyes closed blissfully. Rex watched sadly.

The insect climbed up the wall, step by step, waving each long, thin leg about as if testing the air before hesitantly placing it down firmly on the white plaster. If you looked closely you could see its eyes move slightly in their sockets.

Perceiving that there was a whole blank space in front of it, it walked faster until finally it came to the join between the wall and the ceiling. Its antennae swayed in blind panic and its right front leg gyrated madly. Tentatively it placed its foot on the ceiling, then removed it. In a painfully slow dance, it put the same foot back on the wall and tried with another leg. The response was the same; the ceiling, apparently, was on the left of the insect too. It shook itself slightly and then bravely put one foot on the ceiling and then another. But as it tried to move a third leg forward, one of the others came unstuck and it hung there, back arched scorpion-like, trembling, before falling and crashing to the ground with a metallic crunch.

'Aw, Hector, honey, you disappoint me,' drawled Kim. 'Don't you know you're on show?'

Kim rarely talked about her work, which was a shame because Sandra found it fascinating. The only way to get any serious kind of explanation from her was to see her in the lab. Since it was Friday, Sandra felt she could take the afternoon off so she'd driven over to the university.

Kim picked up the robot which struggled pathetically in her hand and rather brutally ripped out the battery, severing its heart. It twitched once and was still. 'Not too much damage done,' she said and sighed. 'They never bloody work when you want them to. But come and look at these babies.'

Next to her computer was a huge fish tank. A rustling sound was coming from it. Sandra peered inside. There were two platforms made of Perspex with a thin bridge connecting them. Ants carried bits of leaf from one side to the other, co-operating to pass the pieces over the bridge. They were building a nest on the other side. At the moment it was nearly a foot tall, intricately interlocking and garishly coloured. The 'leaves' were bits of plastic, red, yellow, blue and pink, and the 'ants' were robots too.

'Oh,' she breathed in surprise. 'It's beautiful.'

The nest was made in an almost organic pattern that spiralled up and outwards like a fractal, branching into ferns of pink and blue against the red and yellow background.

'Did they do that themselves?'

'Yup. And look, they work together.'

The ants were communicating by touch, using their thin stick-like arms to guide or pull other ants in the direction they wanted them to go. They all had a small light which they flashed to get the others to follow them.

'Just like real ones!' Sandra said in delight.

'What? Real ones have flashing lights on their foreheads?'

'No, but they do use touch and smell to communicate with each other.'

'You know what? Sometimes when I come in at night, there's patterns in their lights.'

'What do you mean?'

'Well, waves of lights running from one side of the tank to the other. It's like they're . . .'

'Sending messages to each other?'

'Hell, I don't know,' said Kim, suddenly dismissive.

Sandra smiled to herself. It was hard enough for a scientist to suggest that animals could intentionally send messages to each other, let alone robots the size of ants.

'Some time, though, next time we're out on the town

at night, we'll stop by the lab and you can see for yourself,' added Kim.

'Didn't you say you got a new research grant?'

'Yes.' Kim grinned wolfishly. 'Huge amounts of money.'

'So what are you going to do with it?'

'I'm going to spend it on robots that'll eat each other.'

Sandra laughed. 'I bet your head of department loves you.'

'He thinks I'm a real wild child,' said Kim and pulled the band out of her hair. Her black afro exploded out around her like a chrysanthemum opening. 'You can come back and see my predators as soon as they're built. Come on, let's go and eat.'

They went to a balti house. Baltis were two a penny in the Midlands, Sandra had discovered. They were curries served up in cast-iron woks. Balti means bucket in Hindi, and, as one Indian guy had sourly told her, it was like eating your breakfast out of the frying pan. But the food was good and it was cheap although the decor left a little to be desired. Tacky photos of Elvis and John Lennon jostled with newspaper clippings taken from the time of the Raj; the music alternated between Madonna and bhangra and there were fish tanks set into the walls filled with plastic seaweed. Kim immediately switched out of her work mode.

'I would like an orgasm, please.'

'I beg your pardon, madam.' The waiter looked uncomfortable.

'You know, the cocktail, cream, brandy . . .'

'I'm afraid we don't serve alcohol.'

'Oh, you don't?'

Sandra put her head in her hands. Kim did this every time.

'Make it water then. A girl's gotta look after her figure and an orgasm's got a lot of calories.'

The waiter beat a hasty retreat. Kim winked at Sandra and looked brazenly round the room. A couple of men at a nearby table looked as if they might start drooling at any moment.

'Don't,' hissed Sandra, 'you'll only encourage them.' She felt sure Kim's skirt didn't even cover her backside when she was sitting down.

'I have met this adorable man,' she said.

Sandra smiled. She'd heard this before.

'He's tall, dark and handsome.'

'Naturally. Does he work in the robotics department?'

'Give me a break. They're all dead from the neck down. A girl's gotta have some fun, you know. No, he's a builder.'

Sandra groaned.

'Don't be such a snob. I met him at a club. He's taking me out tomorrow. Builders get loads of money, so drinks are definitely on him.'

'Well, do you have anything in common with him? You're hardly likely to be able to talk about DOS and silicon circuitry, are you?'

'Don't need to talk. Girls don't have to. You listen while they witter on about beer and football and EastEnders and then you fuck 'em. Simple. You really need a lesson or two, sweetie.'

Kim seemed to have a whole string of relationships that normally lasted a week at the most. She got excited about whoever she was seeing, no matter who they were, and then it would be finished, she'd be terribly hurt, and it would begin all over again. Sandra thought it must be soul-destroying, but still, it was Kim's life and she got some pleasure out of her one, maximum two, night stands. She would have disapproved more, but Kim's predatory instinct came out as soon as any man showed a slight interest in her; she loved to flirt. Sandra was happy for her at this point, although she knew she'd be consoling her in a couple of days' time and saying yes, she was beautiful and no, there was absolutely nothing wrong with her personality and yes, she was incredibly intelligent. Shades of talking to her sister Lisa, she thought wryly.

'Flirtation is the promise of something which will not be fulfilled,' Kim had once said, 'but there's no harm in keeping a promise once in a while.'

'And how's lover boy?' she asked now.

'Oh, Corin's fine. Busy as ever. We're going to see Lisa next weekend.'

Kim looked at her shrewdly. In the dim interior of the restaurant, she seemed to suck light into herself. Her eyes were so dark that you were only aware of their existence by the faint sparkle on her retina and the twin crescents of white that gleamed above her high cheekbones.

Kim raised one eyebrow and said, 'Let's hope lover-boy can out-flirt big sis.'

That night, after she left Kim, she couldn't sleep. Her room became light very early in the morning and a gaggle of magpies started chattering fiercely. She got up, dressed and went into the garage. She almost always parked her car in the drive because the garage was full of rusting scrap metal and welding equipment. It was one of the few pleasures of living in the Midlands; she'd been able to bring all her junk up from her parents' house and could make her sculptures whenever she felt like it. That first year in London, she'd had to escape back home for the odd weekend and it was always frustrating. She liked being able to make things when she felt like it, rather than having to plan it.

The tongue of flame from the blowtorch was blue and sharp as a lizard's. It licked the metal and the solder melted beneath its touch in a thin silver strip, sealing the edges of the two metal plates together. Her sculptures twisted and grew beneath her hands. There was a sudden movement and she jumped. It was Corin. Her heart started racing. She turned the torch off and yanked the visor up.

'I didn't think you were going to come up this weekend,' she said, smiling. 'How lovely to see you.'

She held out her arms to him and realized how stiff she was. It was way past lunchtime.

'Mind my oily gloves,' she said, as he wrapped his arms around her.

He said nothing for a moment but held her and rocked slowly. Then he said, 'Let's get married.'

She looked at him in surprise and he looked taken aback too, but then he laughed and kissed her deeply and she felt like the solder, molten beneath his tongue.

'It'll have to be when you come back to London after you've finished working at the zoo, of course. Maybe next summer. You'd look fantastic, a long white dress and your short white hair. You could wear bright red lipstick - something a bit devilish.'

'And my boots?'

'Don't be silly, darling, you're going to a wedding, not a demonstration.'

'Don't you want to see what I'm making?'

'Later, sweetheart, later.' He pulled her gloves and visor off and half carried her up the stairs to her studio flat above the garage.

'I was watching you,' he said as her hands travelled the length of his ribs, the curve of his spine. 'I watched you for a long time and you didn't notice.'

She looked up at him carefully. He looked as if he were proud of her, but there was a hint of something else. Perhaps, she thought, she'd hurt his pride by being so engrossed in her welding that she hadn't even seen him arrive. But then she remembered that he'd asked her to marry him and she felt as if her heart would burst. He'd put his hair in a ponytail; she pulled out the band and let his hair slide over their faces, cool and smooth.

He brushed his lips across hers. They were dry as the harsh kites of bougainvillea flowers. He dipped his tongue between her teeth and smoothed her mouth as if it were a pebble, drawing water from dry stone. He slid his hand down her body and watched as her eyes closed and she lay, her head cradled in the crook of his arm. He moved his hands firmly and she writhed beside him like a flailing butterfly that cannot escape because it is pinned down and that, despite the beating of its coloured wings, does not want to fly away.

They made love slowly and leisurely. The afternoon sun glowed through conical flasks and Liebig condensers and cast lozenges of stained-glass light on the carpet. Sandra had pilfered a whole collection of glassware from the chemical lab at the university, connected them up to each other and filled them with coloured liquid. Corin's suit lay in a puddle of black silk, the coloured light highlighting the creases as if they were waves of iridescence in oil. Her sculptures, hanging from the ceiling and the walls, formed a forest of shadows. It was hard to tell what was metal and what was the opposite of light. She watched them dreamily through half-closed eyes over Corin's shoulder. They moved strangely. They were like something organic that had died; it was as if an alien spore had settled in an acorn. It had bided its time and waited and the tree had grown up and grown old, its roots a tangle of twisted bark. And then the spore had germinated and the wood had become transformed into base metal; the alien had taken on the shape of the tree's roots and slowly strangled it, killing it with cold, hard steel. This new creature was not content to lie dormant in the soil and suck up nutrients, it wanted flesh. Unwary animals were trapped in its coils and bled dry. Some of these alien life forms turned cannibal and were in the process of devouring each other, and some of them contained animals that contained animals, a food chain feasting where greed is the fuel that lubricates the parts.

To Sandra they represented nature, raw and cruel and ultimately amoral.

Corin raised his head to look at her, his eyes dark in the dim light. 'I will never let you go,' he whispered as he watched her, his breath hot on the pulse of her throat.

Chapter Five

At any moment, her car might fall to bits, split into two and roll into its constituent parts right in the middle of the M5. Even at this comparatively slow speed, her wing mirror was singing in the wind with the soft staccato chirp of a brood of woodpecker fledglings. Corin had arranged to meet her at Lisa's house; it was easier for him to drive to Bristol from London than meet her in the Midlands and drive back down, he said.

She overtook a lorry which flashed at her. She wondered what they meant, these sudden angry, silent hoots. It seemed to her that it was a language in its own right whose meaning was sometimes plain because of the human intention behind it. Remove that intention and the same symbol was meaningless. But quite often she had no idea what the intention was. Like this lorry driver. Was he saying, "You have no right to overtake", or was he saying,

"You cut in too close"? Sometimes she wished there was a little screen in every car and she could speak to the person in front and her words would appear on his screen. She would say, "What"? or, "I'm sorry", but she knew her screen and most other people's would be full of messages like: "You stupid bitch"; "Get off the road", dumb bastard.

The fields on either side of the road were filled with the first bales of hay: great round Swiss rolls of straw, cream the colour of corn; above the stubble, kestrels hovered on scimitar-shaped wings. A lorry pulled out right in front of her and as she was about to move into the far lane the first car in a line of five tore past. She slammed on the brakes and cursed. Her mind was suddenly filled with flames and the hairs on the back of her neck rose. She had a vision of two cars heading towards one another in dangerous slow motion. She quickly snapped on the tape deck and Billy Idol's raw voice filled the car. It was a recurring waking nightmare, this ballet dance of cars, and were she to allow it to play itself out she would have to pull over until she'd psyched herself up to go back on the road. Lisa and Corin couldn't understand this fear she had. She turned the volume up and 'White Wedding' blared out.

Lisa and Corin were already sitting chatting when she arrived. Anger momentarily flashed through her. Corin, who was always late to see her, had actually arrived early for once. But, she reminded herself, it was Saturday lunchtime and not late Friday night. Both Corin and Lisa gave her a brief peck on the cheek and turned back to their conversation. They were talking about television, surprise, surprise, she thought nastily. Lisa poured out white wine and put garlic bread and nibbles on the coffee table. Sandra ate and drank steadily and watched them. It was as if there was an electric current passing between them, they were so perfectly in tune. They gazed steadily into each other's eyes, lifted their glasses at the same time and laughed together as if they were the most amusing couple in the world and she wasn't even there.

Lisa was only slightly taller than her, but she was wearing high heels and was exactly level with Corin when they stood up. Sandra's heart started beating when she remembered Corin telling her that he had a thing for brunettes. And it was clear that Corin had a lot in common with Lisa. Sandra could make sympathetic noises about how tired and stressed Corin was, how everyone who worked for him was a complete tosser and didn't know the first thing about documentary filming, how the contributors were just not what was required, but she didn't really know, she hadn't been there. Lisa had. When she nodded her head she meant yes, I know exactly what you mean, and she would then recount an anecdote about a similar experience of her own, and Corin would nod and laugh and touch her knee (touch her knee? Well, he did touch people a lot when he was talking to them).

Corin was talking about his Oxbridge researcher and imitating her posh accent, although he did not have to make much of an effort to alter his own voice. 'I asked her to find me two families. I said, I don't want stereotypes of poor people. You'd think that was a simple instruction to follow, wouldn't you?'

Lisa nodded understandingly. She knew all too well about researchers who never did what you wanted them to.

'So what does she come back with? Frank and Mildred, that's who. Frank, typical bloke, beer gut out here, string vest, would you believe. Mildred, well, she's got the original cantilever suspension strapped to her chest, flowery pinny, goes to the shops for custard creams in her slippers. Both unemployed, of course. It's like something out of a bleedin' cartoon.'

Lisa smirked. 'Did she do any better with the other family?'

Corin took a big gulp of wine and shook his head. 'Single mother. Always a bad start. The house reeked of incense. Five - five - girls. Three girls sleep in one room, the other two sleep with their mother in her bed. And there are blue Jesuses - blue for Christ's sake! - with red Christmas tree lights stuck on where their hearts should be, with all this sticky stuff piled up at the feet.'

'What religion are they?'

'Well, they're from India, but, get this, they're Catholic. And the baby keeps eating the sweets, offerings I suppose, when its mother isn't looking.'

Lisa was laughing. Lisa always did this, Sandra thought angrily. Whenever any of her boyfriend's met Lisa they were mesmerized by her looks and charm and her high-powered, supposedly glamorous job, and she flirted shamelessly with them. There was no other word for it, Sandra thought. And she didn't know what was worse: Lisa merely playing at flirting with Corin; or the awful possibility that she was seriously pursuing him. For Christ's sake, she thought, they were at a party together, Corin was a friend of a friend, they hardly spoke a word to each other, and now they're acting like old-time buddies.

She had mentioned Lisa's attitude towards her boyfriends at home once but her mother had simply given her that reproving look and said it was just Lisa's way. She was an extrovert, she liked to talk to people and of course anyone would be impressed by the fact that she was a producer at the BBC (this in hushed tones as if she were a direct descendant of the Messiah), and wasn't Sandra being unreasonable, wouldn't she hate it if her sister was unpleasant to her boyfriends, and wasn't it ungrateful when Lisa put herself out (and she knew how busy Lisa was) to go out for a drink with them or cook them a meal? She'd been left feeling like a complete heel, but a part of her had still protested, although in a quieter and quieter voice. You have to understand that Lisa is different, her mother had said.

It had begun a long time before Lisa started at the BBC. Lisa had always been different. She'd never had to work hard for exams, and she'd excelled at the arts subjects she'd picked. It was a known fact in the Roberts family that Lisa was Talented, Ambitious, Beautiful, Would Go a Long Way and Needed Special Treatment. You have to understand, their mother had said to Sandra, Lisa might seem confident, but underneath she isn't really. You can't tease Lisa; you must always keep telling her how good she is because in the kind of career she'll have she'll need to project confidence. Of course, she has the ability (you have to keep reminding her of that) but confidence is what counts. You have to understand the kind of stresses that Lisa is going through. You have to see things from her perspective.

It was as if the family was divided into two. On one side were Lisa and their father, on the other her mother and Sandra. Lisa is so like me, her dad had said. By which he meant high-flying and talented, Sandra thought. Certainly Lisa was as temperamental and highly strung as he was. Most of the time Lisa and her father got on incredibly well, and Sandra had always felt excluded. Her mother felt her role was to sort out her husband's life and back him up in countless ways, from cooking meals and ironing shirts to working part time as a lab assistant and unofficial secretary in his pharmaceutical company. We have to be sympathetic, said her mother, when either Lisa or her father had a tantrum or walked round in a preoccupied daze barely acknowledging anyone else's presence for hours. Her mother, at least, was proud of her, but Sandra couldn't help feeling that her father was slightly disappointed. After all, it was not particularly glamorous to say to your friends that your daughter was looking at chimpanzees in a zoo, and no, she doesn't really have any plans about what she's going to do next.

Empathy, thought Sandra, was the social glue that bound families together. Her mother had an unlimited supply of it and expected Sandra to be the same. We need to support them, her mother kept saying. Lisa, apparently, didn't need empathy. Compassion helped few careers.

Chimpanzees were just like people, she thought: they lived in large social groups, but within the group they got together in families, they had special friends; some males and females were inherently attracted to others, and some relationships were based only on brute force or Machiavellian manipulation. They had a vegetarian diet most of the time, but they would hunt monkeys and kill chimps who didn't belong to their group. Do chimps have empathy, Sandra wondered, as she looked at her sister engrossed in conversation with Corin.

Now Lisa had put a video on and the two of them were looking at it. At least, the picture was on the screen and presumably there was sound to go with it, but both of them were talking over it. Corin was holding his head, grabbing handfuls of his hair and saying Exactly, and See what I mean? and Lisa was gesticulating with her perfectly manicured hands and occasionally rewinding and pausing so that they could dissect the film, shot by shot.

'Look at that. That's not the sort of thing people want to see on a Sunday night at eight p.m. It's simply not BBC!,' said Lisa. And you would know, Sandra thought bitterly. They said that academics weren't in touch with the real world, but neither were they. They might film the real world, but the very act of filming altered that world, and it was changed even more by the editing process, by adding narration and the drama of music. You could make a picture say anything you liked. They had the audacity to claim they knew what people wanted, they who were so far removed from the people whose opinions they purported to report. Sandra had once said this to Corin. He had quoted Flaubert at her: 'The public wants works which flatter its illusions.' He added that he knew better than they did what their illusions were and how best to flatter them. 'Through our films we'll teach them what they want to see and that in turn will influence what they think they want to see in future.'

They were sitting on the edge of the coffee table, side by side, touching. She saw two cars hurtling towards one another in slow motion. She was watching and she could do nothing. In a strange and graceful dance, they drew nearer, the fronts of the bonnets connected and the metal concertinaed, folding into creases as delicate as origami. In her mind, the faces of the people flashed over the crumpling cars like a slow dissolve, eyes wide, mouths drawn into Os, she felt their fear, their panic, their disbelief. The cars bounced back away from each other and the heads of the people lolled like flowers heavy with dew bending on fragile stalks, snapping, splashing rain like tears. And then the cars exploded into flames, crimson and mustard gas yellow, and she felt their searing pain for one brief moment, felt the heat hot on her face, felt the choking clench of the poisonous smoke and then someone was holding her hand, pulling her away, and her face was wet with salted water.

'Are you all right?'

For a moment their faces looked identical, twins staring at her. They blurred, re-formed, took on definition. Of course, how could they be the same, one had copper-coloured hair and the other was dark. Different. Two different people. They were looking at her seriously. What was it, a dream, a childhood memory? She shivered.

'Yes, yes, I'm all right,' she said, and they glanced at each other and she was transported back to being five years old, and Lisa was a mature ten, siding with her parents, sharing stares with them and saying, 'She can't help being so childish, she's only a kid.' Their look spoke volumes in a language whose meaning she did not fully understand. She was seized with the desire to say, 'What exactly do you mean? What is your intention? Tell me so that I can note it down and I'll know for next time.' It felt as alien as the flashing lorries on the motorway, but tinged with the same sense of contempt and disapproval.

'I had a great time. Thank you very much. It's a real pleasure to have made your acquaintance,' said Corin, kissing Lisa as they left the next morning.

'You've been behaving oddly,' he said, turning to Sandra after Lisa had gone inside. 'What was the matter?'

She shook her head dumbly. He sighed and she wasn't sure whether he was looking at her or his car. She half expected him to say, ''Why can't you be more like your sister?" Lisa certainly wouldn't have stood there mute, she'd have said exactly what she felt in no uncertain terms and she would have been admired for it. Sandra didn't want to upset anyone, and in any case she wasn't really having a legitimate feeling, was she? It wasn't as if Corin had actually said or done anything wrong.

But he only said he'd see her next week in London and gave her one of his goodbye kisses that was like a push.

And she went back to work where in the early morning the lion roared with a sound that should shatter rock and the gibbons were singing to one another, beautifully, melodically, males and females, some the colour of cream, some as dark as coffee; they sang of life amidst trees as tall as church spires when all they had was wire and sawdust.

She was staring intently at Tracey, trying to make out exactly who the chimp was looking at as her dark eyes flickered from Kevin to Ted and back again without focusing on either of them. Suddenly she felt something cold trickling into her shoe. She looked down. A child had dropped ice cream on her foot. She was calmly standing there licking the remaining drips running down the cone. Sandra looked down at the mess on her trainer and angrily back up at the child who only now noticed that the top portion of her ice cream had gone. She started to cry and ran wailing over to the teacher.

'Miss, miss, that girl knocked me and made me spill my ice cream and now I haven't any left.' She burst into heavy sobs.

Sandra scuffed her foot against the side of the chimp cage and let the worst of the strawberry goo dribble off.

'I'm sure the lady didn't mean to do it,' said the teacher.

'I want another one, I want a . . .'

'Well, if you have any more money you can go and buy yourself another one.'

'But I haven't . . .'

Sandra jammed her Walkman on and turned the volume up as high as she could without deafening herself. Corin had said he would like children soon. He'd said that perhaps they ought to start thinking about it when she was writing up her thesis. If they could get the timing right, she would be pregnant, nothing dramatic, just a couple of months or so, when she was submitting and then she would have no ties or commitments during the rest of her pregnancy or when the baby was born.

Sandra hadn't said anything. Corin hadn't noticed. He'd been too busy trying out names. He'd rejected Daisy

Douglas as twee, but thought Jack or Francis would go well. But my name's Roberts, Sandra had thought.

The advantage of having a baby, though, was that you could watch it right from day one and give it tests and things to see if it measured up to all the psychology experiments she'd read about in books. In fact, she thought, if she got pregnant now, she'd have a few months to do tests on it before she had to write it up and it could give her a greater insight into . . . She dismissed the idea quickly. It would be far too hard to look after a baby and finish her thesis and right now the latter was more important.

She looked around at the gaggle of schoolchildren who were moving slowly and noisily away. They almost, but not quite, looked like miniature adults. It lulled you into a false sense of security. And you had to be on your guard, because these were not just baby humans, they were a whole separate tribe. They thought differently, they saw the world in an alien way, and the rules by which they lived had no place in the adult one.

You could stuff a hungry child full of biscuits until she was nearly sick and the child would tell you that she felt sick, that she had always felt sick and she always would feel sick. Hunger was a foreign land for forty minutes.

You could show a child a tube of Smarties and ask her what was in it and like any self-respecting child she would tell you, Smarties, of course. But then you would open the orange plastic cap and tip birthday cake candles into her palm, pastel blue and pink with icing sugar stripes, and when you snapped the lid back on and asked her what she'd thought was in the tube she'd say, Birthday cake candles, of course; I always thought it was full of birthday cake candles.

And Paul? Sandra suddenly remembered the strange little boy with his adult-like face. He seemed to have no concept of other people or how to deal with them. Here was a child, she thought, who was doomed to exist in the present tense. For ever.

Chapter Six

Paul had been swinging. When he came home, someone was sitting on the sofa next to his mother. She jumped up quickly.

'Are you going to be my next father?' he asked.

'I think you'd better go now,' Meg said to the man.

Paul stood and watched as the man gathered his things together. Paul's hands twitched slightly. He put them in his pockets. The man left. Meg was looking at him nervously. He went up to his room and took out his books. Just before Meg went to bed, at around ten, she came up to say good night to him.

'Who was that man?'

'A friend, darling. He came over to have a chat with Mummy.'

'Will you tell me what I'm going to do in the morning?'

'I always tell you, Paul. You'll get up in the morning

and you'll brush your teeth and wash your face and go to the toilet.'

'No, no, go to the toilet first, and *then* wash my hands and face and brush my teeth.'

'Yes, you'll do that, and then you'll get dressed and come downstairs for breakfast and I will make you a boiled egg with soldiers to dip into it.'

'Mother's Pride white bread soldiers toasted on one side only.'

'Toasted on one side only. And I will go to the zoo and you will read for half an hour and then you'll go to school. And after school you'll come home and play in the zoo playground, and have your tea and go to bed.'

'You forgot the reading.'

'Yes, you'll do lots of reading. Good night, sleep tight, don't let the . . .'

'There aren't any bugs,' said Paul matter-of-factly. 'Not in my bed there aren't. Or at least, not ones big enough to be seen with the naked eye, although there are millions of house mites.'

At midnight sharp, he came downstairs as he always did and made himself a hot chocolate. He didn't like hot chocolate that much, but he'd read that it was good to drink before you went to bed as it helped you sleep. He stayed awake until one and then put the lights out. He would get up at six the next morning, half an hour before his mother.

Once he'd had a father. He wasn't his real father; he was just pretending. His name was Darren and in Paul's head he always called him Darren, but out loud he had to call him Dad. Sometimes he struggled to say it and the effort made him stutter. Darren got cross if he didn't call him Dad.

He said, 'The other children have got daddies. You don't want to be called a bastard, do you?'

And Paul replied, 'But a bastard means you haven't got a real father, so I am a bastard.'

And Darren hit him.

He hit him quite often. Sometimes he hit Meg too. Afterwards he'd see Darren holding Meg and saying Sorry, sorry, over and over again, as if it were a song, but then that seemed to make him angry again. Paul wondered if repeating a word made you act like that. He looked it up in his books. He read that you could hypnotize yourself by repeating a word, or else you could go into transcendental meditation. Perhaps that's what Darren was trying to do? The encyclopedia said meditation was good for stress. He mustn't be doing it properly, Paul concluded.

One day he came home in the evening earlier than usual because some of Claire's friends were in the zoo playground and he didn't like to be around strange children. The house was all dark but there were some funny noises coming from the sofa. Paul walked over and turned the lamp on. Darren and his mother were lying on the sofa with no clothes on. Darren was lying on top of her and she had her face all screwed up. He bent closer to see what they were doing. Of course, now he would have known straight away. They were reproducing. But then he was only six.

'Jesus Christ, what's the little fucker doing here?' shouted Darren.

'I . . . he . . .'

'I thought you said he never comes back before eight.'

'He normally doesn't.'

He climbed off Meg and started pulling his clothes on. Meg wrapped her dressing gown around herself.

'Go to your room.'

'Why?' asked Paul. He went and stood by the fire.

'Because I told you to. Do it now.'

'I don't think that's a valid reason.'

'Don't be so cheeky. Get upstairs.' Darren's face was all red and blotched.

'Why?' asked Paul again.

'You don't walk in on people like that,' said Darren, making an effort to speak more calmly.

Paul's hands were starting to twitch. He thought he might overbalance. He moved them further out to help him stay upright. They started to flap a bit. That helped keep him stable.

'And stop waving your bloody hands about.'

His hands started to flap even more. Darren grabbed hold of him and started to push him roughly towards the stairs.

'Why are you doing this? I don't want to go upstairs.' He was shaking all over.

'Darren, Darren, leave the boy alone,' said his mother.

'Shut your mouth. And as for you, you fucking insolent little... Darren screamed and threw him against the wall.

He landed in a heap at the foot of the stairs. For a moment his vision was all black, then it started to clear in patches of red.

'Get to your room.'

'I don't want to,' Paul managed to say.

'You little bastard,' Darren said, and then he was hitting him, over and over again with his belt. He lay on the stairs and listened to the whistle of the leather through the air and the thud as the buckle hit his skin and bit into the flesh. Darren was still shouting and his mother was screaming and pulling at him. The noise was deafening. His ears were ringing with it. He wanted to put his hands over his ears to stop the noise getting in but he couldn't move his arms.

Then the hitting stopped and he saw Darren holding his mother and shaking her. He pushed her against the door and then he pulled back his fist and punched her in the mouth. Paul saw some blood. It collected in a little pool and then her mouth went slack and it poured over and ran down her chin like when you make a mini-dam in a stream and the water builds up behind it and then spills over.

The next thing he remembered was feeling something hot falling on him. He opened his eyes and his mother was bending over him. There was water running out of her eyes and dripping onto his chest. The bottom half of her face was all swollen up and puffy. Her mouth was split and it was turning a livid purple colour. She was dabbing at his cuts with something that smelt funny. He supposed it was antiseptic. She began to put cream and plasters on too. She was making sharp little inhalations as she did this. He wondered why, but it wasn't really that interesting.

'Where's Darren?' he asked.

'He's gone out.'

'What time is it?'

'Twelve thirty. You poor little thing. We'll have you fixed

up in no time.' Her breath came in big juddering sobs as she spoke.

'Twelve thirty? But it's past the time for my hot chocolate. Why haven't you brought it for me?'

'You weren't awake.'

'But I always have hot chocolate at twelve o'clock. You should have woken me up if I'd fallen asleep.' He got up and pushed her away. She grabbed hold of him.

'Hold still, you'll pull your plasters off.'

'But I must have hot chocolate. I'm late for it.' He pushed her again and when she wouldn't let go he hit her in the mouth.

She bent over in a crouch nearly touching the floor, and made a funny noise. He started walking towards his bedroom door. Suddenly she took hold of his arm and spun him round.

'You must never do that. That's not nice, to hurt Mummy.'

'I wanted my hot chocolate and you wouldn't let me go-'

She took a deep breath. 'I must explain this to you. Paul, love, hurting people is wrong.'

'But how do I know what hurts them? And why shouldn't I do it?'

'It's wrong. It's ... it damages them. You shouldn't damage someone. And if you hit someone, or push them, you might damage them. And they may cry or scream, and that's how you know.'

Paul took a step towards her and deliberately pinched her arm hard. She cried out and had to restrain herself from slapping him.

He nodded and said in a singsong voice, 'Damaging people makes them cry, I must not damage other people's bodies.' He nodded again. 'OK, Mummy, I won't "hurt" you.'

He went downstairs to make his hot chocolate. When he got to the kitchen he remembered that he hadn't had any tea either. He toasted some bread on one side and spread Marmite on the untoasted side and added some pickled gherkins. He put slices of cheese on top. He put the two pieces of bread under the grill until the cheese had melted and was just starting to go brown. Then he ate this meal which he had eaten every day of his life for as long as he could remember except 16 November when he was three and a half years old and his mother hadn't been able to get him any gherkins. He hadn't eaten anything then, but he'd cried a lot.

Chapter Seven

'Adults are supposed to hold children's hands when they're crossing the road,' said Paul.

'Sorry, I forgot about that,' said Sandra.

His hand lay loosely in hers, not really holding her at all, and as soon as they got to the other side he let go. They walked along a path through a field full of stubble and thistles the colour of moon dust. Meg had said Paul could go round to her flat for the evening. She seemed almost relieved and yet very worried.

'You're sure you'll be able to cope with him?' she asked anxiously. 'He's very highly strung, you know.'

'I'm sure it'll be fine, and if Paul wants to leave I've no doubt he'll tell me.'

Meg gave a slight smile. She stood at the door of her flat and watched them until they were out of sight.

As they were walking through the village, a car pulled

up beside them. The man in the driver's seat wound down the window and asked directions to the next village. Sandra hesitated, trying to think of the best way to explain the maze of twisty roads.

Paul stared straight in front of him, and said, to no-one in particular it seemed, 'You go past the 126, straight on to the 121, take the left turning by the 122, keep going till you get to the 12, take a right at the 17 and carry on and the village begins with the 29.'

The man looked from Sandra to the boy and back again.

'What do the numbers refer to, Paul?' she asked.

'Lamp posts, of course.'

She tried to smother a smile and then said seriously, 'I don't think this gentleman is quite as observant as you are.' She turned to him and explained the directions. He nodded curtly and drove away. The expression on his face made Sandra feel cold, and as she watched the car disappear round a bend in the road it suddenly came home to her how alone Paul would be for the rest of his life. Now he was little and thin, and could easily be hurt, but when he was older he would still act in such a strange manner, so unconnected from other people. What, she wondered, would the future hold for him? And what, she thought with a shudder, might he be capable of?

She took his hand and said, 'What's the number of that lamp post over there?'

He didn't look where she was pointing. '125.'

'And that one?'

'121. The problem here is that such a lot of the roads don't have them. It's an awful predicament when you want to explain to someone how to get to a place. He was lucky because there are no gaps on his route.'

Back in her flat, she took off her jacket and shoes and socks. Paul dived at her feet and licked her toes. She gave a little cry.

'You have such beautiful toes,' he said, and licked them again. 'When I was little my mother used to paint her toes. Sometimes she painted them silver and sometimes red, and if she was in a good mood she would paint mine too. The paint is like a kind of varnish, it's thick and chips off and then you have to remove it with an ethanol-based substance that can dissolve it. It smelt of apples and that smell on Darren's mouth when he'd been drinking. But I remember when I was even younger, two years old, I think, and my mother used to bath me and she would say, "Paul, what beautiful toes you have," and she would put my toes in her mouth and pretend to bite them and I would laugh. My mother was happy then.'

Sandra didn't quite know how to respond. She put her socks back on and said, 'Paul, would you like to eat something?'

'Is it time to eat?'

'Yes,' she said firmly, 'not time for your cheese sandwich, but time for some biscuits and milk.'

As she was putting the biscuits on a plate and making herself a cup of coffee, he walked round her bedsit, running his hands over everything and humming tunelessly under his breath. When he got to her chest of drawers, he opened the top one and took out a handful of her knickers. He held them up to the light and looked at each pair individually, shuffling them as though they were a deck of cards.

'You have much more grown-up knickers than Claire has.'

'Who's Claire?'

'You must know who Claire is.'

'No, I don't. Tell me.'

'Oh, she's a little girl. We might be friends.'

'Well, are you or aren't you?'

He put his head on one side. 'That depends what you mean by friendship. In the true sense of the word, I don't have any friends. But maybe you'll be my friend.'

He dropped her underwear on the floor and helped himself to the biscuits.

'Does it bother you that you don't have any friends?'

'Yes, yes, it does. I'm like a reed that grows pointedly on its own when actually reeds are meant to grow in big groups, all pointy together.'

'Paul,' said Sandra. 'It's usual that when two people are having a conversation, like us, the person who is listening looks into the eyes of the person who is speaking, and the person who is speaking looks at the listener, but not all the time. They keep looking away. Now why don't you tell me what you're interested in? Your mum says you read a lot.'

Paul's hands seemed to float in front of him. He flapped them once or twice and then put them in his pockets where they twitched a little. He started to hum and then suddenly he stopped and ran clumsily over to her bookcase and began pulling books out in great haste.

'You have lots of books on chimps, and this one's all

about animals.' He looked up at her for the first time from the heap of books. He folded his hands in his lap and started to speak, keeping his hands immobile the whole time.

'I'm interested in biology. All aspects of the human body in particular and especially the heart. The heart has two beats. It is made of myocardium muscle which twitches on its own and then that's co-ordinated by the central nervous system so your heart can beat faster or slower but it will never stop, unless, of course, you have a stroke or a heart attack. There are two cavities in the heart. The one to the left contains oxygenated blood, which is pumped from the aorta to the rest of the body, and when it comes back from the body it has waste products and carbon dioxide in it and it goes up the pulmonary artery to the lungs and gets purified and oxygenated. The artery has flaps to stop the blood running back down . . .'

He talked steadily and looked her full in the eyes, every few seconds deliberately glancing away and looking back at her. He was like a robot who was being taught how to be human.

'Paul,' she said, interrupting him, 'I want to ask you something.' She fetched two of her stuffed teddy bears from the end of the bed. 'This one is called Beanie and this one is Chris. Chris is hiding here, behind the sofa, peeking out,' she mimed the action, 'and he's watching Beanie. Beanie doesn't know Chris is watching and he takes a biscuit, the last one . . .'

'They can't watch each other, they're . . .'

'Stupid stuffed bears, yes, I know, but we're pretending that they can see, we're going to act as if they're people.

So Beanie takes this biscuit and he decides he's going to hide it from Chris, because he doesn't want Chris to eat it. He puts it here.' She lifted up the cushion on the sofa and slipped the biscuit underneath. 'Beanie goes off to read a book out of sight.' She moved him behind the armchair. 'Now Chris comes out and he thinks he'll play a trick on Beanie. He saw Beanie hide the biscuit under the cushion, so he takes it out and hides it here.' She put the biscuit under the sofa. 'Chris goes away and Beanie comes back. Beanie is getting hungry and he wants his biscuit. Where will Beanie look for the biscuit?'

'There.' Paul pointed to the biscuit where it was hidden under the sofa.

The biscuit certainly was under the sofa, but most people would have pointed to the cushion: that was where Beanie had put it and he didn't know that Chris had hidden it. Beanie had a false belief about where the biscuit was. Paul couldn't put himself in someone else's shoes, so he didn't have Theory of Mind. She was puzzled, because he wasn't autistic. This was the classic test for autism. Most autistics did not have Theory of Mind, and many of them were mentally retarded. Paul obviously had a high IQ. And he was learning, or trying to learn, how to look at her. Autistics couldn't do that. Neither could they understand the use of metaphor. Paul did or he wouldn't have described himself as being like a reed.

He was eating the last biscuit and reading her books, completely ignoring her and dropping crumbs all over them. She smiled. He reminded her of Professor Dickinson. His office was strewn with sweet and biscuit wrappers and half-drunk cups of tea. Sometimes in the middle of their discussions he'd get side-tracked by a book or a paper and start reading it. She'd have to remind him that she was still there.

She'd done a bit of research into autism and she vaguely remembered reading something about people who weren't quite autistic. She rummaged through some old science journals until eventually she found the article she was looking for and started to flick through it. It described a rare condition that was like autism. 'Almost all of these people are male: the male pattern is exaggerated to the extreme. In general, abstraction is congenial to male thought processes, and in these individual's abstraction is so highly developed that the relationship to people has largely been lost. To put it bluntly, these disturbed children are like intelligent automata. They have to learn everything-with the intellect. But even those individuals who are very able intellectually will strike one as strange. This strangeness may be perceived as anything from chilling cold-bloodedness to endearingly old-fashioned pedantry.'

She continued reading, becoming more and more uneasy. She looked across at Paul. He scarcely seemed to notice her; he was slowly working his way through her textbooks, building up piles of them on the floor. She rubbed her eyes tiredly. The boy had Asperger's syndrome. It was worse than straightforward autism in some ways because he was clearly intelligent enough to realize that he had no real friends and might never have any. Still, she'd heard that some people with Asperger's syndrome were able to go to university. Their social life was pretty non-existent but at least they could have some measure of independence and in some cases were successful in their chosen field. Usually an academic one, she thought. She smiled slightly to herself. It was hardly a surprise that a person with no Theory of Mind should do well in academia.

'Come on, Paul. It's time to go home.'

He stood up to go and she saw he was clutching one of her books under his arm. It was on animal behaviour. She wouldn't need it for a while so she didn't say anything. She held his hand as he'd requested all the way back to his house. He skipped along next to her in his ungainly way, but said nothing. She didn't mind; she was thinking about what she should say to Meg.

Meg opened the door even before they arrived. Paul ran in without saying goodbye to Sandra or greeting his mother.

'Was he good? Did you manage? He wasn't too naughty, was he?' Her face was white and tense.

'He was fine. Very quiet. He read my books.'

'Yes, he's fascinated by biology, isn't he?' The muscles in Meg's face relaxed slightly.

'Meg,' said Sandra awkwardly. 'Have you thought of taking Paul to see a child psychologist?'

Meg looked tight and pinched, as if she were going to reject out of hand what Sandra was about to say. 'He's a little eccentric, that's all. But he's terribly smart,' she said defensively.

'Oh yes, he's incredibly intelligent. That's going to help him. But he may need some specialist help . . .' She realized she sounded incoherent.

Meg was looking at her coldly. 'Paul and I don't have

any problems. He's a little difficult, but nothing that I can't deal with.'

'Oh, I wasn't saying you couldn't . . . it's just that . . .'

'And Paul is doing well at school.'

Sandra realized she wasn't going to get anywhere. It must be tough for Meg, she thought, especially as she had to bring Paul up on her own. She would hardly welcome some upstart student telling her what she should do.

'Well, I liked having Paul. Any time you want to let him come round, he'll be most welcome.'

Meg nodded and Sandra walked slowly back home feeling downcast. It was Friday: gingerbread day. It was a little ritual she had. At the end of the week she almost always made a loaf of gingerbread. When she was a child, about eight or so, her mother had made gingerbread on Fridays. She remembered the winters most clearly. It would be dark when she came home from school and the walk back was long and cold. But at the end of the road was their house with all the windows lit, and as soon as she opened the door the sweet, spicy smell of hot gingerbread would envelop her. Her mother would come rushing forward and take her coat. She'd give her a glass of milk and a slice of gingerbread, so fresh from the oven that the knife had melted the cake together in places. The scent of ginger was one of comfort and safety, but it was a sad smell in some ways. It was a reminder of the end of childhood.

The smell filled the whole flat. She started to cheer up a little. She hadn't handled Meg very well. She should try again, she thought, maybe take her for coffee and talk to her about it in a more relaxed way. She tasted the cake, she loved the hot, treacly taste of the uncooked mixture. Amazing really, that this sticky goo could (on good days) turn into a light and springy cake. Who ever thought of it? Who could have invented cake, she wondered as she stirred the pan.

While she waited for the gingerbread to cook, she tidied up the mess that Paul had made. There were knickers, books and papers everywhere. Corin had bought her one of the books that Paul had been looking at. He'd given it to her just after they started going out with each other, she remembered, opening it. She soon became engrossed. It was a book of paintings and drawings of chimpanzees. It was such a sweet thing for him to have given her, it was like rediscovering an old friend. Her favourite was a pencil drawing by Gary Hodges of a chimp side-on, hugging herself like someone with her arms crossed. She was staring pensively into the distance and Sandra always wondered what she was looking at. But perhaps the best were the paintings chimps had done themselves. Some were garish, a riot of colour in glorious chaos; others were tastefully minimal: black backgrounds with thick, bold strokes across the paper in red, yellow and white. None of them would have been out of place in a contemporary art gallery.

★ ★ ★

'Desire?' said Professor Dickinson, 'Desire, yes, indeed.' He had stood so close to her she could feel the heat of his breath. He'd picked up a human skull and fondled it. 'Desire is the first step, then comes an understanding of beliefs.' His hand passed over the cranium like the slither of tissue paper slipping from a present.

Had he been helpful? She'd gone down to London to discuss her next experiment with him. She sighed. He made her feel so uneasy. Even thinking about her talk with him was enough to start the muscles in her shoulders tensing up.

He'd said, 'You want to know if chimpanzees can comprehend desires in another chimpanzee and you want to know how to find this out. Mmm. That is a tricky one. Can't ask them, can you?' He'd replaced the skull and sat down opposite her.

'And what are the desires? The desire for food, for warmth, for shelter, for sex. Same as our own really.'

'Surely we have more?'

'What can be more important than food and sex?'

Sandra had blushed and he'd leant forward and tapped her on the knee. 'Man and beast, it's all the same. Tea, my dear?'

She forced herself to relax and swung her arms vigorously as she walked along the tow-path. The movement startled a heron which rose up in front of her and flapped its wings slowly, painstakingly. The canal was heavy with mud, its banks choked with clay and fringed with bulrushes and irises, the leaves sword sharp, the blades collapsing in on themselves. Their dead flowers hung down, finely veined as dragonfly wings; the new seed pods were swelling, the seeds within still green and shiny. Deadly nightshade, the tomato-gold berries held in crows' feet pewter clasps, garlanded the hedges and old man's beard drifted on the wind like a swan-feather fog. The leaves remaining on the trees were gold and green, the green leached to the leaves' arteries, pooling at their wrists: it was as if the roots were sucking the trees' blood to store in vats beneath the soil where it would glow in the dark with the fire and brilliance of bottled Chartreuse maturing for spring.

She wrapped her coat around her more tightly. Every half-mile or so there was a bridge over the canal: a perfect bow made out of red brick turning burgundy along the lintel stones, sprouting moss, ivy with its crowns of lethal black berries and strangleholds of dying buddleia.

She'd been thinking about this problem for weeks and now the idea started to germinate in her mind, no doubt encouraged by her chat with her supervisor. She could ask the chimps if they understood the desires of another. She could build a box with two little drawers side by side and she could put a picture above each drawer. One would be a picture of a chimp wanting something, reaching out for a banana, and the other would be of the chimp not wanting anything, looking disdainfully away from the fruit. She would put sweets in the drawer where the picture of the desirous chimp was, and once they learnt this association she'd test them. She'd put a series of different pictures above the drawers, and if they understood why they were picking the right drawer (because it had a picture above it showing a chimp who wanted something) they'd be able to pick the right drawer in the test. Of course, there was always the possibility that the chimps would be picking up on some kind of clue; for instance, that all the correct pictures showed a chimp with one arm outstretched. She'd have to be very careful to make sure there were no features that were the same in all the pictures, because otherwise, if the chimps got the test right, she'd think they could understand desires when, in fact, all they might be doing was recognizing a shape. But if they really could understand that other chimps wanted things, well, that was halfway to understanding beliefs, halfway to having Theory of Mind. She smiled to herself. It was as if a tremendous weight had been lifted off her shoulders.

Over the next couple of weeks, she built the box out of sturdy wood with nuts and bolts for handles; they had to be strong enough to withstand the chimps' savage yanking. She made the drawers themselves shallow with curving bottoms so that sweets put in at the back would roll to the front and could easily be scooped out by thick chimp fingers. She photocopied pictures of chimps and made four sets of cards showing apes wanting or not wanting brightly painted bananas and balls. If the chimps could understand another chimp's desire, they would have the same degree of empathy as a three-year-old child.

To Pat's obvious surprise, Miss Williams agreed in her creaky voice that if that was what Sandra wanted to do it was fine by her, only she must never, repeat never, put her fingers through the bars.

'You may start with Jessica,' said Miss Williams, opening the outer door for her. She released the catch on the door to Jessica's night pen and pulled it open. Jessica bounded out and raced round the indoor enclosure, scattering sawdust in her wake. She dashed over to the window and pressed herself against the glass.

'I'll be back in half an hour. Wait until I've driven away before you go in.'

She folded herself into her Mini, dwarfed by her two white dogs, and drove back towards her house at the edge of the zoo. Sandra took a deep breath and went in. She placed the box in front of the wire mesh door that led from the chimp kitchen into the indoor enclosure and shut the outer door behind her. It was so hot, even the floor was warm. The small kitchen where she was faced the indoor pen and to her right were the night pens. The chimps were in separate pens and were released into the indoor enclosure just before the zoo opened in the morning. Ferguson was still in one of the pens. He couldn't see her properly, but he was moving about curiously. She got out her check sheet and her bag of sweets and placed the first pair of pictures on the box above the drawers.

Jessica had come over to see what she was doing. She stood and watched and was about to walk away again when Sandra opened the bag of jelly babies. Immediately she started to make little high-pitched grunts of excitement and pushed her fingers through the wire as far as they would go. Sandra tore the head off one of the jelly babies and threw it gently towards her. Jessica scrabbled frantically in the sawdust and bit into the head with relish, squeaking even more and shuffling about on her bottom. She was much smaller than she looked from the outside. She was only six years old, barely a teenager, and if Sandra were to have picked her up, she would have fitted comfortably into her arms.

Sandra put the baby's torso into the drawer beneath the picture showing a chimp with a half-peeled banana in its fist and pushed the box next to the wire. Jessica touched both of the handles and bent down to sniff them. She took one gingerly in her mouth and sucked it. Sandra pushed the drawer through from the other side and Jessica shrieked. She fumbled in the drawer in her haste, trying to get the sweet out, and when she succeeded put it greedily in her mouth and looked up at Sandra with an expression of satisfaction.

Sandra put in another sweet and Jessica opened the drawer, took out the sweet and ran round her cage twice. She slithered to a halt in front of the box and tried to push her fingers through the wire, but she couldn't reach. Sandra decided to start on the training phase properly. She spoke softly to the chimp and explained that she needed to watch carefully. She swapped the pictures round and put another baby torso in the other drawer. Jessica opened the first drawer and peered perplexedly into it. She then opened the other and, grunting happily, removed the sweet. Sandra changed round the pictures and again Jessica got it wrong. After a few goes, she started to realize that the sweet wouldn't always be where it had been. Now, as soon as Sandra had put in a sweet and pushed the box close enough for her to reach, she made a grab for both drawers simultaneously and yanked them open. Sandra tried to pull the box away, but even this diminutive chimp holding on to nut and bolt handles was too strong for her. She gave in and relaxed her grip. Jessica held on to the drawer with the sweet in it and took it out with her other hand. She popped it in her mouth and looked up at Sandra smugly. For the next twenty minutes it became a competition to see if Sandra could pull the box away before Jessica grabbed both handles; Jessica settled for one drawer on the rare occasions when she wasn't fast enough.

There was a crunch of wheels on the gravel and Jessica looked up, pouted her lips and hooted. Sandra picked up her data sheets and went outside.

'She is very smart, you know.' Miss Williams was talking to her before she was even halfway out of the car. 'You only have to watch how she interacts with Ferguson to know how clever she is. He bullies her and pulls her around, but most of the time she manages to avoid him and keep well clear of trouble. That kind of thing shows far more intelligence than anything you're doing with her. Anyway, I shall let you have a go with Ferguson and see how you get on with him.'

She went inside, locked the door behind her, and went into the indoor enclosure. Jessica came over and held up her arms to the old woman. Sandra watched them through the window. Miss Williams bent down and kissed Jessica on the lips. The chimp put her arms around her and then started rummaging in her pockets. Miss Williams produced a bag of crisps which she gave to the young female, who opened it and offered the bag to Miss Williams. Sandra, watching through the window, was astonished.

Chimps very rarely shared their food. Miss Williams took a crisp and patted Jessica on her head, then led her by the hand to her night pen. Of course, she may have been trained to do that, Sandra thought, since she was one of the ones the director had hand-reared and still had daily contact with. Either that or being brought up as a human baby for the first two years of her life had given her some pretty unchimpanzee-like characteristics.

Miss Williams now led Ferguson in on a lead. He was a year older than Jessica and a good deal bigger and heavier. She stroked his head and undid the lead. As soon as the director had left, promising to give Sandra half an hour, the chimp's hair rose all over his body, he pursed his lips and panthooted, then rushed round the cage, slamming his barrel against every wall. Sandra went in. The noise, which had been cushioned by the glass surrounding the indoor enclosure, was deafening and even increased in volume as she encroached on his territory. He ran from one end of the cage directly towards her, trailing his hand on the ground. When he was about a metre away from her he raised his hand and showered her with sawdust and then leapt onto the wire mesh of the door screaming and baring his teeth. She kept looking down at the box and putting out the pictures. She threw him a jelly baby, but he only rattled the metal door and hooted even more. After a moment or two, he climbed down, retrieved the jelly baby and rushed back to his barrel slamming.

She pushed the box, now with a sweet in it, up against the wire. Ferguson shoved the barrel from one side of the cage directly into the door. The metal frame reverberated. He pushed the barrel out of the way, grabbed both handles of the box and tried to drag it through the door. When that failed, he slammed it from side to side as well as he was able given the small leverage he had; his hair bristling, he continued to scream and stared straight into her eyes. The noise and his closeness frightened her but she tried not to show it. With a final wrench, shouting even louder, he rattled the door in his massive hands and then dashed round his cage again. She sighed and swapped the cards round, put in a jelly baby and pushed the box forwards again. Ferguson launched himself towards her and repeated the whole procedure all over again. This time he noticed that one of the drawers had something red and squishy in it. His hair flattened and quietly he removed the head; its stump was gummed up with sawdust and it no longer bled artificially coloured juices. Then slowly and in complete silence he walked round his enclosure. When he approached Sandra again, his lip curled in a malicious sneer and he glared malevolently. He threw a double handful of sawdust at her. Some of it went in her eye and stung. She remained crouched down where she was though, swapped the cards over and started to pull the head off another baby.

Ferguson almost casually reached up the door, rested his feet on the metal bar halfway across it and started to pee on her head. She jumped up and backed to the sink, but he only stared at her intently and thrust his pelvis harder so that his pee arced towards her, wetting her trousers and covering the box, the pictures and the jelly babies. It was at this point that Miss Williams appeared.

'Has he been throwing?' she said sweetly, as if the answer were not obvious. Sandra stood in front of her, hair and trousers wet, covered from head to foot in sawdust. Miss Williams's lipstick was smeared on her teeth and Sandra thought she looked like a vampire who had just taken her last meal and was about to flap back with a cackle into her tomb to hide from the day.

'Come along tomorrow morning, the same time,' she said and went into the cage. Ferguson, almost panting like a dog, had an angelic and benevolent expression on his face as she patted his head and gave him a bar of chocolate.

'Little bastard,' Sandra muttered under her breath.

★ ★ ★

'Hey, guess what,' said Annie, running over to her. She stopped short and said, 'What's happened to you, then?'

'I had a little showdown with young Ferguson. I think he thinks he's superior to me.'

Annie leant towards her and sniffed. 'I think he's right. You can't do that to him.'

'It's not funny,' said Sandra. 'I'm going over to the toilets to get cleaned up, but I think an all over body rub in Dettol might be more appropriate.'

'Yeah, chimps' piss really stinks. You just can't get the smell off your clothes.'

'Thanks, Annie, that's cheered me up no end.'

'I was going to tell you, the new keeper Lee told us about, he's just started today.'

'Oh yeah?'

'He's working on chimps and monkeys. He'll be helping Teresa part of the time. And the best bit is, he's pretty good-looking.'

'I see. Got your sights on him already, have you? You'll be fighting off the rest of the zoo if he's even halfway decent.'

'Not me, stupid. If he's working with Teresa, he might, well, you know, she might fall for him.'

Sandra stared at her blankly for a moment and then it clicked. 'Aah, and if Teresa goes off with him, then you'll have Lee to yourself.'

Twin pink spots appeared on Annie's cheeks.

'You know, you're too good for him. You shouldn't let him . . . oh, what the hell. It's none of my business.'

'I wish she'd die,' Annie said vehemently.

Sandra looked at her in surprise. She'd never seen Annie lose her temper, nor say a cross word to anyone.

'I can't sleep at nights when he's at her house. I lie there an' I think what he's saying to her, what he's doing to her. He could be slagging me off for all I know; he could be telling her she's the best thing that's ever happened to him. I don't know, do I? And I can't say anything 'cos he'll go and spend more time with her if I start complaining. And she's such a nasty piece of work. Why did he have to pick her? Sometimes I think of all the ways I could kill her. Like let the chimps out on her. Serve her bloody well right. He was mine before he was ever hers.'

There was a hard core inside this girl, whom Sandra had always considered to be a bit wet for letting Lee treat her like that. And as she spoke, Sandra could imagine her taking a horrible revenge on Teresa, one of blood and madness born of passion and possession; one which she would never have imagined Annie capable of.

'They'd rip her apart, the chimps - they hate her too.'

Sandra touched her arm. 'Shall we go to the canteen and get a cup of tea?'

'It's not open yet.'

'Well, how about the staffroom, or the Portakabin?'

'Thanks, but I can't stand around anymore. I'll get into trouble. His name's Ryan,' she said dully; and then, with a glimmer of her usual self, 'Put in a good word for Teresa.

I'd choke or crack up laughing if I was to try and tell him what a corker she is.' She smiled and then added bitterly, 'Better get Lee to tell him how good she is in bed.'

The next morning Sandra waited at half past seven for Miss Williams, her box tucked under her arm. She felt slightly uneasy because both Ferguson and Jessica had been let out. Ferguson pounded on the glass with his fist and spat at her. He licked his spit and left tongue marks smeared across the window. At this time of the morning, his behaviour made her feel even more queasy than usual.

Fifteen minutes later Miss Williams drove by and poked her head out of the window. 'Sorry, I'm simply too busy to help you today.' She started to wind up the window.

'How about tomorrow?'

Miss Williams shook her head and continued winding.

'But what about the other chimps? You said I could do this with six chimps. Teresa or Annie can let me in to the other chimp enclosure,' she said desperately.

'No, that's far too dangerous.'

'But you said . . .'

'No. They're too busy and it's too dangerous.'

'But Annie said . . .'

'That's final.'

'All right, all right.' The window was almost shut now. 'When shall I come back?'

Miss Williams unwound a fraction and said, 'You'll need to get in touch with my secretary, but I should imagine not for another three weeks.'

'Three weeks! Three sodding weeks!' Sandra stomped across the Portakabin.

'Told you so,' said Pat calmly, pouring a double measure of whisky into her coffee. She took a mouthful and spluttered all over her rainbow-striped jumper.

'She said I could do this experiment with six chimps - that's a small enough sample size as it is, but it's forgivable in this field - but two? I'll be laughed out of town. How can I possibly present a paper on two chimps?'

'Be thankful for what you've got,' said Pat, adding a bit more whisky to cool her coffee.

'Yes, but two?'

'I saw a paper the other day on deception in primates, based on observing one gorilla.'

'Well, that's ridiculous. That's like me writing a paper about a boil on my bum and linking it to wider implications of boils on the bum for the population at large.'

'How much oil could a gum boil boil if a gum boil could boil oil?' sang Pat.

'Anyway, in another three weeks she may change her mind or she might even say come back in another five weeks. "Ask my secretary exactly when."' She imitated the high-pitched creak of Miss Williams's voice. 'It's important to do it regularly. They'll never learn what they're supposed to do if I don't do it every day.'

'Don't say I didn't warn you.'

'Why don't you go and talk to her? You could tell her how wonderful my research is and how important it's going to be - in terms of publicity for her zoo if nothing else.'

'Me?' squeaked Pat. 'Not on your life. I'd rather hand-feed the lions. And your work isn't important as far as she's concerned. What publicity will you bring her? A bit of academic repute, maybe, but she doesn't like scientists and it won't get bums on seats which is all she's bothered about, boils or no boils.'

'She's only an old woman. What can she do to you?'

Pat refused to answer. She started to remove the baby slugs from their bed of moss with forceps.

'You've sure got a steady hand for someone who's having a bit of coffee with her whisky.'

'Now don't you take it out on me, girl. Besides, I haven't drunk it yet.'

Sandra snorted. Pat sprayed water wildly in the air. At least, she was meant to be targeting a piece of tissue paper to give the slugs a moist atmosphere, but in the cage behind the slug container Zarathustra and Nietzsche, the teenage white rats, started to sneeze.

'If they'd wanted a shower, I'm sure they would have asked you for one.'

'It's not the water they're turning their noses up at, it's the smell,' said Pat pointedly.

Sandra grabbed her bag and slammed out of the Portakabin. She had put on the same clothes that she'd been wearing the day before, thinking she might be in for another drenching. She might as well go home and get changed, she thought, and then continue with her chimp-watching in the afternoon.

She walked along, head bowed, scuffing drifts of leaves with her trainers. She felt she was being watched and looked up sharply. Two beady eyes stared back at her. It was a meerkat. She was perched on top of a stump of wood, standing on her hind legs, her front paws resting on her stomach, peering curiously about. The rest of her family were rooting around in the grass and nettles looking for mealworms, backs arched and stripy as armadillos, pointed tails erect, waving like flags. In the wild, one member of the group would act as a look-out, standing on a log or a stone and surveying the desert sand all around them for the rustle of a snake or the kite-shaped shadow of a black harrier hawk. If she saw something dangerous, she'd give an alarm call, alerting the rest of the group to the threat but also unfortunately attracting the predator's attention to herself. A risky business, this saving of lives.

As she turned the corner of the Meerkats' enclosure she saw a man kneeling on the ground cutting the grass verge round a flower bed with a pair of clippers. The verge was too narrow for the zoo's huge lawn- mower, and this job looked like a thankless task. One might as well use a pair of nail scissors. He'd nearly finished and the grass was short and fine, a sprinkling of cuttings scattered about like green hair. In the middle of the verge was a single wild flower: it looked like a tiny mauve version of a forget-me-not, and he was carefully trimming the grass all around it. He was wearing black Wellington boots, dirty, dark brown checked trousers and a black knitted hat. He didn't look like any of the other maintenance men she knew. She thought he might be Craven, the guy Annie said Paul got on well with.

As she was passing he knelt back to admire his handiwork, and then with one snip severed the flower's stem. He looked directly up at her with his one good eye. The other had a black patch over it. 'Never,' he said, 'be a slave to compassion.'

Chapter Eight

It was getting chilly these days, but the reptile house was always warm with a thick, muggy heat. Inside, the light was muted and the dense air smelt like a jungle sharply permeated with the thin odour of animals. It contained a bizarre collection of ill-assorted creatures. A label scribbled in red felt-tip pen and wrapped in a plastic bag was stuck to each vivarium. By the door and in front of a pool of crocodilians were two baby albino coral snakes. They were pure white and little thicker than hiking boot laces; if you looked closely you could see where their stripes were, paler shades of pale: wedding white and old ivory. But their eyes were red as if a vein had been punctured and the sockets had filled with blood that threatened to spill over at any moment.

To one side of the crocodilians, terrapins hung

immobile in a greasy pool covered by a scum of water-weed. When they poked their heads through the film, they were crowned, braceleted and given a necklace and nose ring in chains of clover-shaped plates. They looked like seedy old men with their loose throats, gulping Adam's apples and shifted cravats in Protestant orange and citron yellow. They had such fine paws, Paul thought, the palms jade green with thin, ebony nails. He wanted to have one of their hands curled round his finger.

He wandered over to the other side of the room where there was a tank of marine exotica, so new that nothing in it had been named. A giant sea anemone of a diaphanous mushroom-cream colour with purple - tipped tentacles cradled a garishly painted clown fish in its arms. A cross between a steamroller and an inflated circus tent, a sea slug patrolled the fake sea floor, huge blobs of colour dripping over it as if a child had slapped paint upon its back with a wide, soft brush; grenadine pink, galliano yellow, blue curagao and coconut-cream white. A fistful of air-filled fingers waved madly from its rear end, undulating in the artificial current, and a shoal of minute fish flashed past like a flicker in the neon light.

Paul walked round to Jeffs door. It was next to the rattlesnake's enclosure. He peered in at the snake which lay in great smooth oiled coils of sleek muscle and fine-boned ribs that trapped its one lung and long string of gut in a curved grip as tight as a bird in a gilt birdcage. A mouse was gnawing at its scales. Prey turned predator. Paul opened the door and went in.

'Ah, Paul. Here again, are we?'

Jeffs trousers, as always, were at half-mast showing the

cleavage in his buttocks, his grubby white T-shirt was untucked and his sage-green jumper with holes in the elbows had shrunk in the wash and barely reached his belly button. A long dark line of hair ran in a straight line down his stomach, broken only by his navel where it congealed into a thicker knot. He'd long since lost his keeper's shirt. Miss Williams had given up telling him to dress smartly. It didn't really matter as he remained in the reptile kitchen all day and didn't emerge until the last visitors had gone. Paul perched on a stool and looked round the room; at least, his eyes roved around, but he was watching Jeff.

Jeff was skinning mice, peeling the pelt as if removing a white fur coat, pulling it a little way from the ribs before taking one arm out and then the other. He wheezed a bit and sucked a boiled sweet with his mouth open, making a small sound like a baby rat nibbling on a nut with soft milk teeth. The naked mice were pink and smooth; their yellowed incisors bit their lips in consternation. Jeff finished peeling one and chopped it up. Paul could hear the grind of small bones. Jeffs knife wasn't sharp enough. He'd told him that last week.

Sometimes he spent a long time talking to Jeff. Jeff would listen and nod and say, You're right there, or My! I didn't know that. Is that a fact? and sometimes he'd add things that Paul hadn't heard of. Paul never paused when he was speaking, but he remembered what Jeff said and wrote it down in one of his notebooks and later he would say what Jeff had said back to him, only then it didn't feel like it had ever been Jeffs idea, and Jeff would nod and say, You're right there. But today he didn't feel like talking.

'Now what have we here?' Jeff wiped his hands on his trousers and pulled down a black bin bag from a shelf. Paul's heart started beating faster. Carefully Paul opened the bag and slid it off the body. It was an iguana. It hadn't been dead long for although its body was cool its limbs were not yet stiff with rigor mortis; he could still move them up and down in a parody of waving. Its eyes were covered with opaque white nictitating membranes; it looked as if the lizard had turned its eyeballs inside its skull in its death throes. Paul ran his hand along the skin. The scales were greygreen and its crest hung raggedly. He liked watching the creatures raise these cocks' combs at each other and gulp crickets, their throats as voluminous as carpet bags, the lining of their mouths the colour of a slit strawberry.

Paul wrapped the lizard up again and left. Jeff watched him go. The boy picked up his khaki - coloured holdall from where he'd hidden it in the hedge between the sea otters and the tapirs; he walked straight up to the tigers and darted between the lions and the cheetah and crawled through a hole in the hedge.

The zoo was like the whole world, the playground and the keepers' flats a floating satellite station attached by a potholed umbilical cord. But this was the universe. This was the space beyond the confines marked out by the boundaries of the hedge. Here the universe sloped away from his feet in corn-coloured stripes curving round an old elm in the middle of the field, swollen with botanical gout, its limbs long since amputated, and here in his corner were tall sycamores shedding leaves like tears, their bark mottled with green scabs and white encrustations as if some foul and alien creature had smeared excrement over their trunks.

As he approached the trees, a cloud of crows rose into the sky, cawed and wheeled away to settle, heavy as stones, amongst the stubble. He crouched down and brushed the leaves away from a bare patch of flattened earth in the centre of die ring of trees. He undid the tie on his holdall and unrolled it. It was a piece of heavy duty canvas with a series of pockets of differing sizes. He took out a little hardbacked black notebook and a pen that was only three inches long and had You can come to the zoo too! written on it in yellow italics. Then he unwrapped the lizard and laid it on its back on the hard ground. In the second smallest pocket were some large nails held together by an elastic band. He removed four and put the rest back. He trapped the body beneath his leg to prevent it rolling over and placed the nail point to its wrist. Then he hammered it home. He shifted his weight slightly and stretched out the leg on the opposite side. He hammered a nail through its ankle and crouched in front of the lizard. He could now nail its other two limbs out and it was there, cruciform in front of him, the tip of its tongue protruding from its mouth, turgid and black.

He took out the stem of his scalpel and fitted it with a blade, then slit the lizard from its throat to the base of its tail. Green plasma welled up where his knife bit into the skin. He quivered with excitement at the ease with which the knife parted the reptile's scales, almost as if he were not moving his hand at all. The layer of fat below put up a bit more resistance, clinging webbily to the blade and stretching like a membrane.

The next layer was muscle. He pinned the flaps of flesh back with thin dissection pins. Now he was working faster, winkling apart the rib cage, the edge of the knife skittering on bone and grating the red away to reveal white cartilage. And here, here was the heart. He sliced through the veins and arteries that led to it, cutting it loose from its moorings as if he were prising out a precious stone. He held it in his fist, wet and leaking reptilian blood down the creases of his palm and over the pulse of his wrist. He laid it on the ground and bent over it, cutting it open. It was a special heart. It had not two but three chambers and the walls were smooth and they bowed to the pressure of his fingers.

He put it tenderly to one side and carried on with his investigations. The gut was all one long tube leading from the throat into the J-shaped stomach, coiling as it became the intestine and ending in the cloaca. He pressed it and ran his fingers gently along his glistening surface, but did not disturb it any more than that.

Above him the crows had returned and were flapping and cawing in anticipation. They shifted their weight from thin twig to thin twig and angled their heads, peering down at him like old women favouring one eye and then the other, trying to focus over beaks as sharp as knitting needles.

The lungs seemed to fall apart of their own accord when he touched the tip of his scalpel to their spongy surface, and they bubbled and frothed; manifold compartments packed with air sacs like blister-wrap. Down near the tail end were a few smooth white globes. He scooped them out. They were as frail as the inner casing of a hen's egg, the sac of silk that tears when the shell is peeled away. He tried to cut one open, but it spewed out a jet of blood and yolk like an eyeball being pierced. Once the pressure inside had dropped, he made a larger slit in the calcareous shell and allowed the gummy liquid to seep into the soil. Inside was a tiny mutated blob, a dollop of flesh with stumpy appendages and a bulging network of capillaries where its eyes would have been. So the lizard was a she.

He wiped his hands and his blade on a piece of lens cleaning tissue and scrutinized her fingers. They were long in comparison with her hands, the skin tough and wrinkled, folded in creases round the knuckles. He cut each one off separately. He took some of the very fine pins he'd used to stretch back the canvas of the lizard's skin, and carried the pins and the fingers over to the fence behind the trees. He nailed each finger into the wood, pushing the pin in with the ball of his thumb. He cut all her toes off and sliced away the hooked nails that were as black and shiny as if they'd been varnished. Then he ate each toe individually, chewing hard to grind down the tiny toe bones. The crows had now settled on the ground between the trees as if they knew that he was at an end.

Chapter Nine

Susie was sucking Jo-Lee's toes. One by one. Ten little piggies. She got bored by the time she reached 'And this little piggy had no roast beef,' and went to try to fondle her brother through the wire. Jo-Lee pressed her face against the window. She stared into Sandra's eyes and put her head on one side, then touched her lips to the glass in a kiss.

Sandra felt tears prick the back of her throat. She wanted to kiss the glass back but there were visitors. She swallowed hard. It reminded her of Asian movies where even kissing was a screen taboo so film directors had come up with a more inventive way of showing it. A sensual heroine would press her luscious and heavily lipsticked mouth against an apple, gazing mistily and adoringly into her suitor's eyes. She would turn the apple round and pass it to him and he would ardently smother the apple's skin with his own lips. It was thought highly shocking when it was first done.

Two weeks had gone past since she had last seen Miss Williams and she felt as if her mind were an edifice concocted from icing sugar which might, at any minute, crumble or melt. She was still carrying on with her behavioural observations but what would happen when she finished them? What would she do next? What if Miss Williams kept acting like this? What if she wouldn't let her continue her experiment? She felt sick to the pit of her stomach and her hands trembled at odd moments. This was the most important thing she had ever done and it was going to be screwed up, stillborn before it had taken its first breath. It was crucial for the animals to be taught on a regular basis, otherwise they'd never learn, and they'd get tired of doing the experiment and bored with jelly babies. If they were only allowed to practise choosing the right drawer now and again, she'd never get on to the really interesting part: showing whether they could understand desires or not. And understanding desires was the first rung on the ladder that led to the dizzy heights from which one could survey the mind of another person. This was the first time anyone had ever tried to ask another species what they thought.

In fact, she reflected, it wasn't just the most important thing she'd ever done, it was vital work in its own right. People had to recognize how closely chimps were related to them, not just the abstract theoretical concept but what 'being related' actually meant. The tragedy of it was that she was being thwarted in such a petty way. Corin said she shouldn't worry, it would all turn out for the best (without saying what the best might be), and then proceeded to tell her all about Frank and Mildred and Anjou and her daughters whom he just called one to five because he could never remember their names.

Pat said, Yes, it's hard isn't it, but that's what it's like for the rest of us, and she then reeled off a whole series of anecdotes about Miss Williams, ranging from her docking someone's pay by half for three weeks because he'd left a green parakeet outside and it had died, to a story about her tearing down the curtains in one of the keeper's flats because they weren't the ones Miss Williams had originally hung there. Since Pat had been at the zoo for fifteen years, she had an endless supply of examples.

I don't want to be told that it will all be all right, thought Sandra, and I don't want to be told that it's been so much worse for other people. I just want some sympathy. And I want someone to wave a magic wand and make it better.

Instead all she could do was carry on collecting data on gaze direction, working her way through the hours and the animals, trying not to think in the spaces between and going for long walks by the canal. There was a nip in the air and she had to wear fingerless gloves and a jumper and raincoat. She didn't know what to do with herself. The sick feeling had settled for good. She thought she exuded it like a cloud and it trailed vaporously behind her.

One of the things that had helped, though, was a card from her father which arrived that morning. That in itself was a rare event; usually he just signed his name at the bottom of her mother's letters, and he almost never spoke to her on the phone. Her mother must have told him she was having a tough time and perhaps, she thought cynically, asked him to send the card. But even so, it was a great comfort to her. It said, in a typically terse way, to keep her chin up and that her mother and he were proud of her. It made her feel a bit better. Maybe he did grudgingly admire what she was doing, or, at the very least, her tenacity.

Now she could understand why all the keepers' major topic of conversation was when Miss Williams might die and how to hasten her departure. What was so unbearable was being completely powerless in the face of Miss Williams's irrational decisions. Perhaps, she thought, people felt like this in the past when they were tied to the land and were caught in the thrall of the weather, of plagues of pests and freak deaths of crops and animals. Then they must have thought the gods cruel and unfathomable. But the irony of it, she thought, was that then they worshipped this capriciousness and now the keeper tribe hated it with a hatred that was very nearly palpable.

There were far fewer visitors now, which was a blessing. The end of the sun and the holiday were like a tourniquet; the arterial flow of people stopped and only leaked in gouts occasionally as they spurted into the zoo in one-off coach loads and clotted round the tea bar.

As usual, when she wasn't worrying or writing down what the chimps were doing, she slipped into a fantasy about the wedding. She saw herself walking gracefully down the aisle in a riot of white lace and watered silk, trailing ivy and stargazer lilies from a huge bouquet, the air dense with the smell of cold stone and incense. She would glide across flags dusted with lozenges of red and orange, turquoise and pink flowers: an overspill of light from the stained glass windows. She would stand before the priest and her breath would cause her veil to tremble and she'd listen to Corin's footsteps as he came closer, and then, brushing her slightly, but enough to make her arm tingle, he'd be beside her. He'd wink at her with his crazy eye and turn to face the priest, his expression solemn again. They would start to kneel, she'd tuck up her skirts and then, By God, Sandra, she'd hear him hiss and her blood would run cold, you've got your trainers on.

She sighed and looked at Tracey, who was picking her teeth. Somehow, she could never get past this bit. Try as she might, she could not imagine him slipping a ring on her finger, and as far as the reception went she could only picture him drinking copious quantities of champagne and getting aggressively drunk, which, she thought, hardly needed much imagination at all. And she knew she'd be in a cold sweat the whole time, constantly picking up her skirts just to check she hadn't left her trainers on or they hadn't miraculously reappeared.

She suddenly became aware of another person, further down the corridor. She looked at his reflection in the glass. He was a young man in a keeper's uniform and he was standing staring into the cage. She couldn't stop looking at his image. There was such pain in his face. He rubbed his temples tiredly and when he looked up again, his eyes met hers. It was as if they had spoken out loud.

'I think we ought to get some toys and things in here,' he said, gesturing to the cage, which was bare apart from a couple of dismantled cardboard boxes and some shredded bedding paper. 'That is, if the chimps' sudden playing activity won't disrupt your data collecting.'

She wasn't sure whether he was being sarcastic or not. She said carefully, 'I'd prefer it if they were doing something. I've just spent an hour watching Kevin and he sat there and stared into space the whole time - apart from looking at his toes now and again.'

'He had to peer over the top of his balls, no doubt,' he said in a deadpan way.

She giggled and he smiled widely, showing big, even, white teeth.

'Ryan O'Friel,' he said, walking over to her and extending his hand. 'At your service. Sandra,' he added when she put her hand in his.

His hand was very warm and large and he held hers fractionally too long. She was taken aback. Keepers round here did not behave like this. They barely acknowledged her presence and when she smiled or waved, they generally grimaced or looked the other way. Still, he was new. He had blue eyes, collar-length black hair and a little beard, quite closely shaven.

'You don't have much of an accent,' she said.

He pushed his baseball cap to the back of his head and said with a thick Southern Irish lilt, 'There's queer few people living in Lancashire with a touch of the brogue.'

She smiled and said, 'So that's where you're from. I've never been that far north.'

'No, well, you'd not get past customs without your passport.'

He stuck his hands in his pockets and looked over her

shoulder at her notes. 'Gobbledygook's what it looks like. What are you doing?'

She took a breath to start to explain, but he said quickly, 'No, don't tell me.'

She looked up at him sharply.

'I'd like to know properly. I know what you scientists are like. You dismiss us poor bastard lay- people with a couple of baby words or else you go on for hours in jargon because you don't want to be misquoted or misunderstood. I'll treat you to a cup of tea in the salmonella bar one of these fine days and you can give me the quotable version.'

She laughed. He could only have been here for a short time and yet he already knew that there had been an outbreak of food poisoning in the cafe a year ago. Pat and Annie were her sources of gossip, but on any other subject apart from Miss Williams the other keepers were strangely reticent. She couldn't imagine Teresa telling him. She wouldn't have thought it proper, much less funny. Perhaps Annie was going to foil her own plans and accidentally make Ryan fall for her.

He raised his hand, palm towards her, and walked away.

When the three weeks were up, Miss Williams announced that she was still busy. Sandra grouched round the zoo for another week and then was unexpectedly cornered by the director in her Mini who shouted above the rattle of the decaying engine that she could start again the next day. Sandra rushed over to tell Ryan. She knew if she went to see Pat she'd only sniff and say, That's Miss Williams for you. Unpredictable. She'll think of some excuse to stop you again; and Sandra would be deflated. Ryan, she knew, would be enthusiastic. She'd taken to having tea with him in the hot chimp kitchen in the afternoons while Teresa was in the staffroom. By that stage in the day, Pat was usually either comatose, incomprehensible or insensible. She'd held her up at broom point the other day and demanded a toll of a shot of whisky or she wouldn't let her in to use the kettle for coffee. When Sandra had protested that she didn't usually carry measures of liquor around, Pat had slammed the door in her face and locked it from the inside.

She'd told Ryan about the desire experiment and how frustrating it was that she couldn't do it. He'd just said, Bummer, and nothing else, but she could feel his sympathy. She was thankful he hadn't tried to make her feel bad by telling her how well off she was compared to others, or said it would all be OK. He'd patted her on the shoulder when she left.

'Come and look at this,' said Ryan excitedly, pulling her into the chimp house when he saw her. 'Look.' He pointed proudly.

In the cage with the large group of chimps was a brightly painted toy car with outsize plastic wheels, a lime-green body, and grape-purple bumpers. Ted was holding it in one hand and running it along the floor. She almost expected him to be making broom- broom noises as well. The others were gathered in a semi-circle around him, looking at the car curiously. Joseph had climbed down from his mother and was stretching his arms out to the car, whilst his mother was standing nervously behind him, her hands hovering above his back, ready to pull him out of danger if need be.

Ted turned the car over on its back as if it were a beetle, grabbed it at either end and pulled. The muscles in his arms bulged but the expression on his face didn't change. The plastic went white at the joins and then ripped. He delicately removed the body of the car and proceeded to pull the wheels off.

Sandra started to laugh at Ryan's outraged expression.

'I bought that with my own money. I put it in with them not ten minutes ago and look at it. It looks like it's just been down the M25.'

Ted had now succeeded in pulling one of the wheels off and was holding the other in the palm of his hand, a long bit of wire protruding. Joseph patted the bust-up pile of plastic and moved it experimentally along the floor.

'Oh shit,' whispered Ryan. Ted was now picking his teeth with the wire. There was blood on his thumb. 'My life will not be worth living. Come on.' He grabbed her arm and pulled her down the corridor. When they got outside he gave her a little push. 'Go and stand outside the enclosure and call them.'

'Ted,' she shouted, 'Tracey.' She felt stupid.

Ryan emerged from the kitchen a couple of minutes later with a washing-up bowl of tomatoes and oranges. 'Here, chuck these over. I'm going inside to shut the inner door when they go out. Holy Joe. They'd better get their asses outside before the witch comes back.'

Teresa? Did he mean Teresa? Quite an apt description,

she thought, smiling, but an opinion that was going to disappoint Annie. 'Ted, come here,' she yelled and threw some tomatoes over the wire mesh. There was a steep trench with a moat on the other side of the wire and at first her tomatoes didn't make it and bobbed around in the water like buoys. Tracey and Sally wandered out and started stuffing their faces on the fruit that had floated towards them. There was no sign of the others. Her arm ached. She threw the last orange in and leant against the wire mesh.

Ryan came out, his brow wrinkled. 'Bastards. You try to be nice to them and what do they do? Poke their eyes out and blame it on you.'

At that moment, Ted hobbled out on three legs, still clutching his wire. Ryan swore. The others followed, apart from Chrissie and Joseph who stubbornly refused to budge. Joseph was engrossed with the garish carnage on the cage floor and Chrissie sat next to him with a bored, but presumably maternal, expression on her face.

'I can't even get the other wire and bits of car with them in there. Incriminating bloody evidence, that's what,' he muttered.

Ted scooped most of the fruit up and squashed half into his mouth and half into one hand. He hobbled back in again, tomato juice dribbling from one fist, blood from the other. In the distance Sandra could see Teresa walking towards them, hair swaying, eyes cast down.

'Oh brother.' He looked at Sandra and then winked. 'Better go and meet my maker. Shame to get sacked after such a promising start. You better make yourself scarce. You know what she thinks of students; she'll think you egged me on and I'm such a soft bastard I'll carry the can.'

She nodded. 'I expect you're right. Good luck.'

Jessica was so excited to see her clutching her box in one hand and her bag of jelly babies from Scoop 'n' Save in the other that she started running round the cage, squeaking wildly. Sandra was touched at this show of affection, but reminded herself that it was probably induced by E numbers.

'You, my dear,' she said to the chimp, 'are going to get so many cavities in your teeth, you'll be sorry.'

Jessica stretched her fingers through the bars while she waited for Sandra to get ready. Jessica wasn't just smart, she was eager, and it only took a couple of days before they were able to go onto the second pair of cards. But here she had a few problems. The first set had shown a chimp about to eat a banana with a gleeful expression on his face, and one who was not interested. Jessica had to pick the chimp stretching for the fruit. Of course, for the first two pairs of cards, the chimps only had to learn that choosing one card out of the pair would always mean they found a sweet in the drawer beneath that card. But Sandra was hoping that, by the time they got on to the third pair, they would understand why one card was the correct one. The second pair showed a chimp wanting to be groomed. He lolled back with one arm raised like a Roman emperor, gazing into the middle distance, and a female, practically crouched underneath his armpit, was about to groom him. Jessica reverted back to her grab-both-drawers strategy.

As for Ferguson, her hopes of his calming down and accepting her were dashed. Absence had not made his heart grow fonder. She had to brace herself to go in with him and look unconcerned as he savagely pounded on the metal door, hooted and tossed his barrel round the room. It was quite amazing how much a young chimp could store in his bladder and release over the course of half an hour. The day she managed, eventually, to get his score above a random level and they were able to try out the wants-to-be-groomed pair of cards, he opted for a new tactic. He ran towards her at a slow lollop, but instead of gathering handfuls of sawdust to spray at her like stinging confetti he rolled some of his shit in the sawdust, as if he were dusting a dough ball in icing sugar, and threw that at her. It was quite soft and spattered over the door, splashing down upon her and the data sheets.

She gritted her teeth and put another jelly baby head in the box. She felt like walking out, but that would only make him worse.

Ryan was looking gloomy too when she saw him. He was pushing a wheelbarrow full of fruit and vegetables over to the primate house where he worked when he wasn't helping Teresa.

'Oh, hello,' he said, putting the barrow down. 'Taken up carpentry, have we?' He sniffed the sawdust. 'Maybe not. Aren't many carpenters smell like that. I won't ask.'

'What did Teresa say?'

'She was very snooty about it and said that perhaps I shouldn't be left on my own with the chimps, but that she wouldn't tell Miss Williams about it this time. Two-faced little bitch. Miss Williams drives over the next morning, gunning down the path in her Mini as if she's the reincarnation of Senna, Teresa skedaddles sharpish and

Miss Williams proceeds to harangue me for the next fifteen minutes about the dangers of toys, my general ignorance and untrustworthiness and how I'd only been given the job out of the goodness of her heart. Not much good in that clapped-out organ when it comes to pay day, if you ask me.

'Anyway, I said they needed something to play with - after apologizing profusely and doing a bit of the old grovelling - but she says, "they've got a climbing frame and cardboard boxes."' He imitated her for the last bit. 'Then Teresa comes back and when I says, What did you go and tell her for? she acts all innocent and then goes off in a real old stonk and wouldn't speak to me for the rest of the day.'

'How about hiding their food for them? You could put fruit in the grass outside and peanut butter and things in the trees and scatter sunflower seeds about. They'd have to search for their food and it would be a bit unpredictable like real life.'

'What, a jar of Sunpat stuck in the fork of a tree? That'd look a bit daft.'

'No, you noodle, just a small bit smeared into the cracks so they'd have to get it out with twigs the way they fish for termites in the wild.'

He nodded. 'Yes. I think it's a good idea. The only problem is Jo-Lee and Susie. They only go outside for half an hour and then they're inside getting bored the rest of the time.'

'We'll have to think about that one. Maybe you could persuade them to put the whole group together.' She hesitated and then said, 'Perhaps you shouldn't push too hard now. Miss Williams is funny. Once she dislikes someone, she doesn't change her opinion of them. You don't want to lose your job before you can start to do any good.'

'That's not important. It's the animals that count,' he said sharply and picked up the wheelbarrow.

She followed him to the primate house; she had to do some data collection on the spider monkeys anyway. His broad back seemed set in reproach. She trailed along behind him. Men were so temperamental.

By the time they reached the enclosure, he seemed to be in a good humour again. He pushed open the kitchen door and, making his fists into a trumpet, heralded the coming of the sprouts.

'Daft thing,' said Dawn, the monkey keeper. 'Get in here and get them veggies chopped.'

Dawn was brusque but not quite as sour as some of the others. The closest she ever came to smiling was when Ryan was around. Sandra wondered how long it would be before he was fighting off hordes of women.

One of the monkeys was pregnant. Dawn said she'd give birth in a month or so, but it was hard to predict accurately. When Sandra had first started watching them, she'd thought there were eight males and two females, which was a highly unusual social system. One of the males looked rather fat too, but in an odd sort of way. After watching them mating a couple of times, with the female behind pumping into the male, she realized that what she'd thought were males were actually females. The fat one was pregnant and their pink 'penises' were elongated clitorises. She'd told Kim who'd shrieked with laughter and said, 'But honey, don't you know, mine's that size too?'

She only gave Jessica and Ferguson ten goes each on the test cards. This was to see if they'd understood what was going on: why they were meant to be choosing the desire card. Any more trials and they might start to learn blindly which was the right one to pick without any understanding of why. Jessica scored seven out of ten on both pairs of pictures. Ferguson got three out of ten and five out of ten right. Because five out of ten right would be random, Ferguson's scores were simply at a chance level.

She was frustrated. She felt that he was actually intelligent but wasn't trying, and he certainly hadn't been concentrating. And Jessica's results were disappointing too. For them to be accepted on a scientific basis she should have got at least eight out of ten right.

'Maybe it's your pictures,' said Ryan, but he wasn't being completely serious. 'How does desire work? I mean, how do they know that other people want things?'

'Imagination,' said Sandra. 'Children start to imagine what it's like to want things and then they imagine what it's like to be another person and for that person to want something. It's the ability to put yourself in someone else's shoes. Like empathy - you can show empathy that's compassion, or you can show empathy where you understand what another person feels. You need to be able to imagine what it's like to be that person or you can't empathize with them and you can't understand what they might be thinking.'

'What about compassion? Surely you need imagination

for that too.'

She shrugged. 'Maybe. You could just remember what pain was like for you and then assume that's what it's like for everyone else without imagining anything.'

'I think therefore I am is the statement of an intellectual who underrates toothache.' He smiled. 'Milan Kundera. I'm not sure that we can remember pain very well,' he said after a pause. 'If we did, we wouldn't be able to function. We'd be paralysed in case we hurt ourselves. We'd never take risks. Kundera also said "Suffering is the university of egocentrism." I think compassion is the ultimate in imagination. Imagination for your own pain since you can't remember what it was like, and for someone else's pain because you can never know how their pain feels.' He shrugged and grinned. 'But then, what do I know, I'm only a monkey keeper. Stop looking at me like that.' He gave her a nudge and she blushed and smiled.

'You're wasting your brain here,' she said.

'I don't think so,' he said coolly. He seemed to wrestle with something inside himself. She could almost see the tug-of-war taking place on his face. When he turned back to her, he said casually, 'There's not much to do round here.'

She smirked and then tried to wipe the smile from her face because she knew what he was going to say and didn't want him to know she knew in case it made him uneasy. But in his straightforward way he continued without a pause, 'You know that's a preamble to asking if you'll go out for a drink with me. And you know where I live so it's up to you.'

He was about to walk away but she grabbed his arm.

'I can't make most weekends. I usually see my boyfriend.'

'Typical,' he said gruffly. 'Why are no good-looking women footloose and fancy free? Ach,' he said, putting on his Irish accent, 'only an eejit like himself would keep having to ask that one.'

'So you don't want to go for a drink, then?'

'Don't be so daft. I don't just want to get in your knickers - although I wouldn't say no if you offered - but you're not about to, so any time during the week. Well, maybe Monday to Wednesday. I'm trying not to sound too desperate here.'

She laughed in spite of herself. Corin would heartily disapprove, she thought. Not just that she was going to go out for a drink with someone who was attracted to her, but that he would be so blunt about it. But Corin wasn't able to see her this weekend. Too busy. She missed him with an ache that was tangible. She missed the feel of him, his milky smoothness in her arms, the way his skin seemed to unroll before her as she ran her hands along his torso like a chart to an exotic land printed on raw satin: there would be a mermaid and there would be dragons; there would be fish leaping from unknown waters and a compass sailing on its own circumference without reference to a magnetic north that was yet to be discovered.

Ryan was staring at her. His eyes were very pale and there was a dark ring of indigo round the iris. 'Monday then. I'll come round and pick you up.'

'Monday it is.'

She left him and as she was walking home, thinking of Corin, she thought, well, why not go and see him? He had to film at the weekend, he'd said, but she could still have an evening with him. Suddenly excited by the prospect, she ran the last bit home, showered and got changed. Her hands were trembling.

It was almost ten by the time she reached his house. The traffic had been a nightmare. She had played her Billy Idol tape over and over. It was dark and cold and she was hungry but she smiled when she thought how his expression would change as she walked in. She crossed over the street humming 'Don't need a gun'. His flat was on the top floor of one of those old, tall, thin houses in South Kensington. She reached the landing slightly out of breath and, as she was about to put the key in the lock, she thought she heard voices. She leant forward and pressed her ear to the door. Sure enough there were voices. Perhaps it was the TV? But it wasn't the TV. She could clearly hear Corin's voice. She wondered who he was with. Now he was laughing and someone else was laughing with him. A woman. He hadn't said that he was going to see anyone tonight. She stood and listened.

Corin was talking about his film. 'Frank was completely apoplectic. He was yelling "Don't you ever do that again, you little bastard," at his son Bobbie, holding him by the hair with one hand and hitting him with the other. Bobbie was screaming "Let go, let me go". Jesus, you know, you just don't know what to do. You can't interfere - and I wasn't filming at the time. I know it goes on - Mildred is always covered with bruises - but I can't show it because as soon as the camera's running they're on their best bloody behaviour and nothing happens for hours. I'm bored out of my tiny mind.'

There was a sympathetic murmur. Lisa, thought Sandra with a sinking feeling. Her whole body went completely cold and her stomach felt like lead. She was just about to push open the door when Corin started speaking again. Sandra stood transfixed. She had a strange feeling that this was the kind of thing he would not have said to her.

'. . . so I think that's the best way round it. I annoyed the hell out of Frank all day - he was ready to explode. Dave, the cameraman, was clutching his mobile the whole time as if it were King Arthur's sword and was going to save his skin. So I've got him on the edge of his chair, stewing in his own juice, and then I kicked over his tea. Well, you wouldn't believe it, he was effing and blinding - "You come into my fuckin' house and drink my fuckin' tea and say you're from the lah-dee-dah BB fuckin' C and you can't even sit still and give a man some peace" ... I made sure that Dave filmed him from a low angle and then later on I filmed Bobbie when he was watching "Child's Play" — poor kid, looked scared out of his wits - and I also filmed Bobbie running down the hall when he was late for school. And . . .'

'You'll edit the three sequences together.'

'Yeah. Exactly.'

'Like a wildlife film. That's what we do when we're trying to film a hunting scene. I mean, you know it happens, everyone knows it happens. It's the law of nature, big things eat little things, but they don't always do it on cue.'

Sandra stared at the wood grain of the door. She felt sick.

Lisa was still talking. 'Interesting, interesting technique. I'm not sure many - if any - directors have done that with what's supposed to be a fly-on-the-wall documentary. Do you think you'll tell anyone?'

Sandra didn't want to know the answer. She unlocked the door and went in.

Corin was half out of his seat, a startled expression on his face. The only light in the room came from a candelabra she'd made him for Christmas, the strands of steel all gathered in one central bunch before spreading out in a circle. On the table in front of him were two balloon glasses full of brandy and sitting opposite Corin was Lisa. Corin grinned and opened his arms. She allowed herself to be embraced, but her body was stiff.

'What a surprise. I didn't expect to see you here. You do know I'm filming tomorrow, don't you?'

'And I expect you didn't expect me.' Lisa smiled sardonically.

Sandra could only shake her head dumbly.

'Lisa was down here doing a recce and I said she could stay over. Cheaper than staying in a hotel.'

'Of course, I'll claim it on expenses anyway,' said Lisa, looking at Corin and they both laughed. 'So, little sister, how's it going with your chimps?'

'Fine,' said Sandra woodenly.

Lisa glanced over at Corin as if they were exchanging looks about an unruly child. 'I'm going to hit the sack and leave you two guys to smooch away. I'll see you before I go - I don't have to leave particularly early, unlike lover boy.' She kissed Sandra on the cheek and then Corin. Even her goodbye kisses are like Corin's, she thought. Small shoves with lips.

As soon as Lisa had left the room, Corin said, 'Wait a sec,' and rushed after her. She could hear them talking in low voices in the hall. She stood feeling forlorn. For some reason both glasses had lipstick prints on them. She heard Corin say good night and give Lisa another kiss. She felt as if she might cry.

Corin came back in. 'What's the matter?'

'Why didn't you tell me she was staying?' she asked.

'I didn't know until this afternoon. For Christ's sake, she's your sister.'

'I'd just like to have known, that's all,' Sandra muttered sulkily. Somehow Corin always made her feel in the wrong.

'Bath time,' said Corin. 'Stay right here.'

He ran a bath that was oily with Fenjal and filled with a mountain of bubbles. He lit a couple of candles and brought in a bottle of champagne in an ice bucket.

Corin always had champagne, bottles of beer and film spools in the fridge, but not much else. He undressed her like a child and poured her out a glass that was as frothy as the bath.

She drew a cross on his body with bubbles. It was meant to be a kiss. 'Sorry for being silly,' she said, smiling at him. It was an effort to smile. Was she imagining it or was he being distant? Was he seriously put out because she was disturbing his tete-a-tete with her sister? And shouldn't he have been more pleased to see her? There was a funny ache in her chest and it felt hard to breathe.

'I've forgotten already,' he replied and she could feel the champagne coat her tongue with a caress as icy as a thousand needles.

But it wasn't long before he'd managed to down most of the bottle and was splashing about, glancing at the clock on the wall and saying he had to be up early and shouldn't they go to bed? Sandra closed her eyes and sighed inwardly. Her bones felt weary. Where did Corin get his manic energy from? Why couldn't he just relax?

'You stay a bit if you want,' he said, towelling himself vigorously, when it was obvious she wasn't about to leap out after him.

She lay in the warm water. The temperature felt like body heat; if she lay still she couldn't tell where her body ended and the water began. The bubbles had mostly melted and their shadows grazed her skin like clouds casting clouds upon the sea. The ticking of the clock reverberated against the wall; an Edgar Allan Poe heart sealed into the brickwork. Lisa was in the spare room. She felt a little jealous. It was in that room that Corin had first made love to her. She told herself not to be so silly. Finally, she heaved herself up and got dried. She padded wetly into the bedroom.

'Can't you dry your feet?' asked Corin irritably. He was always telling her off about it.

She picked up the T-shirt she normally wore in bed at his house. The neck of it smelt funny. She sniffed it deeply.

'What are you doing?'

It didn't smell clean and fresh like the freesia perfume

she wore. In fact, the cloying floral scent was totally foreign. She took another deep sniff. It didn't smell of her, the mixture of perfume, rosewood soap, Body Shop deodorant and peach and apricot cream that was her composite odour. Her heart started to beat faster. Surely not. Surely he hadn't slept with her? In her T-shirt? In this bed? That was absurd. But . . .

She was holding the neck of the shirt over half her face now, breathing it in lest the smell evaporate before she deciphered it.

'Sandra?'

Then suddenly she remembered. Last time she was here Corin had given her a massage. He'd rubbed some cream on her, the remnants of a bottle belonging to an ex-girlfriend. She relaxed her tense body and grinned at him with relief.

'Absolutely nothing,' she said and stretched out her arms to him. In the dim light, the colours of his eyes seemed to separate, the brown became almost black, the green lighter. As she started to drift asleep, the image of his eyes slid into a vision of a narrow stream, its surface bright green with water-weed. Two small boats built like miniature Viking ships were floating down it, one after the other; they left lines of black water bare of water-weed and they were filled with flames.

Chapter Ten

The crow had been electrocuted. Half its feathers were daubed with red mud like war paint. It had flown into the elephants' electric fence. He cradled its head in his palm and felt the fragile bones of its skull. The body lay along his arm and the wings opened and hung down on either side like a corvid Christ. Its eyes were glazed. They reminded him of the swollen sultanas coated in honey that his mother put in apple pies. The ones on top of the pie got burnt, and when you stuck your fork in them they were hollow.

Paul put the bird in his rucksack and went to retrieve his holdall from where it was hidden in the hedge by the otters. It was amazing how light the bird was. All those feathers. They were just a bluff. He crossed the magpie field: the early morning frost had made the grass stiff and the blades fenced ineffectually with his shoes. Jeff was standing on the far side, waiting for him. He was holding the handles of his wheelbarrow but he put it down when Paul reached him. The barrow was full of frozen fish and the bottom of it was a mess of congealed blood with ice and clear scales floating in it like toe nails that had been ripped off.

'What've you got there?'

'A dead bird.'

'My reptiles not good enough for you?'

'I need something else to practise on.'

'Practice makes perfect, boy. But what will you be when you're perfect?'

'I don't know what you mean,' said Paul.

'I've got a surprise for you,' said Jeff, clearing his throat and changing the subject.

'What is it?'

'It wouldn't be a surprise if I told you, would it?'

Paul said nothing. Jeff bent down to him. 'Please come and look at my surprise.' His breath stank and he reeked, a sweetish smell of unwashed decay laced with the savage aroma of dead fish. 'Please?'

'Why?' asked Paul. 'I'm busy.'

'It won't take long.' Jeff stood up, suddenly brisk and authoritative, as if he knew that Paul would do anything as long as his sentences had the ring of commandments written in stone. His hand on Paul's shoulder shook. He steered him towards the Enchanted Forest.

'Now,' he said as he pushed him inside, 'you go round as you always do and I'll see you here afterwards.' He locked the door behind them and disappeared into the gloom with a lumbering skip, his cluster of keys jangling like a gaoler's.

It was dark inside the Enchanted Forest and the corridor was narrow. Paul waited for his eyes to adjust to the dimness. He could hear the small stirrings of small animals. Still clutching his rucksack, he started walking down the corridor. The walls were heavily painted with emulsion, slapped on by Pat's thick brush, canopy running into understorey, understorey dripping into undergrowth. The greens, he knew, were all greener than green and the flowers were larger than life. He ran his hand along the wall and felt the forest in clots of paint, reading its history like Braille. His fingers came to the edge of the first flap which said 'Lift me'.

Things that were written down were bound to be right. He lifted the flap and behind it was a pane of glass and a bush baby, blinking with large, dumb eyes. It regarded him balefully and chewed mournfully on some kind of pellet as if it were singularly unappetizing and it was having difficulty swallowing. He let the flap drop.

The next one was a window into the fruit bats' cage.

They hung upside down, completely wrapped in their wings like membranous shrouds. One unwrapped slightly and poked his foxy head out. His eyes blazed in the dark. He unfurled his wings some more and yawned, licking his lips. The small, sharp canine teeth glinted and Paul noticed how extraordinarily long and thin the bat's tongue was.

Paul stood quite still. He could hear something being scraped across the floor. The scraping stopped. There was hoarse breathing. He carried on opening the flaps. Past the hissing cockroach, he opened what should have been the giant African scorpion but it wasn't in its glass tank. The glass wasn't there either. Instead there was another kind of creature that hung limply at the back of the box and gleamed whitely. He put his hand in and touched it. It was soft and warm. He held it a little more firmly in his hand and squeezed. There was a sound like the wind moving in the trees. He felt it harden. He took his hand away and watched as it grew and expanded, curling up towards the roof of the tank like the scorpion's arching tail.

He touched it again, just with the tip of his finger, and it was completely hard and knotty. There was a low moaning sound. A bead of liquid glistened at the end of it. He put his finger to it and when he pulled it away a viscous thread stretched between his finger and the thing. He smelt it. His hand didn't smell nice. He was disappointed the scorpion wasn't there. Normally there was an ultraviolet light and the scorpion glowed bright orange. All scorpions fluoresce: green, orange, yellow, violet. Bored, he turned away and headed for the door.

It was locked. He waited beside it. He put his hand in his rucksack and felt the crow, the fragile heat that was almost extinguished, the dry oiliness of its feathers, the mud, crumbling beneath his fingers. Eventually he heard footsteps. They approached him slowly, drawing nearer and nearer. He took his hand out from his rucksack.

Jeff stepped out from the shadows. He was staring at him. He walked over to him, so close that his smell enveloped Paul. He reached out and brushed his cheek with his hand. The keys jangled and the door swung open a little way. Paul slipped out and ran across to the otters.

The sun was a ball above the horizon. Too late, too late,

he sang in his mind. But still, this was only a practice. He could afford to continue even though the flames of sun no longer burned the frost from the edge of the field. The old dead elm was like a finger pointing at the sky. Too late, too late, the crows all cried.

He pegged out the bird and the cawing crows had cannibalism in their eyes. Carefully he sliced away the feathers at their shafts in a line down the bird's stomach. He was getting good at this, he knew. He looked in his biology textbook before and after, and now his dissections resembled the ones in the old, yellowing book, its paper thick, its anatomical diagrams drawn in spare black lines. He cut open the bird and parted its ribcage, severing the delicate connection at the wishbone. Slowly the bird's heart beat once, twice and then stopped.

Chapter Eleven

It was freezing. She felt she had never been so cold in all her life; she couldn't stay outside for longer than an hour at a time. She dressed in so many layers of clothes she could hardly move. Her fingers would become too cramped to write and it hurt to walk on her numbed feet. She imagined them glowing palely in lumps of ice like frozen fish arriving at a fishmonger's. Every half-hour she would rush to the toilet and hold her hands under the hot air dryer until her flesh had softened enough for her to carry on recording data. More often than not she'd lift her boots up to the jet of air but it did little good other than to thaw the rubber soles somewhat.

The keepers walked round, heads bowed, hugging themselves. They had to stay outside for far less time than she did, but they felt the cold more since the kitchens and cages were warm. Even at home she could get little respite.

There was only one gas fire for the whole flat. The shower and bathroom were downstairs at the back of the garage and there was no heating. Her breath froze in front of her face and it was torture to have to take her clothes off. And if that was bad, emerging hot and glowing from the shower was even worse. She'd shake uncontrollably as she put her clothes back on and ran upstairs to the only slightly warmer flat.

It was dark when she got up in the mornings and by the time she arrived at the zoo the sun would be a red ball on the horizon, its rays spilling on grass iced sharp as daggers, their edges slick with clotting blood. Once she woke and every branch and twig had been coated in ice. She walked to work beneath a white sky, wheeling crows and white trees that glittered sinisterly in the grey dawn. By about lunchtime the following day, the ice had started to melt and shards of ice, moulded in the shape of branches, came raining down and shattered on the ground, littering the roads with broken bottles; nature's answer to the Night of the Long Knives.

She'd taped a programme about chimpanzees and decided to show it to the chimps at the zoo. She wondered whether the chimps would recognize their own kind. They had, after all, never been in the wild, and the only chimps they'd ever known were the ones they shared a cage with. Surprisingly Miss Williams had raised no objections, probably because she'd allowed the chimps to watch TV in her house when they were babies, Sandra thought grimly. It was as cold as ever, the sky dark grey. She rested her small TV and video on an upside down dustbin and fed the extension cables in through the window of the chimp kitchen. Ferguson and Jessica came to see what she was up to. Ferguson, in an amicable mood because she was outside and no longer trespassing on his territory and annoying him by hiding headless jelly babies in drawers, simply nodded at her kindly and swung on the wooden bars in his indoor enclosure. When she turned the TV on he came and stood in front of it, pressing his freckled nose against the glass and leaning his elbows on the window sill like a schoolboy. Jessica sat cross-legged on a wooden beam a discreet distance behind him. Sandra switched on the tape.

The section she had chosen to show them was a hunt. Chimps will often hunt colobus monkeys and mangabeys. They don't run blindly after their prey; instead a beater flushes the animal out as the others silently encircle the hapless victim, and then they rush out from their ambush, exploding into bloodthirsty cries, and rip the monkey limb from limb while it's still alive. They divide out the spoil, the females and infants begging for food, the males squabbling amongst themselves. Whoever gets the head scoops the brains out and wipes the inside of the skull with a leaf to soak up the last cranial juices. They also use leaves to wipe the blood from their faces.

She watched Ferguson through the glass. Superimposed upon his face was the reflection of the frozen world, a line of bare, dead elms like broken teeth in a mouth whose tongue had been cut out, and the brilliant green lushness of the rainforest. Fleeting images of the tense chimps gazing into the canopy were moonlighters from another world chasing through ghost images of winter. The shadow chimps stole across his face and the hairs on Ferguson's head and back slowly rose and he pouted his pink lips slightly and silently. The hunters tore after the colobus. Black and white and alien to them, it struggled between its captors, and they screamed and fought and dismembered it. Their faces were lathered with blood and the monkey's oil-paint-blue intestine coiled onto the forest floor. Ferguson could not take his eyes from the screen. It was as if he were mesmerized.

Finally, he tore himself away and ran frantically round the cage, no longer able to contain his emotions. He came back and pressed himself up against the glass again. His hair bristled even more and he swayed from side to side. After another minute he let out a shriek and ran round the cage before returning to the hunt. Some ancestral memory had been resurrected in this chimp who had never seen anything other than the inside of his cage and English soil: his blood pounded at the sight of blood and his hands itched to kill.

It was only when she turned off the video that he looked up at her and stared directly and searchingly into her eyes. As his hair wilted, she felt the hairs on the back of her neck prickle. She shuddered. Perhaps showing a volatile young male chimp a hunting scene had not been such a good idea. She turned away from him and hastily unplugged the TV.

At lunchtime she went over to the chimp house and tapped on the kitchen window. There was a sticker on the glass saying '*Homo sapiens*: the world's most dangerous creature'. Ryan's head popped up from below it and he mouthed, 'Be with you in a minute.' He disappeared again.

She stamped her feet in a vague attempt to get the circulation going, but it was too painful. He came out, clutching his lunch box, and they half ran, half staggered through the bitter cold over to the Portakabin. Sandra held her hands over the steam from the kettle until it started to burn her.

'Tomorrow's the big day,' said Ryan, putting a stick insect on his face.

Pat was cleaning them out. She picked up a female, disentangling it from a withered bramble stalk, and added it to the one on Ryan's cheek. It walked into his hair, bent its spine back, and held its front legs up in praying mantis fashion. The first insect stuck one of its legs out and swayed from side to side as if it were a twig blowing in the wind, clinging to Ryan's skin with its other five sticky toes. Sandra shuddered.

'What do you mean?' asked Pat, whose alcoholic frenzy seemed to have calmed down somewhat now that there were almost no children around.

'Jo-Lee and Susie are going to be released into the main group.'

Pat snorted. Sandra smiled at him.

Ryan turned to her and said, 'They want you to be there tomorrow. If you're standing around collecting data you can keep an eye on them and get me or Teresa if anything goes wrong.'

She nodded. 'Fine by me.'

'I'm sure it will be all right. Susie has always got on reasonably well with the others - she is Chrissie and Ted's daughter, after all. Jo-Lee's the one we have to be worried about and Chrissie has stopped trying to attack her through the wire - she's really the only one who hated her.'

He removed the stick insects which were still clinging tenaciously to him and put them on some fresh bramble, although it didn't look much more alive than the pieces Pat had removed. He made coffee for the three of them. Sandra watched him covertly. He had strong, masculine hands. She couldn't help comparing them to Corin's which were thin and almost spidery: pianist's fingers. He was about the same size as Corin but looked bigger since he was broader and more muscular.

'What on earth are you eating?' asked Pat incredulously.

'A vegan pepperoni, avocado, alfalfa and humus sandwich,' said Ryan through a large mouthful.

'I didn't know you were a vegan,' Sandra said, and when he gave her a smile full of food she added, 'I thought they were supposed to be skinny.'

'You calling me fat?' he said in mock belligerence, swallowing. He turned to Pat. 'So tell me, Patricia, what have you been up to lately?'

'Last night I was hunting wolves.'

'Aye, an' you drained more than one whisky bottle dry.'

Pat took a swipe at him. 'Cheeky bastard. Let's not exaggerate. One wolf.'

'Go on.'

'Do you know about the wolf project?'

They shook their heads.

'A former member of the military's anti-terrorist squad took early retirement and is breeding wolves in Templar forest. It's not that far from the zoo, actually. Have you been there?'

'I've walked a little way into it, but it's private, isn't it?' said Sandra.

'Yes. You can follow that footpath straight through it, but you can't go anywhere else in the forest. He lives in the middle with his wolves and one of them is tame - her mother was killed and he brought her up. Normally he walks her in the wood and I've told him time and time again that it's not one of the world's most clever things to do . . .'

'What's wrong with taking her out?' interrupted Ryan. 'Presumably she's cooped up in a cage the rest of the time.'

'Yes, but wolves aren't dogs and you can't really treat them as if they are. The inevitable happened last night. She realized - took her bloody long enough - that she's stronger than Martin and she just ran off into the forest, trailing her lead behind her. Martin thought she'd come back straight away but she didn't. Eventually he drove over and picked me up and the two of us wandered round the forest until three a.m. calling for her and brandishing bits of meat like psychos.'

'Did you find her?'

'Yes, finally. She came back to Martin and played catch with him - she'd come up close enough for him to grab her lead and when he made a lunge for it she'd run off. She got hungry in the end, though, and allowed herself to be caught. I don't think he'll be taking her out again. At least, I hope the man's got more sense.'

'How many does he keep?' asked Sandra.

'Two females and a male. One of the females is pregnant.'

'What's he got them for?' said Ryan.

'He wants to release them.'

Ryan snorted. 'That'll go down well with the villagers.'

'Wolves used to roam all over Britain and most of Europe. He wants to reintroduce them in Scotland - the only chance he's got is to try on the Island of Rhum since then they'd be self-contained.'

'Well, he can't really do it anywhere else - he'll come into conflict with the farmers,' said Sandra.

'Rubbish,' Ryan replied. 'Wolves are shy creatures. If they had the whole of the wilds of Scotland to run around in, they'd hardly hang round people with shotguns. Besides, there are so many deer they're culling them. The wolves would keep the population down easily.'

Pat nodded in agreement. Sandra felt a little uneasy but she didn't say anything.

'I'll take you both along to meet Martin and his wolves if you like.'

Ryan hesitated and then said slowly, 'Yes, I'd like that. It would be useful.'

Sandra looked at him strangely. She wondered why he hesitated when a moment before he'd been so keen to see them released. Surely he couldn't be scared? She looked outside at the miserable wintry day and decided that she really couldn't bear going out into the cold again - especially when she was going to have to spend the whole of the following day in front of the chimp house. She'd bring a hot water bottle with her, she decided, but now she was definitely going home.

When she got up and announced her intention to the others, they looked at each other and with one accord sighed heavily and said, 'Bloody students.'

'Thanks for the sympathy, pals,' she said, and left.

She didn't go home, though. The thought of her cold flat was too depressing for words. Instead she drove over to Birmingham. Much as Kim liked to give the impression that she was wild and spontaneous, she was a creature of habit. At the time when most people were going home from work, Kim went swimming. Sandra looked at her watch. If she hurried, she'd just catch her. She didn't particularly like swimming, but the thought of a pool full of warm water suddenly seemed very appealing.

She loved the feeling of the water against her skin, sliding into its warm, intimate embrace. She watched Kim launch into a slick front crawl. She wouldn't stop until she'd clocked up a hundred lengths. Sandra was content to amble slowly about until the water no longer felt warm and then get out. Just watching Kim made her feel tired.

Most of the women in the pool were old; their flesh hung in thick folds, heavy and sagging, and even in this watery environment they did not seem buoyant. The lot of a swimming pool attendant was an odd one, she thought. It must be one of the most boring jobs in the world, and yet strangely fascinating: they sat in their high chairs and the human body in all its shapes and sizes was paraded in front of them. Did it disgust them? Did it put them off sex? Did they think, Dear God, that's how I'll be when I'm old? Did they lust after those whose clothing, pared to the bone, revealed their perfect figures?

There was a thin white girl swimming in the lane next to her. Her hair was piled on top of her head, and even though she was doing the crawl she craned her head out of the water like a tortoise stretching and not a hair was wet. She placed the palms of her hands flat on the surface of the water with the utmost precision, and with each stroke her heels bobbed to the surface, white as the empty egg-cases of cuttlefish.

To take her mind off the boredom of physical exercise, she thought about beliefs. The ability to understand that another being had beliefs, and, moreover, that their beliefs could be mistaken, was the crucial hallmark of having Theory of Mind. Her desire experiment hadn't worked particularly well, but that might have been a failing of the experiment itself rather than because the chimps lacked an understanding of desires. What she needed was an experiment that was unambiguous. It was a tough one. How do you communicate with a creature that has no language to find out if they understand that you have a mistaken belief? But as she swam, she thought she might just have an idea.

She was having a cup of tea and a sticky bun in the cafe above the pool when Kim flung herself into the chair next to her.

'Well, don't overdo it, honey,' she said, eyeing the bun with misgiving.

'I need the fat to keep warm,' said Sandra, biting into it. 'Some of us have to work in the great outdoors,' she added with her mouth full.

Kim made a face. 'Hardly the Serengeti, is it, sweetie?'

'More like the Antarctic.'

Kim snorted and then said, 'Talking of zoos, I've built one of my own.' She arched one eyebrow. 'It looks rather good, actually. Care to take a look?'

They walked over to the lab. Kim explained that in five days' time there was going to be a press conference. Not for anyone of great significance, just science writers and local hacks, but they might get the odd assistant producer from the Open University if they were lucky. Kim thought it was a hoot and was going along with the head of the department's plans because her robots were going to be the first thing anyone saw. Big tanks had been put in the lobby for the ants and her insects and there was a much larger enclosure for the robot prey, which Kim called her rabots, and their predators. Next to the rabots drinks and nibbles would be served and then people would be shepherded through to see what the head referred to as more serious work.

Kim stood in one corner of the lobby and Sandra was aware that she was watching her as she walked between the tanks. Her footsteps echoed hollowly. In the semi-dark the ants were winking, waves of their semaphore messages flashing from one end of their tank to the other. The nest they'd been building had grown larger, the pattern more complicated. The insects cast spooky daddy-long-leg shadows and made curious plucking, sucking and scratching sounds as they negotiated the walls and ceilings of their giant glass tank.

Sandra shivered. 'They're just like stick insects at the zoo, always wandering around looking for a way out. It's as if they're feeling every side of their glass case and thinking "We must be able to escape somewhere", but they can't find out where and they're too dull to realize they've been over every inch of their tank already.'

She moved on to a pen with a big sign saying 'Rabots'. Kim beamed proudly.

'Ah, so that's what you've blown your postdoctoral budget on.'

The pen was open plan like a nursery crèche; a barrier about half a metre high hemmed in part of the corridor. Bits of sawdust and grit were strewn across the floor. In the middle of the pen was the sun, a bright light set in the floor, and radiating from it were the feeder stations for the rabots to recharge themselves.

'The rabots are solar powered,' explained Kim.

Lush green potted plants had been placed here and there inside the enclosure, along with a scattering of pebbles and bits of driftwood.

'Didn't realize you had such a talent for interior design,' said Sandra with a smile.

The rabots looked as if they were cobbled together from bits of Lego, and scuttled busily about like tinker toys. The predators, also cylinder-shaped and just as haphazardly put together, or so it seemed, moved in a more measured way. They were distinguished from the rabots by a large protruding metal spike. Sandra succumbed to her natural fascination for observing behaviour. Within a couple of minutes, she was kneeling on the floor staring intently into the pen.

The rabots seemed to spend a lot of their time in groups. They sucked up the grit and sawdust using some mechanism attached to their underside and left clear trails of clean floor behind them, but they could switch this device off, as Sandra discovered later. It was almost as if they were acting as a herd, she thought. They moved in unison, cautiously clinging to the shelter of the plants and the driftwood. The two predators were next to each other at the far end. They hardly stirred. After some time the rabots edged away from their cover and started to head for the sun. One of the predators moved slightly and immediately some of the rabots froze. The others broke away and skittered back to the comparative safety of a spider plant, stirring up the dust as they went. In their fear, they stopped hoovering. The group that most needed to recharge their batteries picked up courage and continued towards the sun. Both the predators started to move this time, but instead of going straight for the rabots they slid sideways in opposite directions. The rabots advanced, less worried about the predators' movements. When they reached the sun, they jostled each other for the position furthest from the predators. They connected little devices just above their wheels to the feeding stations and started to hum as they recharged. The predators inched closer. One of the rabots broke away and beetled back to the others cowering beneath the pot plants.

Suddenly both predators increased their speed dramatically and homed in on their prey. There was pandemonium. The rabots struggled to withdraw their charging devices and bumped into each other in their haste to escape. One rabot wasn't quick enough. The predator that reached it first sunk its long metal proboscis into a hole in the rabot. There was a thin whine and the rabot buzzed frantically. After about thirty seconds the rabot became completely still and the predator removed its blade and disappeared into its lair at the far end.

'Amazing!' said Sandra. 'So the predator's stolen the electricity the rabot charged itself up with?'

'Yes.'

'Is the rabot dead?'

'It's lifeless, not dead. I can repower it. But what often happens is that when the next lot of rabots comes down to recharge, one of the others gives it a quick boost from its own batteries - not much, but enough to allow it to get to the sun and mainline some more for itself.'

'That's incredible. How altruistic. It's like vampire bats. They feed on blood and if one of them can't feed for three days, she'll die, so what happens is that one of the other females will regurgitate blood for her.'

'How disgusting.'

'It's fascinating. These groups of bats live together for up to thirteen years and they have special friends - two of them will share blood over the years when things go badly for them. So does that happen with the rabots? Are there special friends who charge each other up? And do any of them cheat - like not charge up a rabot that's charged them up?'

'I've no idea. I thought you might know.'

'Me? How could I? I've only just seen them.'

'Well, that's why I brought you here. The thing is, there's a lot of behaviour in the rabots - and in the robot ants - that wasn't programmed. It's evolved. I simply put in the basics to allow them to function. It's taken fucking months to get all the bugs out.'

'But why couldn't you program it? I mean, you could write a program, allowing them to recognize that one of their companions wasn't moving . . .'

'Honey,' drawled Kim, 'I might be a genius, but I'm not that clever. If you knew how backward robotics really was, you wouldn't say that kind of thing. Even recognizing the difference between a square and a triangle is tough as hell to program. And anyway, that's boring. If I'm going to create robots that do the housework, they have to *want* to do it. They have to be selfishly motivated - and selfishness can lead to altruism.'

'Yeah, I guess so. The bats do it because they'll get fed by their friend when they haven't had a meal for a few days. They're not doing it because they have an overwhelming urge to show empathy.'

'Exactly,' agreed Kim. 'So if I knew more about what's going on and what kind of behaviour you could expect when you haven't pre-programmed it, it would help me design the next lot of robots. And I wondered whether someone who has training in animal behaviour could do it. I don't know anything about how you collect data . . .'

'Well, you follow one focal individual for about an hour at a time, and every minute - or whatever time scale you want—'

'And I don't need to know,' Kim interrupted. 'What I want to know is whether it's a really barmy idea or whether it would be feasible and interesting for someone to do. I mean, obviously I think it's a brilliant idea, but would anyone else?'

'Oh, yes, definitely.'

'Well, in that case, I'll put in a proposal for a grant. Do you want to work on it with me? I can do the robot bit and you can write more of the animal side of it.'

'Sure,' said Sandra enthusiastically.

'Doing anything after your Ph.D.?'

'I've no idea. I don't know what I want to do.'

'Don't you want to stay in academia?'

'I don't know,' said Sandra slowly.

'Well, if we get the grant, it would be a great opportunity for you. Think about it.'

Sandra nodded. Kim was looking at her impatiently. She knew what she was thinking. Kim had always known what she wanted to do and she had a very low tolerance for those who were less decisive.

'OK, sweetheart, get off your knees,' she said, snapping out of her serious mode. 'I'm not leaving you with the animals all night. We've got some heavy drinking to do and it's closing time in half an hour.'

The following day Teresa let Jo-Lee and Susie into the main enclosure with Ted. Normally they were allowed an hour together before the youngsters were packed back into their own area. He usually displayed for a couple of minutes, swaggering around as if the cage were a person who had to be reminded who was boss. Once he'd reclaimed the space the night had stolen from him, he ate a few sunflower seeds, strolled round outside and climbed up a tree to peer in a lordly fashion over the rest of the zoo. At this height he was level with the giraffes' heads. He ignored the others, occasionally cuffing or patting Susie gently.

This morning was no different except that Ted displayed for longer. Ryan and Teresa were tense and he could feel it. Jo-Lee skirted carefully round him and Susie darted in front of her, diving between her legs in her haste to get outside. Sandra was watching and he was showing off. He calmed down shortly as if nothing had happened and came over to tap the glass with his fingernail. It looked as if he were beckoning her.

The order in which the chimps were to be released from their night pens had been very carefully chosen. It had meant that the night before they had to be put to bed in the reverse order and it had taken Ryan and Teresa two hours to do it. The chimps had refused to go where the keepers wanted them to.

Tracey was released next. She bounded in, gauche as a puppy, half slithered into Ted and ran excitedly round Jo-Lee. She and Jo-Lee had been let out together recently, just the two of them. Tracey had expected to dominate since she was from the big group, and she had been full of naive enthusiasm. But Jo-Lee had been hand-reared and she was used to getting her own way. She didn't know chimp etiquette. It wasn't that she ignored the possibility that Tracey might be dominant, it was just that the thought never crossed her mind. Within minutes Tracey was cowed and fawning. She skittered about Jo-Lee, half wanting to play, half afraid she might be rebuffed and a little uncertain about this change to their routine.

Jo-Lee eyed her condescendingly, but she was a young chimp too. She put out her hand and stroked Tracey in a gruff way, half shove, half stroke. She started to pull Tracey round the cage by one arm. Sandra had decided that she couldn't use this data in her study as it might be abnormal, but she collected it anyway and made copious notes in the margins. It might make a 'short communication' to a zoo journal, she thought, and she could always write it up with

Ryan. It would do him good, she concluded, to be able to use his brain and get a publication out. He'd been very vague about what he'd been doing up until now. He'd said something about college, travelling and voluntary work, but he was good at evading questions. His answers melted like coconut cream at the touch of a finger, and it was only later that she was aware of how easily he had fobbed her off, distracting her attention with bright baubles of conversation. Strange, she thought, when he was normally so blunt.

Jo-Lee and Tracey were still playing in a wary kind of way when Kevin was released. He slithered into the cage and half sat down on his haunches. He scratched his head perplexedly and stared about worriedly. He would probably spend the day pulling his hair out, she thought; he was a nervy chimp and he hated change. Ted yawned, displaying all his teeth, in Kevin's direction, and the subordinate chimp cringed. Tracey, as if to show Jo-Lee just where her allegiance lay and to remind her that she was an outsider, dashed over to Kevin. The two of them embraced like long-lost lovers. They kissed briefly and Tracey started to groom him. Jo-Lee, jilted, watched them. A normal chimp would go her own way and ignore them. But not Jo-Lee. After only a moment's hesitation she sidled over to them. She didn't make any gestures to ask them to play, she simply tried to tug Tracey away. Tracey let herself be pulled. Perhaps she wasn't used to being so much in demand. Kevin watched her go and halfheartedly picked his teeth.

Susie followed Tracey and Jo-Lee around, trying to get in on their game, and like the teenagers they were they did not take too kindly to a little snot-nosed kid trying to muscle in on their act and remind them that barely a year or so ago they'd been like that too. They pushed her away and held her head to the floor. Jo-Lee only used Susie for friendship when she had to. Susie went to sit in Kevin's lap and he held her awkwardly with the embarrassed pleasure of a bachelor who's been presented with a baby.

Sally came next. Kevin stretched out his hand to her and made a gesture of subordination, but she swept past, regally ignoring him as if she were a dowager duchess, her large and saggy belly swinging. She greeted Ted and then froze at the sight of Jo-Lee. Tracey seemed to shrink in on herself and crouched closer to the ground, looking fear-stricken. Tracey was the most junior female, hence her friendship with Kevin who, despite being a male, was below everyone in rank except Tracey. And Chrissie and Sally were best friends and Chrissie hated Jo-Lee. It was as if Tracey had been caught red-handed fraternizing with the enemy.

Sally started at Jo-Lee with what might have been anger. Then she let out a shriek and ran straight at her. Even her breasts wobbled. Jo-Lee looked scared. She stood transfixed for a moment and then ran, pushing Tracey out of the way and darting round Kevin to dive through the door. Sally lumbered after her, still screaming. Sandra got up and rushed outside. By the time she'd run down the corridor and round the chimp house to the outdoor enclosure, Jo-Lee was at the very top of one of the trees and Kevin, Tracey and Susie were peering outside from the relative safety and warmth of the indoor cage. Sally thundered up and down below the tree and then ran round the edge of the moat giving panthoot cries. Finally, winded, she stopped and sprawled across one of the ropes that was stretched between the trees. She'd carved a green path in the iced grass. She looked like a smoker trying to get her breath back. The others stared for a bit longer then turned and went back inside with both the disappointed and relieved air of spectators in a pub where there might have been a brawl.

Sandra rubbed her gloves over her face; her skin felt raw. The two chimps ignored one another pointedly. Jo-Lee clung to her tree perch and pretended to be terribly interested in the giraffes. Sally walked along the rope, but without elegance. She could not balance on two legs, and even using all four limbs she kept slipping off. The rope would twist to one side and she would remain clinging to it until she practically touched the ground and would then fall ungracefully onto the grass.

'Are they OK?'

It was Teresa.

'I think they're all right now. They've calmed down a bit, and the others showed no signs of joining in when Sally went for her.'

'I saw that.'

'You could leave them for a bit before you put Chrissie in.'

'Mm. Might do that. I think I'll let her out after the coffee break.'

'Susie seems to be doing well,' said Sandra cheerfully, trying to generate some kind of enthusiastic response from Teresa, but she only nodded dourly and went back inside. Sandra shivered and blew on her fingers.

Eventually Sally went indoors. Jo-Lee stayed in the tree until Susie came out. Then she climbed down and hugged Susie, who, without rancour for the way she'd been treated earlier, hugged her back. The two of them hovered nervously at the door for a few moments and then eventually darted inside. Sandra, when she returned to the corridor, saw that Jo-Lee was shaking, partly from the cold, but partly, no doubt, because of the stress. But although all of them were a little tense, there were no further incidents. Until Chrissie appeared.

Chrissie stalked into the cage and glared at the others. Sandra had the distinct impression that she was mightily displeased about being kept in her night pen for so long. Her son, Joseph, clutched her chest, but as soon as he saw his sister Susie he let go and scampered over to her. Chrissie made a move to grab him but, recognizing her daughter, she let him go. It was strange how little maternal affection she showed for Susie, and Susie played with Joseph as if she were blind to everyone else, as if she were frightened of showing that she'd seen her mother in case she had to accept that her mother didn't care. But in the days to come, Chrissie did acknowledge her daughter and even allowed her to carry Joseph around and babysit him for long periods on her own.

Now, however, Chrissie's eyes, hard as chips of dark stained glass, glittered round the cage. Jo-Lee, no longer her usual brash self, was cowering in one corner. Tracey had traitorously moved to sit next to Kevin. Only mad Sally was braving the cold outside. Chrissie did nothing, though. She greeted Ted like an equal and he responded with the deference of a king to a queen.

Sandra put her hot water bottle in her rucksack. It was cold and the water rolled in it as if it were a dead and waterlogged squid. She ate her dry sandwiches and hoped Ryan would come round so she could ask him to fill up the water bottle and bring her a cup of coffee. She needed to go to the loo, but she didn't want to leave the chimps just when Chrissie had been let in. There were orange traffic cones round the enclosure and a sign asking people not to enter. It was eerie being in the dimly lit visitors' corridor with no-one in it, like being in a museum at night with the exhibits still lit up in front of you.

Chrissie gave no indication that she had seen Jo-Lee, although every time she moved Jo-Lee flinched. After about an hour, Jo-Lee visibly relaxed and presented herself to Tracey to be groomed. Tracey obliged. Sandra cursed Ryan. Where the hell had he gone? He and Teresa had let Chrissie out and then skedaddled. What if something had gone wrong? She wandered outside and peered in the chimp kitchen. It was empty. She tried the door half-heartedly expecting it to be locked, but it was open. A radio hissed and crackled on the work surface and there was a hastily scrawled note next to it.

It said, Sandy, sorry, got called over to see Miss Williams, she wants to know how it's all progressing. We'll be back after lunch. Call us on the radio if there's any problem. R.

There was no kettle in the kitchen so she ran the water until it got hot and soaked her hands in its warmth. The running water made her even more uncomfortable. She went back inside the chimp house. Nothing had changed. The chimps hadn't even shifted position. She felt as if she might have an accident if she stayed. She glanced round at them all again, and then checked on Sally. She was slumped in a crook in one of the trees licking her lips noisily. Perhaps she had found a cache of frozen peanut butter.

She walked as quickly as she could. She thought that if she ran, she might wet herself. The sky was dark grey and there was a loose bandage of white clouds stretched across it through which the sun, yellow and watery as pus, was seeping. The toilets were fractionally warmer than outside, but only by virtue of being covered; there was no heating and to take off her layers of trousers and thermal long johns and expose her naked flesh to the bitter air was a small torture. Neither was there any hot water. She switched the hand dryer on three times before her hands were thawed.

It was only when she was level with the magpie field that she realized Sally was no longer outside. And then the screaming began. It was high-pitched and rang through the zoo, splintering the frozen air into ice- white shards sharp as knives. She broke into a run and her blood went cold as numerous other voices joined in. From way over on the other side of the zoo the cries of the older chimps echoed, serrated with bloodthirstiness.

She grabbed the radio from the kitchen and ran into the chimp house. The din was tremendous. She was sweating now and she could feel moisture puddling at the crooks of her knees and elbows, cold and clammy. She was terrified of what she was going to see. She depressed the button on the radio and shouted over the noise,

'Emergency at the chimp house. Someone get over here quickly. Get to the chimp house.'

She ran down the corridor. The sound bounced off the walls, ricocheted from the sterile tiles, vibrated in her ears like tinnitus. Jo-Lee was clinging to the top of the wire that separated the group cage from her old home. Sally and Chrissie stood beneath her and Tracey hung back behind them. Kevin was crouched at the far end underneath a low shelf holding Joseph and Susie in his arms and rocking back and forwards. Jo-Lee was shrieking in fear. The whites of her eyes rolled. The other three females were barking and screaming, their lips pulled back to expose gums as pink as flayed flesh and teeth as thick and square as tombstones. Chrissie and Sally were jumping up the wire and trying to grab Jo-Lee who was screaming even louder and attempting to climb higher. She scrabbled at the ceiling as if she'd cling to that if she could. There was a long gash down her ankle through which the white of bone showed and her foot was dark with blood.

'For God's sake, someone get over here,' shouted Sandra down the radio.

Then both Chrissie and Sally leapt onto the wire at the same time, one either side of Jo-Lee. They each seized one of her legs and pulled. Jo-Lee clung desperately to the wire but under the force of their weight she started to lose her grip. Her fingers skittered over the mesh, the nails catching. Sally sank her teeth into her thigh and Jo-Lee's screaming became even more high-pitched. She tumbled to the ground and the two females fell on top of her. Ted was panthooting, all his hair standing on end. He flung himself from one side of the cage to the other, hurtling into the window which vibrated in its frame and then crashing into the wall. He seemed powerless to stop the females but also excited by them.

Tracey, Sally and Chrissie all started to attack Jo- Lee, biting her and tearing at her flesh with their big, strong teeth, the muscles in their arms bulging as they dragged her across the floor. Sally climbed onto a shelf and jumped, landing with both feet on her head. There was a sickening crunch. Sandra started to scream. A pool of blood spread across half the cage and the three attacking females were covered in it, their cries becoming more hysterical. Ted slipped on the advancing pool and fell, righted himself and slipped again, sending blood-red skid marks across the floor. Jo-Lee didn't seem to be moving any more.

Sandra shouted and banged on the glass but they took no notice. It was unlikely they could even hear her.

'Oh Christ.' It was Ryan. He put his arm round her. 'Quick, come away from here. Teresa,' he shouted, 'you go down the other end. I'll open up the doors this side.'

He led Sandra back up the corridor. She was crying and shaking. He pushed her into a chair in the kitchen and ran to open the holding pen that separated the night pens from the indoor cage. There was a hiss and a clunk as the door to the holding pen opened. Kevin hobbled in, clutching both Susie and Joseph to his chest. They were whimpering and his teeth were chattering. His liver-coloured eyes rolled, the whites yellow. Ryan shut the door behind them. He opened the door into the night cage.

'Go down, go on, right down.'

Kevin obeyed, walking right down the row of night pens to the end one. Ryan ran after him and shut the three of them in. Then he ran back and opened the holding pen again. Sandra wiped her eyes and told herself to stop being so pathetic. She went and stood behind Ryan. His knuckles looked skinless as he gripped the control panel, white as a skeleton dipped in an acid bath.

'They're not coming, they're not coming,' he muttered.

They could hear Teresa calling the chimps. Sandra peered through the grille. Then a surprising thing happened. Ted advanced on the group of females. Tracey immediately ran over to the holding pen and Ryan pressed a button and the door slid shut behind her.

'Check they're getting a vet,' he shouted to Sandra.

She realized she was still gripping the radio so tightly that the imprint from the receiver was etched into the palm of her hand. She spoke to the secretaries, but in a disjointed way. She was watching what was happening.

Ted forcibly picked Sally up and hurled her towards the door of the holding pen. She landed several metres away. He turned to Chrissie. She backed off and skirted round the edge of the cage until she was standing by Sally. He charged at them, his roar growing louder as he picked up speed. They turned and fled, both trying to get into the holding pen at the same time. He pulled up short and stood with his arms either side of the door, barring their exit.

'Thank God,' said Ryan. He quickly closed the door to the night pen that Tracey was in. Chrissie and Sally stole into the adjoining cage like thieves.

'If we don't get her out bloody fast she's going to die. If she isn't dead already. Ted, come on, mate, you're going to have to come in too because we can't go in there with you still around, however sweet and lovely you might be.'

But Ted was walking back towards Jo-Lee. He bent down and sniffed at her body. Sandra could hardly look. Jo-Lee was covered in blood and completely inert. There were huge gaping wounds all over her arms and legs and one eye was obscured by a swelling as raw as pulverized meat.

'Shit,' Ryan swore. 'Come on, Ted, come out.'

But Ted bent down and picked Jo-Lee up in his arms. He stood up on two legs as well as he was able and staggered over towards the holding pen with her. He'd almost reached it when he slipped on some blood and fell to the floor. But he kept hold of her. He laid her down carefully and pushed her into the pen. Sandra caught her breath as Jo-Lee's arm snagged on the door but Ted picked it up and stuffed it in after her a little roughly. Then he sat down a little way away and looked up expectantly.

Ryan had frozen. 'Jesus,' he whispered, 'you don't need to be doing all them fucking tests.' He punched the holding pen button and the door sealed Ted off on his own. They looked down at Jo-Lee's mangled body lying in front of them.

Chapter Twelve

Two things remained with her after the chimps' fight. A feeling of sickness and a handprint. Jo-Lee was still alive when the vet arrived and put her under anaesthetic so he could stitch her up. Sandra only stayed long enough to see that she'd survived and then went to the canal to try to walk the attack out of her system.

There was a thin film of ice on the surface. She trudged along the path feeling the scalloped mud splinter and the black pools that had frozen in the ruts and were as misshapen as deformed eyes grind into shattered sightlessness beneath her boots.

She felt sick to the pit of her stomach and couldn't help thinking, if only I'd stayed it might not have happened. It reminded her of *Lord of the Flies*; there was the same childish savagery about it. At the same time, a little voice was whispering that she could write about it in her thesis. She could have a chapter on anecdotal evidence with examples like Jessica pretending she wasn't interested in the toy but attempting to play with it when she thought Ferguson wasn't looking, and this incident with Ted. Unheard of, to have anecdotes rather than real data, but still, if the other chapters were scientifically rigorous . . .

She started thinking about the accident again. After the vet had arrived, Ryan had turned to her, wordless, and pressed her forehead to his chest. His hand cupped the back of her head. His hands were so large that her skull fitted neatly into his palm. Even now with her hat on and the wind nicking her ears with bat-small claws, she could still feel it.

It started to hail, the stones of ice making her cheeks smart. Someone had once told her that somewhere the hailstones were as big as oranges. She imagined an African country, the sky blue, raining down ice oranges. Some people would shelter under cardboard boxes and some would pick them up in their hands and polish them in their palms as one does with pebbles wet and worn by salt water.

The walk didn't really help. She decided to stay with Corin for a couple of days. She'd almost finished collecting data on the chimps' gaze so could start to analyse it during the day, and the calm and quiet would help prepare her for the evenings when Corin would blow in and whistle round the flat like a wild winter wind.

But it didn't turn out like that.

She cut her hair specially, with her clippers, and redyed it white blonde. Her bedsit was cloudy with the smell of peroxide and its acidity burnt her fingers. She took the train down, not wanting to skid on the roads, and walked from the tube station. Her feet knew the route unconsciously; the pattern of the flagstones was tattooed into their soles. Once she looked around and didn't know where she was and her heart rose like yeast, the blood seeming to froth in her mouth. She walked on a little way and then recognized a hydrangea bush, the flowers transmuted into dead brown moths. She relaxed and let her body lead the way in its own unseeing manner.

Corin had always been light. Sometimes it was hard to stare directly at him in case he blinded you. Now his gaze had been channelled through a prism and as it refracted outwards it scattered across the walls and diffused into cracks in the plaster. He had become brittle. His spindly fingers were all of a piece with how thin his arms had become. She felt if she touched him he might break and if she spoke to him he might fragment. She kept her voice low and quiet.

He said he had to finish the filming soon and he had nothing worthwhile. He said it was a crime that they had made him do the programme. He knew that he was good, but in this business you were only as good as your last programme, and if it was bad how was he going to convince everyone else?

His hair had changed. It had become dry as wheat. She imagined a fire crackling through it, leaping into existence from the heat of a light bulb and reducing his crop of hair to blackened stubble. There was a hunted look in his eyes and his face looked bruised. The bones had risen to the surface like something that had sunk out of sight but now, unpleasantly, is reminding you of its existence.

The fridge had edible things in it for a change: olives, Camembert, blue cheese dip (nothing to dip in it, though), Salsa salad and, amazingly, strawberries. She was touched because she knew how busy he was. He opened a bottle of champagne and dropped a strawberry in her glass. It was a glass with a long stem into which the liquid could run and the strawberry choked it. The champagne finally bubbled up from beneath and the strawberry rose to the top, fizzing like a time bomb.

'Here,' he said. I've already asked you so it doesn't need to be too romantic.' He pushed a little box over to her.

She smiled and opened it. A gold ring with a single diamond. She put it on and it fit perfectly. It looked strange on her hand, cold and alien. She didn't normally wear rings.

'Thank you,' she said and leaned over to kiss him.

'So have you decided what you're going to wear?'

She looked blankly at him.

'For the wedding,' he said irritably.

'But I thought you said it wasn't going to be until summer.'

'Yes, but you need to plan these things. I haven't seen you buying any of those wedding mags. Isn't that what girlies are meant to do?'

He was joking but she thought he meant it. She checked. 'I should be buying wedding magazines?' she said a touch sardonically.

'Well, you need something decent to wear,' he said sharply and turned away, as if bored. To lessen the harshness, he added, 'I can't imagine in that wealth of batik, tie-dye and floral print bulging out of your wardrobe you have anything remotely suitable for a reception, never mind a bride's dress. And you need to get some shoes, you can't wear your trainers.' He was smiling but there was a hard edge to it. 'Have you decided who will be the bridesmaids? And do you know where everyone is supposed to sit and what to put on the invitations?'

'But, Corin, we haven't decided anything yet.'

'No, well, you'd better start doing your homework.' He picked up the bottle and went into the sitting room. She heard him turn the TV on.

She sat where she was and looked at her bubble-blistered strawberry. She felt empty inside. Theory of Mind, she thought bitterly, a gift possessed by anyone older than four who was not autistic, a gift that most animals probably didn't have, a gift for communicating and showing empathy, and yet here was Corin, an intelligent man, acting as if he didn't have it, didn't know what she was thinking, and, even worse, didn't care. She thought of Ryan. There was a serene quality to him, the peacefulness you feel swimming in a pool in a hot country. She felt as if being with Ryan was a bit like a bath full of *crème bain* and now Corin was scouring the slickness off her skin with sandpaper. But there was something in Ryan that she hadn't resolved. Beneath the warmth and calm was a hidden current. If she dipped her toes down she might feel it suck at them.

She got up and went into the sitting room. She loved Corin because he was like a comet. He was streaking across the night sky and she was blinded by his afterglow. She didn't want to be left behind. She wanted to be special because she would be lit by his reflection. She peeled all her clothes off, one by one, and the neon light from the TV and his green brown gaze lapped over her. For a long moment he looked at her as if mapping her body and then he picked her up and carried her into the bedroom. He licked the soles of her feet and swallowed her toes whole. He pressed himself between her lips; he tasted of milk and bitter almonds and his breath rasped like the sea when it whispers over the shingle.

But later when he pulled away from her and turned on the bedside lamp, he gave a sharp cry, and then said roughly, 'Why the hell didn't you tell me you had your period?'

'I didn't know,' she said plaintively.

'What the hell you mean you didn't know?' he said savagely. 'Every woman knows when she's got her period.'

'I didn't. I thought it was going to be around now, but I didn't know it was going to start right this very instant.'

She peered down at herself. She looked as if she'd just been violated. Her thighs were smeared with blood and so were the tops of his. The sheet was covered in dying roses, their petals crushed and scattered. A gout of black womb tissue clung to his penis. She felt terrible.

Corin went to the bathroom to wash. When he came back he said, his face carefully neutral, 'There's a party on in Muswell Hill. We need to be quick if we're going to get there before all the drink's gone.' He started to put his clothes back on.

'What time is it?' she asked.

'Midnight,' he said without looking at her.

She washed without turning the light on and then

pulled her clothes on slowly as if she were wrapping porcelain up in brown paper.

★ ★ ★

The day after she got back there was a knock at her door and Ryan walked in. She stood up abruptly. She'd just had a shower and was only wearing her dressing gown.

She pulled it tighter around herself.

'Sorry,' he said. 'You didn't hear me knocking downstairs and you'd left the front door unlocked.' She could see his thought travel across his face slowly as a cloud moving over the sky. He suddenly looked pained and turned away.

'I'll wait on the stairs,' he said.

There was nowhere else to wait in her one- bedroomed flat. She hastily pulled on some clothes and rubbed Dax into her hair. She felt excited by the way he had looked at her, and then immediately guilty.

'You can come in now,' she called. 'Do you want a drink?'

'Tea would be nice.'

'I was thinking of something stronger.'

He grinned. 'Now you're talking.'

He slumped on the sofa and stared morosely out of the window although there was nothing to see except condensation blooming in the shape of cabbage flowers.

'That sounds like one hell of a drink,' he said in the silence when she'd turned off the blender.

'It will be. It's a Sandra special.'

He ran his fingers over her tape collection and she

thought of Paul. She hoped he wasn't going to start rifling through her knickers. He put on Generation X.

'I didn't know you were an Idol fan.'

'One should never touch idols: the gilt may come off on one's hands.' He smiled up at her. 'Flaubert.' But his smile vanished as quickly as it had come.

'There you go.' She handed him a half-pint glass stolen from the local filled with thick brown liquid stiff with ground ice.

'Mmm. It's nice,' he said, taking a sip. 'What's it got in it?'

'Hot chocolate powder, milk, dark rum, white rum and nutmeg.'

'Here's something a little more warming.' He reached into his jacket pocket and drew out some Rizlas, a bit of Lebanese gold wrapped in cling film and a pouch of tobacco.

She passed him a book to roll the joint on and a box of matches. The smell was heavy and resinous. She already felt warm inside. Corin heartily disapproved of drugs in any form and of alcohol other than straight drinks from certified labels. He was horrified when she mentioned she was going to try making homemade wine with leftover fruit from the zoo. It wasn't that she wanted to drink the wine so much as that she wanted to have a row of dusty bottles glowing with the colours of summer distilled.

She watched as Ryan inhaled and the end of the joint winked: the light of a train crackling with electricity as it hurtled down the tunnel of the Rizlas.

'So what is it?'

'What do you mean?' he asked, screwing up his eyes at

the smoke that wound creeper-like round his head. 'I'm sorry. I have to admit, there is something I wanted to talk to you about.' He took another drag and passed the joint to her. 'Things aren't so good at work. Jo-Lee is still in pretty poor shape - though I think she will recover and that's the main thing. But Teresa is mad because I got all the chimps back in and stole the limelight. After all, I am a very junior keeper. She's really twisting the knife. She's reminded Miss Williams on more than one occasion that it was me who suggested putting the group together. Ach, they'd have got round to it in the end, I know, but I did push them or we'd have been waiting until kingdom come. And Miss Williams, the old bat, is happy to forget that and blame it on me. I can't afford to lose this job, Sandy,' he said, leaning forward.

She felt her head fill with air and drift like helium. She passed the joint back.

'You're intelligent enough to do something that pays better.'

'That isn't the point. I wasn't talking about money. This is what I came to tell you. Christ knows why 'cos I'm not supposed to tell any bloody body, but you - you . . .' He paused. 'I want you to know.' He took a deep breath. 'I'm a member of the AZA.'

There was silence while she assimilated this and the floor seemed to dissolve beneath her feet. Any moment now she'd be perched on a rafter suspended above the roof of her clapped-out car. She said nothing and was acutely aware that he was staring hard at her.

'So,' she said eventually, 'you're a member of the Anti-

Zoo Army and you're working at the zoo because you're an infiltrator.'

'Don't look at me like I'm a terrorist.'

She thought of the bombs, the people who'd been hurt, the animals who'd roamed wild and eventually been tranquillized and recaptured, or worse, shot by the police. They had the power to do that once an animal left a zoo.

'What are you going to do?' she said nastily. 'Hand the keys over to them? Tell them to let the tiger walk free?' She suddenly felt she might cry. It was the stress of the fight, the couple of days she'd spent with Corin that had not gone well, and now good old dependable Ryan . . . She felt personally betrayed.

'It's not like that,' he pleaded. 'I want to talk about it with you. Will you listen?'

She took a drag and cupped the smoke against the roof of her mouth with her tongue. She nodded. He'd known she couldn't refuse but now he suddenly looked uncomfortable. He stared at his hands, tightly gripping the glass, and then towards the window again.

'I guess I should go. It's not right to involve you in this. I'm sorry I mentioned it,' he added bitterly and made a move as if to get up.

She held out the joint for him. 'You owe it to me,' she said, a hard edge of anger in her voice.

He looked at her in surprise.

'You can't tell me you're in an organization I despise and expect everything to be all right between us. You might as well justify yourself.'

He sighed and said slowly, 'Well, I believe that no animal should be kept in captivity. It's like house arrest, or prison. It denies animals what is right and natural. They shouldn't be deprived of their liberty. Better death than that,' he said fiercely. 'I believe habitats should be preserved, but if they're not, then those animals shouldn't be kept under lock and key on the off chance that their great-great-grandchildren might be introduced back into the wild. And the argument that zoos are there for education is bollocks. I mean, you can read, you can watch films. You don't learn about *Homo* bloody *sapiens* by staring at cages of them.'

'People did, in the past. They kept Eskimos and Pygmies in cages.'

'I know. But for entertainment, not education. And no-one should be behind bars for a reason as trivial as that.'

She sighed. 'I agree with you so far. Mostly.'

'I knew you would. The point where I'm sure you and the AZA differ is that you wouldn't want these animals to be released.' He held up his hand as if she were about to interrupt him. 'I believe every individual animal has the right to life, liberty and freedom,' he recited, 'but I've realized that it's more complicated than that.'

Now he sighed and drained half his glass at once. His breath steamed the inside and he emerged with the ends of his moustache coated in chocolate. 'You can't really let these animals out. They've become domesticated — almost. They wouldn't survive. The line the AZA takes is that they'd be supremely happy for the last part of their lives and better short, sharp ecstasy than interminable boredom. But I'm no longer sure that's right any more. I don't like the way they're kept, but things could be done to change that. Some of those animals wouldn't leave their cages if the doors were blowing in the wind, some would come back, and the ones that stayed away would starve or get shot. There's nothing ecstatic about that,' he said angrily. 'And I'm getting fond of some of those bastard chimps. Maybe I just don't want to let them go.'

'You know what they can do,' she said quietly. 'To each other or anyone else.'

'I know,' he said helplessly. He looked into her eyes. 'I have no intention of letting the AZA get their hands on this place. But I can't keep stalling. What should I do?'

'Do you really want to know?'

'I like you,' he said, smiling, 'I like you a lot.'

'Don't say it,' she warned.

'I'll say it anyway: pity you're with some other guy. I hope he treats you good.'

'Stall a bit longer,' she said quickly to cover her embarrassment. 'Try to change things from the inside. Then maybe you could leave and join some other organization. Less militant. You'd have insider knowledge and no bombs.'

'Ah, but boys like playing with toys. The bombs were the best bit.'

She hardly heard him. She was looking at her naked fingers. She didn't like wearing rings. She didn't want to lose it at the zoo. She didn't want to advertise . . . what, that she was engaged to Corin? It wasn't that she didn't want people to know, it was that she only wanted the people to know whom she wanted to tell. And with a start she realized she didn't want Ryan to find out. She was shocked at herself and flattered at his frank admission that he liked her.

'I didn't mean it,' he said quickly, mistaking the reason for her silence.

He looked lost. She tried to imagine what it would be like to firmly believe in something and then have the foundations of your belief undermined; to burn to change the world and find you are unable to; to have a vision in black and white and suddenly see that everything has blurred into shades of grey. Somewhere on this continuum lay right and wrong, but every time you pinned them down they escaped like butterflies with torn wings and bleeding throats.

'Thanks for telling me,' she said, because he needed her to reassure him, but inside she felt a great emptiness, as if the one thing she depended on had metamorphosed into something shapeless and nameless. She felt there was nothing solid in her life any more except her work.

Miss Williams wouldn't see her. Not even for the ten minutes Sandra insisted it would take. She phoned every day at four sharp only to be told that there was absolutely no room in Miss Williams's diary except for lunch and she couldn't disturb her then, but why not try phoning the next day?

Sandra told herself not to despair. She spent that week making sculptures in the garage. She wore lots of clothes and the heat of the gas torch warmed her to the core. She loved the way the steel became soft and malleable beneath the flame; how the blue flame kindled a red-hot glow. The red and blue reminded her of lovers: both hot, both working to the same end, one bending to the other's will. But what happened when you turned the gas off and the steel hardened into a brand new shape and had no further need of the flame? She tried not to think of Corin: to think about how it was and remember how it had been.

She made two sculptures that week, twisting spirals of organic metal: creatures within creatures that feasted upon one another, parasitic, carnivorous, cannibalistic. To her it seemed normal: it was biology writ large in metal.

One day the sky became bright blue and she hung her washing out to dry on the line at the back of the garage. It froze into stiff shapes. Towards the end of the week there was a thaw and the world became dirty brown. The field at the back changed from crisp corrugations to a mulch of mud and crows marched in serried ranks down the ploughed rows. The farmhouses looked like water hogs swaddled in soil and about to sink further into the mire. She found a pair of her knickers outside that must have fallen when she was bringing her clothes in. She picked them up intending to wash them again, but they were crawling with thin beetle larvae.

At the end of the week, Corin came to stay and Kim arrived for the evening. She tore up on her motorbike, and when she braked a spray of stones was flung from her back wheel; when she took her helmet off, her hair exploded like a wild animal released.

'Come and meet Corin,' Sandra said, hugging her.

Corin wheeled round as they walked in. He was already smiling, but his grin slowly dissolved. The two of them stared at each other. Kim was a good two inches taller in her high-heeled boots. A slow smile trickled across her face.

'Good God, Kim, you are so beautiful.'

'You remember me, then?'

'I do. So you did it, then?' He stepped forward and shook her hand as if he were shaking a wrestler's.

Sandra expected Kim to withdraw and wince, but it was Corin who let go first.

'Did what?' she asked.

'Grew up,' said Corin, still staring into Kim's eyes, 'became transformed. She wasn't always this beautiful, Sandra. Our ugly duckling's become a swan.'

'Come on, Corin, I wasn't ugly even then.'

'To my eyes, sweetheart, to my eyes,' he replied and they both laughed.

Sandra looked at them in astonishment. What the hell was going on? 'You two know each other?' she asked.

'Not strictly speaking,' said Kim and both she and Corin laughed again. 'We were at college together. I must have been in the first year when you were in the third year.'

Corin nodded.

'Why didn't you tell me?'

'I didn't realize your Corin and the one I knew were the same person,' said Kim smoothly. She and Corin were still staring at each other.

'This needs a toast,' said Corin, suddenly spinning into action. He uncorked a bottle of Rose d' Anjou and poured it. 'To old friends and new-found beauty,' he said, raising his glass.

'Not so new,' said Kim, staring at him. 'It's a good few years since college.'

Sandra chinked her glass against the others', but she found it hard to share in their gaiety. She felt something tight and hard clench in her chest. Corin had never been secretive about his past. Sometimes he was open to the point that she felt salt was being rubbed in a new wound; she really had no interest in his ex-girlfriends and what they had done together. But sometimes, such as now, she felt she was missing out on huge chunks of his past life and couldn't comprehend large portions of his present one.

She sullenly dished up the meal she'd cooked. Corin and Kim were talking nineteen to the dozen about students and lecturers they'd known at Oxford. She ate half-heartedly and twisted her engagement ring nervously. Sometimes she wished the wedding were over and done with and they were married. Then he would be hers and she wouldn't have to worry, would she? She wouldn't have to try to figure out whether things really weren't working or whether he just wasn't enjoying his job.

Kim refused to stay the night. She said she wasn't about to slum it and sleep on the floor, and secretly Sandra was glad. She left at three in the morning, black in her leathers and helmet, driving out into a night punctured with stars, the smoke from her exhaust freezing in her wake.

As Sandra was bending over to clear the table, Corin leant against her from behind. She caught her breath and felt herself become moist as he reached beneath her skirt and pulled her pants off. Her breath choked in her throat as he pushed himself roughly into her and pinned her arms to the table, resting his full weight on her so that she couldn't move. He pushed her legs wider apart with his knees and thrust into her so hard she could feel her pubic bone grinding against the edge of the table. She was at once excited by his force and afraid because she was excited and because he was so much stronger than she was. He was hurting her, and yet it was still pleasurable; he was using her, but he loved her and that made it all right, didn't it?

That night she dreamt of Kim. Kim was taking off her silver lycra top. She stretched upwards and pulled it over her head, the muscles in her arms and shoulders taut, her nipples erect and black as prunes. Her body was the colour of steel in the dark, the light from outside gilding one side blue-black; she was as perfectly made as an iron android.

'You are so beautiful,' Sandra breathed, and she ran her hands in a line from Kim's uptilted throat down to the hard knot of her navel and butterflied them out at her waist. She spun her round and ran her tongue along the groove of her spine between the twin ridges of muscle. Kim's shoulder-blades flexed like budding wings and her ribs slid smooth as a snake's beneath her fingers. Her tongue wandered round to the front again and licked one of her nipples. It trembled in her mouth and her hand slid up the inside of one of those sleek, hard thighs . . .

She woke with a start, one hand resting on Corin's leg, the other pressed against his chest. She felt sick and the wine tasted rotten in the back of her throat. Her jerk into consciousness woke Corin and he misinterpreted the way she was holding him. He rolled her over and himself into her in one smooth oiled movement and she was so tired she could only lie inert beneath him and smell the sleep on his breath.

Miss Williams eventually agreed to see her a couple of days later. The sky was a dazzling blue but it was still cold; there was black ice on the roads, lumps of jet cleaved open, flawless and lethal. As she walked across the zoo towards Miss Williams's house, something blotted out the sun that had shattered like a smashed crystal in the sky and dropped silently and softly towards her. She ducked involuntarily, but the snowy owl fell noiseless in front of her and perched on a bin. It regarded her balefully with one blank sunflower-yellow eye. At first she thought it had escaped, but then she saw the leather jesses trailing from one leg.

As suddenly and silently as it had come, it took off again and she watched it glide over to Craven and settle on his hand. It tore into the flesh of his wrist, the sinew stretching from its beak until it snapped and the owl cocked its head upright, its beak full of pink and red tissue. She realized he was holding a piece of meat in his fist. His shadow was long and thin and his eye sockets were dark so that it looked as if he had a patch over each of them. She turned and hurried away.

Miss Williams was wearing a necklace of moonstones and a brooch with a silver dagger with a hart wound round it. Her red lipstick was smudged over her teeth again. One of her white dogs moulted on Sandra and rooted embarrassingly in her crotch every time she dropped her guard. To Sandra's surprise, Miss Williams said that she could experiment with Jessica and Ferguson, Jo-Lee and a fourth chimp, Fred, who was one of the older ones that up until now Sandra hadn't spent any time watching. The director added that Jo-Lee was in a cage on her own and it might stop her being so bored.

Sandra couldn't believe her luck. The only proviso was

that she wait until after the New Year, when Jo-Lee would have fully recovered. That was fine by her. Christmas was only a few days away and she still had to build the equipment. As she left the house, she saw the shadow of the owl glide across the sky.

Chapter Thirteen

Today he had quite a lot to carry. He took it in two stages. On his way back, he let himself into the monkey house, for no other reason than that the door was open. It was still dark and few of the keepers were up. He found Dawn in the kitchen, though, humming to the radio as it crackled through its tinny litany of songs. She was chopping up prunes, digging the knife into them, pulling the flesh back and gouging out the stones. She looked as if she were flaying an animal.

'So what do you want, weirdo?'

'My Christmas present.'

She looked around. 'Did you leave it here?'

He shook his head. 'I didn't get it.'

She looked at him as if he were mad.

'I wanted a textbook on biology but Mum didn't buy

it for me. She said it was too expensive, but she bought me two jumpers instead and I bet they cost nearly as much as the book.'

'Two jumpers are a lot more useful.'

'I'm never going to wear them.'

'Well, you are an ungrateful little sod, aren't you?'

She hacked another prune in two. Paul sidled round the door and went to watch the spider monkeys.

Dawn hadn't turned on all the lights in the corridor. There was the sharp smell of boiling milk and the acrid odour of monkey sweat. One of the monkeys had her face all twisted up. She was crouched in the corner of the cage. The big male with his troll face and punk hair peered at her and then at Paul. The other two females came up to look at their mother and touch her; they followed their father round the cage. Apart from the female in the corner who hadn't moved around much for a few months, the others were constantly in motion, like gas particles in a small sealed chamber. Sometimes they collided and bumped off one another, mostly they ricocheted off the walls.

She seemed to be having convulsions. She grabbed the side of the ledge she was sitting on and gripped it tightly, looking down between her legs. Something small and red appeared. The female pushed and it moved fractionally. The other three monkeys crowded round her, their heads practically touching her distended vagina. She batted ineffectually at them with her free hand and scrunched up her face even more.

Paul didn't see the baby being born because they were so tightly pressed around her, but after the male had sniffed and touched it he came and spread-eagled himself against the glass in front of Paul and stared with ice-blue eyes into his own. The baby, covered in a film of blood and mucus, was black beneath its amniotic sac. It was so tiny he could have held it in one hand. There was bright blood smeared along the white ledge the female was sitting on. She stretched out one of the baby's arms and then one of its legs like an anxious parent checking her baby has all its fingers. Then she put its hand in her mouth and started to chew. The tiny thing struggled pathetically, but it made no difference. She opened her mouth wide, displaying small, sharp canines, and bit into its head as if it were an apple. The fragile skull burst and oozed a gum of brains and oily blood. It splattered over her fur and the shelf. The others came to look, curious. They dipped their fingers in the mess and licked them. It reminded him of the cannibalistic chimps he'd read about. The mother had eaten some of her own babies and then she and her daughter had eaten the babies of other chimps. That was in the wild, but mothers often ate their babies when they were born in captivity. He couldn't remember where he'd read that and it bothered him.

He watched the baby's other hand clench in a single spasm. Dawn come out of the kitchen and started walking up the corridor towards him.

'You still here?'

He nodded. 'But it's getting light. I'll have to go soon.'

She stopped near him and glanced into the spider monkeys' cage, did a double take, and screamed.

'Why didn't you tell me?' she shouted.

Paul looked up at her in surprise, but she looked as if she were about to hit him so he ran.

The best Christmas present he'd ever got was from his dad. He must have been about three and he remembered his mum saying, That's far too grown-up a present for him, but it wasn't.

It was a kind of doll, a man about a foot tall made of clear Perspex and you could see all his veins in a red and blue branching vine with tendrils extending into his fingertips. Behind the veins was his heart suspended like a cherry stone with wisps of flesh still clinging to it. You could open him down the middle and peel back the veins and the muscle in thick, striated slabs and look at his intestines, his lungs and liver, his gonads and bladder shiny and plastic, slick as skinned grapes. He still played with it sometimes.

The sky looked as if someone had painted it black and spilt a drop of water. The clear liquid bled into the dark one and diluted it. He crouched over his flattened patch of mud patterned with hoar frost fractals and brushed away the debris with his hands: leftover bones, picked clean, and the crow's tattered skin, dusty and ragged. He assembled everything he might need and then set to work.

Really he should be starting lower down the phylogenetic order, but it was difficult to get things like frogs in winter. He had toyed with the idea of stealing one of the cane toads, but in the end he'd decided not to.

They were, after all, larger than rats. Using a Tippex pen, he carefully wrote A on one cockroach and V on the other. He bred the cockroaches in his bedroom. They moved their legs like mechanical toys futilely and incessantly when he held their hard brown carapaces between finger and thumb. They were one of the most primitive beetles in the world, and highly successful as species go. He dropped them both at the same time into his killing jar and screwed on the lid. In the bottom was a wad of cotton wool soaked in chloroform. A stood for Aorta and V for Ventricle: the names of his pet white rats.

He watched the cockroaches struggle to survive, clawing frantically at the sheer glass walls. They lived a long time. But not as long as bdelloid rotifers, which Paul knew could form themselves into comma-shaped cysts during drought and survive being boiled for an hour or kept at one degree below absolute zero, which is minus 272°C. Eventually, Aorta keeled over and lay still. Paul opened the jar and shook out Ventricle. It could go free; that was fair. The cockroach did not move. Perhaps it believed freedom was another of its dying hallucinations. Eventually it staggered off, drunk on the poison.

The cockroach Aorta had died, which meant that the real Ventricle had been chosen. Paul opened the cage he had brought with him and pulled out Ventricle. He held the rat up to his face and she nuzzled her pink nose against his, her whiskers quivering. She was six months old and he'd had her since she was a nude baby.

When he tried to stake her to the ground with his pins, she bit him hard. It was difficult with a live, wriggling creature which didn't want to die. He held her tight and forced her head into the killing jar, but only enough to knock her out for a moment. Then quickly he pinned her to the ground, banging the nails hard with his hammer to drive them into earth solid with frost. He started his stopwatch.

He had just cut into her throat when she came round and opened her mouth. No sound came out: he must have damaged her larynx. She struggled violently. She pulled one paw free, her wrist almost completely severing where the nail had held her down. He placed one hand over her throat to keep her immobile. He could feel the blood squirt out from the slit he had made in her flesh. He held the cotton wool over her mouth as she trembled and when she grew still again he drove in another nail, but further up her forearm. It must have hit a main vein because her white fur immediately stained red.

Now that she was pinned down securely, he could continue with his work. A little later he clicked his stopwatch off and wrote down the numbers in his notebook with his blue pen from the zoo. Three minutes and fifty-eight seconds. That was how long it was until Ventricle's heart stopped beating from when he'd made the first incision.

He cut off all four of her paws, and then, taking the right-hand front paw, he stood up and faced the sun, closed his eyes and turned round three times to the left. He dropped the paw. It took him a little while to find it. It was so tiny. It was like when his mother dropped an earring and she asked him to look for it. She didn't move from the spot she was standing on, and shouted for him to come and help her. He had to crawl around on his hands and knees running his fingers over the carpet because it could be right in front of him but he wouldn't see it.

The paw was lying on the ground, palm uppermost, a bead of blood next to it which had been knocked out of the stump when it hit the earth. A little later it would freeze like the stone in his mother's engagement ring. Palm uppermost. That was good luck. He picked it up and nailed it and the other front paw to the fence. The fingers were too small to cut off and pin up individually, and the toes were so tiny that he didn't need to chew at all, just swallow a couple of times, and they slipped down his throat as if they were uncooked grains of rice.

The day had gone from dark to light with almost no transition. Now it would continue to get lighter in the mornings. He decided that he'd stick to this routine, the third day of every month, because the very first dissection he ever did was on the third day of the third month and it was important to keep these things the same. Then as now it had been just as the sun tipped over the edge of the horizon, but, he thought, his mum would wonder what he was doing if he started leaving the house at three or four in the morning. He felt a slight edge of panic. He tried to calm himself. He could make each new dissection three hours later than the previous one. He looked at his watch and noted the time in his book. Gradually his racing heart stilled. Then he packed his things up and took Aorta home. She was peering through the bars of the cage looking for Ventricle and sneezing with cold.

Chapter Fourteen

'Here.' Sandra tossed a book across to Paul. 'You can't keep it; I borrowed it from college for you. You've got it for a month but I'll try to renew it after that.'

It was the biology textbook Paul had wanted for Christmas. He picked it up and turned it over in his hands. He didn't say anything. Ryan raised his eyebrows at her, but she said, 'He is pleased. Aren't you, Paul?'

He nodded uncertainly.

'Now it's milk and biscuits time and then we're going to play a game.'

'You are so bossy,' said Ryan with a smirk.

She gave him a shove. 'He needs to be told these things.'

He snorted. 'Milk and Biscuits Time, indeed.'

'Are we going to use that thing?' Paul's eyes skittered round the room like frightened butterflies, resting briefly on Sandra before winging away.

He meant the box she had built for her experiment on

beliefs, but he didn't point at it. She thought it might be another of the things he didn't do, but unlike autistic children he might be able to learn.

'You mean this?' said Ryan, and pointed at the large wooden box with four small drawers that stood in the middle of the room.

Paul seemed to hunch into himself and he dropped the biscuit he was holding.

'Just look at the mess you're making, young fellow.' Ryan pointed at the biscuit which had fallen at Paul's feet.

Paul started to shake and his irises disappeared as his eyes, the colour of cabbage whites, rolled.

Sandra pushed Ryan's hand down. 'You don't like pointing, do you, Paul?'

He shook his head. 'He's got hair on his face like my dad. My first dad. He pointed at me and then he hit me, but the others did that as well. All the dads. Of course, the others weren't my real dad but Mum said they were. I don't know why she said they were when they weren't.

'Why are we going to play this game? I don't like tests. Is it like a school test? Once I got eleven out of twenty in spelling and Mrs Malone said I ought to try harder, but if you don't know how to spell a word how do you know you've spelt it wrong? I get all my maths questions right, though. Mrs Malone says it's a wonder because I don't write anything down except for the answer, but it would take too long to explain how I know what the answer is. When I've worked it out, I know it's right because it has the colour of right about it. The number glows all shiny in my mind.' He bit into his biscuit.

Ryan and Sandra glanced at each other.

'Ryan is not your dad, and he's not going to hit you or point at you again. And it's not a test like the ones you do at school. I'm doing an experiment for my university studies. I want to see if it works. There's no wrong or right about it, but maybe I haven't designed my test properly. It would be a real help to me if you'd have a go.'

Paul didn't say anything, but he didn't look as if he were going to get upset again. She took that as a yes.

'OK. Ryan is going to help me, so you just watch the first time.'

Ryan lifted the box onto the table and put the coloured peg above the first drawer and went round the back to put in a sweet. Sandra pulled open the first drawer and took out a blue Smartie.

'All right, now you have a go.'

Ryan picked up the peg and placed it above the third drawer along and then Sandra nudged Paul. He opened the first drawer and carefully shut it again. Sandra opened the one below the peg and showed him the sweet that was inside. Paul got the next five goes right. He made a little pile of Smarties in front of him, separating them by their colours like a mosaic of flattened marbles.

'Paul, you've done really well, so we're going to make it a little bit harder now. Watch carefully.'

Ryan put the peg above the first drawer and, whilst Ryan was watching, Sandra moved it so it was above the fourth drawer along. Ryan went behind the box. Paul stretched out his hand. It hovered, small and white, in front of the drawers, then he pulled open the fourth drawer and took out the Smartie.

'It's orange,' he said and added it to the orange ones.

Ryan placed the peg above the third drawer and went round behind the box. As soon as he'd gone behind the box and could no longer see them, Sandra moved the peg so it was above the second drawer. She elaborately mimed putting her finger to her lips and crouching down so that it would be obvious to Paul that Ryan hadn't seen her. Paul opened the drawer below the peg instead of the third drawer where Ryan thought the peg was, and when the Smartie was not there Paul searched for it with his fingertips as if it were only invisible and not nonexistent.

They continued for a while longer before Sandra said that that was enough. She knew now that Paul did not have Theory of Mind. He did not act as if he understood that because Ryan had not seen where she'd moved the peg to, the sweet was going to be in the drawer that Ryan had originally labelled with the Peg-

'I got Smarties only half the time,' said Paul, 'and he put one in every time.'

'Yes,' said Sandra, 'he did.'

'Give me more goes.'

They repeated the exercise, only this time Paul sat with his face scrunched up in front of the box and thought long and hard as if he were contemplating a chess move. Then he quickly pulled open a drawer. It was the correct one. He took out the Smartie without a change in expression. They carried on but Paul no longer hesitated and unerringly picked the right drawer.

Ryan gave her a broad grin and put a tape on. Paul immediately covered his ears and started rocking. Sandra turned it off.

'Better?'

'It's a hurty thing,' he said, cautiously removing his hands. He picked up the biology textbook and crammed his pile of Smarties into a pocket. He left without saying another word.

'Paul, wait,' she called after him, but it was too late. He'd already gone.

'Holy mother of Jesus, he's one helluva strange kid,' Ryan whistled, and then added, 'Poor sod. I hope he's no father with hair on his face waiting at home for him.'

He stood up and pulled back the curtain a fraction so he could see Paul, a small bent figure, hunched over his book, running awkwardly down the drive. 'I'm going to walk him home,' he said, letting the curtain fall.

He paused halfway through pulling on his jacket. 'He was like a machine,' he said slowly. 'He didn't have this Theory of Mind thing, and then he did. It was as if he learnt rules for what to do and then followed them. Eerie. A person acting like that - like a robot almost.'

'Yeah. Listen, I would come with you, but I'd really like you to talk to Meg. Paul needs help. He should go to a clinician, who'd diagnose him properly and tell Meg about special schools or tutors ... I tried once before but she didn't like me telling her what to do. It might be better coming from you.'

'Do my best.' He shrugged his jacket on and leant over and kissed her on the cheek.

He'd gone before she could thank him for helping. She felt her cheek might be permanently marked. Branded with the imprint of his lips.

'I saw someone do it and it made me think, That's what I

want to do.' Annie swung the axe and there was a sound like breaking glass. 'Course, now I'm doing it, 'snot quite as much fun as it looks.'

'Looks?' said Sandra. 'It doesn't look like much fun at all.'

Annie cut a surreal figure, dressed all in black: thigh-high boots, waterproof and a floppy rain hat, in a world whitened with crystallized snow, standing in the middle of a crescent of holiday-blue water. She wielded the axe with gusto and the ice shattered into fragments.

Sandra walked round the enclosure. Annie had left the door to the keepers' kitchen open so she could meet Fred, Pru and May. She hadn't bothered studying them before because they were old, about thirty-five, which was well into middle age, and they weren't living in a semi-naturalistic group like the others. Ferguson and Jessica weren't either, but at least they were young and active.

She was preoccupied and slightly tense. The next morning, she was to start her test with the chimps, and she envisaged having a tough time again with Ferguson; Fred she didn't know at all and Jo-Lee was a bit of an unknown quantity. How would a recently scarred chimp kept in virtually solitary confinement react to her and her great wooden box?

She rounded the corner, mesmerized by the mica glitter of the iced snow on the path. It was only when she'd almost reached the door that she looked up and jumped. Craven was standing right in front of her. His one good eye was so dark she could see no white in it and he seemed to be staring through her and beyond, his gaze not held by what he saw.

'You'll never find it,' he said and walked past her, missing her by a couple of inches.

She thought he might be speaking to someone else, but there was no-one there, only him trudging away, his boots squeaking in the snow. He gave her the creeps.

She shivered and pushed open the door. The wall immediately opposite her was made up of metal bars and in the cage behind was a huge chimp, the largest she had ever seen, clutching the bars and resting his head against them. Looking at her.

She closed the door and didn't approach too near. She spoke softly and quietly and told him she had come to meet him and work with him and she hoped they would get on well together. He pouted his black lips slightly and tilted his head on one side to listen to her.

He backed off and stood in the middle of his cage, his lips still pouted, black and pink, and swayed from side to side. The two females were sitting on a ledge above him, right at the back, and she couldn't see them very well. Every third sway he lifted his arms and clapped his hands, and he started to make a low moaning sound. The noise increased in volume: it was a keening that spoke of grief and frustration. She imagined early explorers hearing that sound echoing through the jungle, a sound to kill bird song and insect whirr stone dead, spine chilling and desolate; they would think of voodoo and dark spirits, their nightmares returned to stalk the earth.

Fred had worked himself up sufficiently by this stage to burst into a bloodcurdling hooting and wailing. He stood on his legs and clapped his hands together, slapping his feet on the concrete floor, faster and faster until it seemed as if he could barely maintain the rhythm he had created. Finally, he seemed to wear himself out. He stopped.

'Are you practising to be a drummer?' she asked him.

He reached up to a tyre hanging above his head, and with one arm lifted himself bodily from the floor and up to the shelf a good four feet above his head. He grabbed hold of one of the females and dragged her by the hair on her head back down and over towards Sandra.

She was a pitiful specimen, old and thin, her behind half swollen and jelly baby pink; she was whimpering and her lips were pulled back exposing the whole of her gums. She had hardly any teeth left, and those that remained were just stumps, worn almost to the root. She must be May, thought Sandra. Annie had said she was mentally retarded. 'She is so thick, she stares right through you like you're not there, and if you give her a bit of food she watches while the others take it off her and eat it.'

Fred mashed May's head up against the bars and locked his elbow so that his arm was straight and she couldn't move her face, her gums pressed painfully against the metal. He put his other arm underneath her and hoisted her backside up towards him and shoved himself savagely into her. She let out a high-pitched wail and continued to cry whilst he banged her head on the bars with each thrust.

Sandra covered her mouth with her hand and looked away and then back again in horrid fascination. Fred shuddered, pulled out of her and dropped her. She crouched where she was, lips torn open in a silent scream.

A couple of minutes later, his penis, thin, triangular and purple-pink, rose again and he repeated the procedure, more brutally than before if that were possible. She was screaming in earnest now. When he'd come, he sat still for a minute and then patted her gently on the head, as if to quieten her. She continued to cry, rocking backwards and forwards, staring vacantly in front of her. Fred wandered round the small concrete cage, becoming increasingly distracted. None of the chimps could go outside because Annie still hadn't finished de-icing the moat.

As if his patience had finally broken, he punched her hard in the back. His fist was the size of a cabbage. She made a choking sound and fell face down on the floor. She lay there, immobile and silent.

'Is she OK?' Sandra asked in consternation as Annie walked in.

The keeper nodded. 'He's always doing it.' She sighed. 'It's 'cos it's so small in here and they're bored. He doesn't pick on Pru, she keeps out of his way, but May is so dense she can't seem to understand that screaming annoys him. He's not a patient chimp. Pru sometimes gangs up on her too. They carry her up to that ledge and throw her off, and once the two of them took her outside and threw her over the electric fence into the moat. She was so scared she wouldn't go back into their cage, but swam along to the next one and got in there - with the big male orang.'

Annie slid open the outer door and Fred and the shadow in the top corner that was Pru ran outside. May lay where she was, spread-eagled on the concrete.

There's heating under the floor,' said Annie, 'that's why she does it,' but even she no longer sounded certain.

Jessica was a joy. She was always excited to see Sandra, she sat in front of the box and watched her every move, she didn't try to grab the handles before she was meant to and she didn't try grabbing Sandra either.

Surprisingly, Ferguson was also good. Maybe he felt he had exerted his dominance over her, tamed this unruly female, and now he could relax, safe in his masculinity. He wasn't as attentive as Jessica; he kept getting distracted and doing school boyish things such as snorting so that mucus spilled out of his nose. It made Sandra's stomach heave.

The two who turned out to be a problem were Fred and Jo-Lee. When Sandra first saw Jo-Lee, she was in a night pen on her own, hunched miserably in the corner. Her skin was laced with an intaglio of white scar tissue and her eyes were dull. She hunched even further back when Sandra put the box next to her cage.

Sandra left it there for a couple of days, but when she returned there was little change. Jo-Lee sat and rocked and wouldn't come near her, but would sometimes climb up the mesh in the far corner, straining to see Teresa. The plucky, bold chimp had been replaced by a shadow of her former self.

'She's lost all her confidence,' Sandra said to Teresa, who was clanging past with a bucket of water, slopping suds on the floor.

'She's much better now. Far more well behaved. She used to be a real handful but these days she's a piece of cake to deal with. Best thing that could've happened to her.'

Sandra looked angrily at Teresa's back, but said nothing.

'And make sure you don't give her anything sweet,' the keeper tossed over her shoulder before disappearing into the kitchen.

Hand-reared chimps were given sweets and sugar in their drinks at the house. When they got to the real world of cages and sunflower seeds, onions and carrots and monkey food, they had to be weaned off sugar. Teresa and Annie didn't want Fred or Jo-Lee to be given any reminders of their former, sweeter days.

After the fourth day of coaxing, Jo-Lee finally came to look at the box and touch the handles, but she wouldn't open a drawer or even take any of the fruit that Sandra had pushed through the mesh to tempt her over. She simple sat clutching a huge sheaf of shredded paper to her chest, her thumb in her mouth, her legs crossed, rocking and rocking.

Sandra tried everything she could think of: out-of-season pears, mango, coconut, grapes, all to no avail.

And Fred was exactly the same. Sandra paid a visit to the health shop in town and came back loaded with sugar-free carob drops and bars which tasted horribly bitter to her, but Fred went wild for them and openly begged in between grabbing any and every drawer. Even Jo-Lee stirred herself from her stupor, and although she kept her legs crossed, the ball of paper in her lap and her thumb in her mouth, she did manage to open a few drawers and was rewarded with Hartley Hippo Healthy Teeth Drops. Things were going to be all right, Sandra thought. She went back to town that afternoon and bought more carob sweets.

But the next time she visited Fred and Jo-Lee, they showed absolutely no interest in any of the ersatz chocolate. Ferguson and Jessica were slowly progressing and she felt sure that in the not too distant future they would start associating the coloured peg with the correct drawer, and then she could go on to the experimental stage. But Fred and Jo-Lee hadn't even tried more than a few times and it was over three weeks since she'd started the experiment.

'Oh, look,' said Annie, seeing her distress, 'give him some sweets, then. You won't be doing this for ever - he's not going to get fat and need fillings in a few weeks. And if Teresa says anything to you about Jo-Lee, I'll have a word with her.'

The first day she tried sweets with them was a resounding success. Fred had a record number of goes and even Jo-Lee had several. But things still weren't destined to go smoothly. The next time, they wanted nothing to do with the Munchies they had gorged themselves on the day before. She had to change the rewards she gave them every day. She became a newsagent sweet connoisseur and a frequent visitor to Scoop 'n' Save. Her trousers were permanently dusted with sawdust from kneeling on the floor, she exuded an aroma of chocolate and sweet-store toffee and her fingers were sticky with sprinkled sugar and jelly fruit juice. She took to carrying a penknife with her at all times to chop up Twix's and Bounty bars; her pockets rustled with sweet wrappers and the car was sprinkled with chocolate crumbs.

All four chimps were now using the box, but it was a slow process. Not for them the fast and almost intuitive way Paul had picked up the fact that coloured peg equalled sweet-in-drawer. To be fair to them, they were animals, and even though they possessed a lesser intelligence they were far more in tune with their biology than humans. Even if they knew where the sweet should be, they would look in one of the other drawers, just in case she had hidden it somewhere else. In the wild it would be no use relying on one tree that was choked with fruit, because what would happen when you'd eaten it all, or monkeys stole it, or the fruit was no longer in season and you had no idea where there might be any more? In the wild, it paid to be cautious and keep your options open.

They were in Ludmila's. It was Sandra's favourite of all the clubs that Kim frequented. The top part of it was a vegetarian cafe by day and at night you could still sit at the tables hewn from solid lumps of wood, blackened and twisted as if they'd been salvaged from the corrosion of a peat bog. The floor trembled slightly, vibrating to the music from the dance floor downstairs. The walls were painted black and dripped at the tide mark half way down into red. There were fragments of mirrors made into mosaics and the pipes were exposed and wrapped with aluminium foil and chicken wire. A cross between a Gothic cemetery and a beach, bits of driftwood, sanded bottles, lumps of marble and worn parts of rusted wrought-iron gates adorned the walls, and clear glass vodka bottles vomited candle wax onto the tables. It was a relief, thought Sandra, to get away from Hartley Hippo

Healthy Teeth Drops, and smell of perfume rather than chocolate, even if it was only for an evening.

They were drinking wine from plastic beakers and scanning the usual mixed crowd of glittery blacks and drug-pale anarchos. A boy on the next table was staring vacantly into space, but he looked uncannily as if he were gazing right at her. He was dressed all in black so that it seemed as if only his square-jawed face existed, suspended like a Cheshire cat without the grin. He had shaved blond hair and a long black ponytail sprouting from the middle of his head. The roots were dyed pink, as were his eyebrows. He had so many earrings he looked as if someone had put a brace on his ear and he was morosely chewing a bauble attached to a ring through his bottom lip. His black eye-liner had bled a little. Sandra noticed that Kim was watching the boy with an appreciative stare. Sometimes, she thought, she felt on the periphery of life, always watching and trying, somehow, to assemble some kind of meaning from everything she saw. His gaze clicked into focus and he gave Kim a look that would have slit her throat. She blew him a kiss and he snorted.

Sandra took a gulp at her drink and then said, 'Do you think your predator and prey robots will be conscious?'

Kim glanced furtively around her and, leaning forward, said in a loud stage whisper, 'When do you think they'll bring in the next consignment of oranges?'

Sandra wrinkled her forehead and then grinned. 'I was just idly thinking about your robot zoo . . . and what I might do next year when I've finished my thesis.'

'We're out having fun and you're thinking of work,' said

Kim.

'Not all of us have an off button, Kim. We can't look at the clock at five thirty - a.m. in your case - and think, right, time to have fun, no other thoughts allowed to gatecrash the party.'

'I don't know whether they'll be conscious or not. I'm not interested. Christ, I'm starving,' she added. 'Wait a second.'

Kim went over to a machine on the wall and slotted in a few coins. A flake and a Twix tumbled out. She unwound the twist at the top of the flake and slowly peeled away the wrapping, winking at Sandra as she bit into the chocolate. Sandra noticed her catch the eye of a man dressed in red leather, so worn his waistcoat and trousers would have stood up without him. He had a necklace with a silver Chinese symbol that hung down his chest, and his shoulder-length black hair was threaded with feathers. She sighed. She hated the way Kim looked around at everyone else when she was trying to talk. She didn't feel that Kim was listening unless she was staring right at her.

'How can you say that? If they were conscious, you'd be famous. No-one has made a conscious robot before.'

'Would I get lots of men then?' She smiled and added, 'I'm not setting out to try to make them anything other than good robots. And I guess if they were conscious, it would be at a very primitive level - like a rabbit, say.'

'I was just thinking . . . Paul has Asperger's syndrome and he doesn't have Theory of Mind. But people with Asperger's can learn how to act as if they have - as if they really understand that other people have beliefs about the world. Now robots aren't conscious, but if you built one that could learn that people had beliefs and desires it would be fantastic. Whether it was really conscious or not, it would act as if it was.'

Kim thought for a bit and then nodded. 'And if I managed that then I really would be famous and get to sleep with lots of men.'

Sandra flicked some of her wine at her.

'No,' said Kim, slightly more seriously, 'as I said, I'm not interested in making conscious robots, but they might end up that way. See, I want to make ones that do the housework.'

'Yes, and having little metal creatures running round killing other little metal creatures will help you make a robot that'll do the dishes,' said Sandra sarcastically.

'Exactly. A robot that'll do the housework has to want to clear up after you - it has to want to lick your boots. Once you've left for work, it has to decide what order to do things in, whether to sweep the floor and then clear the table, or the other way round, and whether washing the dishes should be done before wiping the windows. And it would have to decide when it ought to recharge its batteries. So my rabots are the first step towards making a much more advanced creature with desires.'

'The desire to do the housework?'

'You still don't see the connection, do you? My rabots have to decide when to recharge their batteries, whether to go without food if there's a predator around - all these major decisions. It's a dog eat dog world out there.'

'Robot eat rabot.'

'Yeah. All the decisions the rabots make, they're the

same kind of decisions a house-cleaning robot would have to make. Now do you see? Well, honey, let us get on and groove.'

They bought more drinks and went downstairs. The walls were black and red in the basement as well. There were dried blood-coloured sofas that exuded the smell of sweat and semen when you sat on them and iron stools round the bar shaped like the Red Queen's crown. Sandra loved to watch Kim dance. She was wearing a short, tight silver lycra top and skirt that left a gap of several inches of hard black stomach, and spiky shoes made of strips of leather criss-crossing over her feet and up her ankles. With her hard, muscular body and her silver clothes, bathed by the blue flashing lights, she looked like some kind of alien machine.

'You are beautiful,' said Sandra, in one of the brief interludes when Kim stopped dancing and came over to sit with her. 'I wish I had a body like yours.'

'No you don't, child,' said Kim softly, and yawned.

'I work out like a dog for it. I do weights every other day and you know how much I swim.'

She was still casting her gaze round the room like a net. Her eyes snagged on a man, tall and thin with long ginger hair. As he danced, the light caught his fingers, fine as those of a pianist. He had his eyes shut, and Sandra half expected them to be greenbrown and uneven.

'You don't stop, do you?' said Sandra. 'Eyeing up the talent,' but even as she said it she felt strangely uncomfortable.

Kim continued to stare and her face softened slightly.

Eventually she said, 'I did once. I did once, sweetie.'

She was quite drunk.

'Were you in a coma or something?'

'Very funny. I had a lover.'

Sandra was about to make another flippant remark about the usual duration of Kim's affairs, but she thought it might be hurtful so she said nothing. Kim continued.

'He was a juggler. I loved him,' she said fiercely, 'with all my heart.'

She had stopped looking at the ginger-haired man, who was bathed in blue light, and her gaze was unfocused.

'He used to work in a circus and he toured all over Europe. I went with him sometimes. I loved that life, you know, its wild, gypsy existence. I loved being surrounded by people who didn't think I was odd.'

'Odd? How could anyone think that? You are stunning.'

'Odd, child, odd, that's what I am.'

Sandra thought about the greasepaint, the big top, the harsh lights round the make-up mirrors, audiences packed together on wooden benches. Yes, Kim would love that life, but, Sandra reflected, she was probably more in love with the idea of it than the reality. Kim liked order, routine, and a slick gloss of exuberance, as shiny and false as nail varnish.

'It must have been difficult. I mean, if he was always away.'

'Yes. It was wonderful when he was over here, but I missed him a helluva lot when he went abroad. Once I flew out to see him in Paris. On the spur of the moment. Caught a plane from Birmingham airport and I was there.'

Sandra smiled at the excitement of it. She could

picture Kim arriving late one evening, the circus all lit up from within, surrounded by tents as bright as sweets. All she had done was go down to London one night to surprise Corin and look how that had turned out.

'Oh, he must have been so pleased to see you.'

'Oh yes,' said Kim bitterly. 'He was pleased as punch.'

'Why?'

'He had a woman with him. A real woman.'

'Oh. I'm sorry.' She wondered at Kim's strange turn of phrase, but decided that it wasn't really the right time to ask about it.

'And so were they,' said Kim viciously.

For some reason Sandra suddenly felt frightened and her heart began to beat faster.

'Why, Kim?' she whispered.

Kim turned and looked her full in the face for the first time that evening. She was pressed very close to Sandra. 'Because,' she said, not taking her eyes away from her, 'I drew a line in the dirt from where I was to their tent. I drew it in kerosene and then I lit a match.' She smiled without mirth and the light caught the tips of her teeth.

She's joking, she doesn't really mean it, she's testing me, thought Sandra, but she knew in her heart of hearts that Kim was telling the truth.

Later they spilled out into the street, sweat freezing on their skin, and flowed with the others in a jagged, flotsam-choked river that swirled and eddied round all-night curry houses and chip shops and branched down dark streets and between bus stops. Above them all the rotunda glowered, only half its sign winking Coca Cola like a foretaste of the dystopia Bladerunner portrayed, and the one-way motorway coiled round the city, bent in on itself in a sinister tangle of intestines, digesting cars, people, sanity.

'Damn birds,' Kim cursed softly; the dawn chorus had already started under the bleary multi-suns of the street lamps.

It was the first time Kim had spoken since they left the club. Why did she tell me? Sandra wondered as they walked back from the bus stop to Kim's flat. It was a test, she thought, a test to see if she'd let Kim down, to see how far Kim could push this friendship, a test to see how sympathetic she, Sandra, really was.

When they got in Kim tore open a plastic wrapper and popped out a fresh needle. She filled it, held it up to the window and squirted a drop from the end, tapped it and eased out another drop, then slid it smoothly into her thigh. Sandra was just about to ask her what she was doing when Kim said, 'I'm diabetic.'

'I didn't realize . . .' she started to say, but Kim had already walked out of the room.

Sandra couldn't sleep. Every time she drifted off she could see a line of flames dancing across the mud in complete silence and, as the first tongues licked the canvas, the rush of air as the flames fireballed filled her head louder than any explosion. She got up. She could hardly see because of the afterimage of fire embossed on her retina. She dressed quietly and let herself out of the flat. The pavement was glassy with ice and there were frost flowers on the windows of her car. It coughed and spluttered when she tried to start it. She prayed Kim wouldn't look out of the window. Finally, the car jerked into life and she drove away, slowly at first, then faster as she hit open, empty roads. She kept her mind carefully blank and her tiredness helped. But if there was one thing she was certain of, it was that after she'd finished her thesis she was not going to be working with robots.

The precision of winter had gone, and in its place was grey spring with sword-sharp bulb leaves thrusting through the soil; the blood-red suns of December, fragile as fertile egg yolks, had smashed and leached stickily into the sky leaving it aching yellow and bruised. The ground beneath the trees round the edge of the Templar forest was carpeted in snowdrops, each bell like a ball gown edged in green brocade. The flowers of the sycamore were starting to emerge; the colour of fluorescent limes, they fell and littered the ground like the tails of dyed lambs.

'Is it going all right?' Ryan poked his head round the door of the kitchen where Sandra was feeding Fred Rolos as fast as she could get the peg set up and the box pushed forward.

'Fine. It's taking a while, though. Ferguson and Jessica are nearly there - it won't be long before they'll be ready. Fred doesn't seem to have quite enough brain cells for this lark. He knows there's a sweet in there somewhere and he's going to do his best to get it, but other than that, not a clue, I'm afraid.'

'Well, let me know when you need me to help with the next bit.'

'Will do,' she said as he left.

Annie was standing leaning on her mop, the end of it floating like seaweed in a puddle of Mersey water.

'He fancies you.'

Sandra coloured. 'I'm not his type.'

'Come off it. You can tell, the way he looks at you and all the stuff he does for you - like putting wire mesh over the bars so Fred can't get his hand through and grab you - and saying he'll help when you get to the experimental part.'

'Yeah, OK, maybe he does. But he's a really nice guy, and he'd do it anyway.'

'And you practically a married woman.'

Sandra sighed and Annie looked at her sharply. 'Not havin' second thoughts, are you?'

'No, nothing like that,' she said a little too vehemently. 'I did try with Ryan, you know, talking about skinny T - but it was quite clear early on that the last person in the world he was going to sleep with would be Teresa.'

Annie laughed. 'Don't blame him.'

'So you and Lee are still . . .?'

'Yeah, we're still . . . Lee is . . .'

'Lee is what?' Bottle-blond hair, tan outrageous orange for spring in the Midlands. Lee.

Annie blushed to the roots of her hair.

'Talking about you, not to you.'

'Must've been good. You wouldn't say anything nasty about me, would you, babe?' He put his arms round her as she held the mop and kissed her, then stuck his tongue in her ear. She screamed and he winked at Sandra.

'Don't believe everything you hear.'

'She don't need to. The walls are so thin, when she walks past the flats she can hear everything she wants - and probably a sight more she doesn't want.'

'When she walks past the keepers' flats,' said Lee, still looking at her. 'And why would she do that? To see Ryan, by any chance?' He laughed at her and said, 'Don't try to look innocent with me. We all know you two've got something going.'

'We're just good friends,' protested Sandra.

'Uh huh. Heard that one before. A degree doesn't make you a better liar. I'll stick with my GCSE French and my YTS Zoo Keeping. I'm a damn good liar, me.'

'It doesn't sound like you need to be,' said Sandra.

He stuck his tongue out at her and then walked over to the bars.

'Come on then, Freddie, come to Daddy. You remember me, Fred, don't you?'

Fred came over and gripped the bars in his huge hands and pressed his face up against them. His eyes became cute and liquid like a spaniel's, something that happened when he liked someone or felt that he wasn't getting enough Maltesers. Lee ran his fingers down one of Fred's thick digits, talking and crooning softly to him all the while.

'I don't know how he dares,' said Annie. 'I've never touched him and I've worked here four years.'

'But he don't like you, do he, he likes me, we're best buddies, aren't we, pal?'

Fred poked his liquorice and ice cream lips through the bars in a pout and Lee stroked the velvety skin on them as if he were a horse. Sandra was about to pack up her stuff because it didn't look as if she was going to get any more work done at this rate when Fred moved suddenly, so swiftly she couldn't be sure she'd seen it, and Lee started to scream. His hand was through the bars up to the knuckle for one long moment, then there was a crunching sound and he staggered back.

Blood spouted everywhere, spraying the white bars and the concrete floor and the screaming went on and on.

'What is it? What's happened?' she cried, but Lee was holding his wrist and shouting.

Annie put her hands up to her mouth and let out an ear-piercing shriek. There was a bloody stump where Lee's index finger had been.

Sandra ran across the kitchen, grabbed a towel and threw it over Lee's hand. She gripped what was left of his finger as tightly as she could but the blood was still pumping out and it soaked the towel within seconds. Lee was green. She pushed him back into a chair and forced his head between his knees and held his hand up in the air. He tried to twist it out of her grip. He was still yelling. Annie continued to scream and all three chimps were wailing and pant- hooting.

'Annie, for fuck's sake, get them out of that cage.'

Annie was shaking and tears were coursing down her face.

'Annie! Annie! Get the chimps out of that cage.'

You were supposed to hit them, weren't you, when they got hysterical like that, but she couldn't leave Lee.

'Annie, you've got to get them out of there. We need to get his finger. To sew back on.'

Abruptly Annie shut up and, pale as marble, she ran

to the back of the cage to lift the hatch up.

The radio was miles away, or so it seemed. It was at the other end of the kitchen. Lee had stopped screaming, but he was sobbing.

'Hold your hand up here, hold it up, don't put it down.'

'It hurts,' he moaned.

'I know, I know, hold it up, it's the best thing to do, and hold this here with your other hand.' She moved his good hand to grip the stump of his finger. He moaned afresh, but she pushed his head further down between his legs.

'Not a bloody contortionist,' he muttered.

She grabbed the radio and made an emergency call, then took the elastic band Annie's hair was tied up in and wrapped it round the remains of Lee's finger.

It was with some difficulty that Annie eventually managed to get the three chimps out. Like bystanders at an accident, they didn't want to leave the scene in the kitchen. An ambulance came and took Lee away, but none of the medics could find his finger.

Annie refused to look.

Sandra went to the toilet and threw up. She was overcome with despondency. It took all her energy to get home and throw her bloody clothes in the bin.

Chapter Fifteen

'Terrible incident. Most unfortunate.' Miss Williams shook her heavy head of black hair. Sandra was reminded of a flower weighted with water trembling on its stalk.

She murmured something in agreement. The clock ticked with quiet resonance and one of Miss Williams's white dogs opened one bloodshot eye to stare at her. She had a vision of Lee shaking in her arms, her hands sticky with warm blood. She shook her head and took a deep breath. 'About my experiment . . .'

'Out of the question. Absolutely not. It would be far too dangerous.'

'But . . .'

'No.'

'I'm not going to stick my fingers in.'

'Fred is bound to be all wound up. Even if you don't get your finger bitten off, you'll excite him. He'll associate you with it.'

'The others are fine, though,' she said, changing her

tactics, 'and they're doing so well.'

'Oh yes, by all means, carry on with the other three. Just keep well away from the bars. I don't think any of them would do that sort of thing, but you never know.'

Sandra heaved a sigh of relief. For one awful minute she'd thought that was the end of her experiment. She talked to Miss Williams for a little longer and then went to find Ryan to ask him to help her with the next stage.

* * *

It had taken the chimps quite a long time to get the hang of associating the peg with the drawer, but now they'd picked it up. Sandra had opted to start with Jessica since she seemed the smartest and the most co-operative. She was intrigued by Ryan being there as well and dashed round the cage in her excitement, then clung to the wire and blew kisses at him.

Sandra put the peg above the third drawer. Ryan immediately moved it to the first drawer along whilst Sandra was watching. She went round the back and put a sweet in the first drawer. She slid the box forward so that Jessica could reach it and she opened the right drawer. But when they repeated the procedure without Sandra's seeing where the peg had been moved to, the chimp still opened the drawer below the peg and looked completely nonplussed to find that there was no sweet in it.

At first all the chimps got that part of the test wrong; although Ryan moved the peg when Sandra was not looking, they still expected the sweet to be in the drawer labelled by the peg as it had been when they were learning.

Ferguson got very angry when the sweet no longer obeyed the rule he'd learnt, and reverted to his former charming habit of peeing on them. Ryan yelled at him and he stopped straight away, although he looked meanly at them and refused to have another go. But very quickly, as if it had suddenly dawned on them what they were supposed to be monitoring, the others looked to see where Sandra was looking and whether she'd seen Ryan moving the peg. They started to pick the right drawer. All three managed to find the sweet. All three could understand her false belief about where the peg was. All three had Theory of Mind.

On the last day, Jo-Lee found the sweet almost every time. Sandra finished the last trial and pulled the box away. Jo-Lee watched her expectantly.

'That's it, Jo-Lee, that's your lot.'

The chimp continued to stare up at her. These days she didn't rock quite so much when Sandra and Ryan were there, or act as scared, but she was still quiet and sucked her thumb and clutched her wad of shredded paper. She came and pressed herself up against the bars when the two of them dragged the box into the kitchen. Sandra clanged the metal barred door behind her, bolted it and fastened the padlock. All the while Jo-Lee watched her, pressed up against the bars of her cage, and it seemed to Sandra that there was unutterable sadness in those eyes. She felt as if the bolt were sliding into her own heart.

What amazed her about London was its lack of homogeneity. It seemed to be made up of a patchwork of places that didn't go together but, like a quilt, formed a composite whole. Take the roundabout near Shepherd's Bush, roads flying out of it in dirty, greasy, car-choked highways, overshadowed by high- rise blocks, ungainly stakes planted in the tarmacked earth, and flanked by sordid pubs whose carpets were stained with beer and old men's lives, and whose poster-covered walls advertised breasts and bands. And yet there was a mosque, perfect as a biscuit, iced in white and gold, and in the corner, right in the lee of the whirlpool of cars, a house tucked away with a green balcony and a wrought-iron winch protruding from the walls. It looked like a cottage industry converted to a country house and the Green Party poster that you would expect was tacked in the upstairs window next to an aspidistra. Alongside it was a property called Ghost Removals.

The rich and the poor lived in discrete sections, but so narrowly confined and dangerously close. The great white houses with their rococo balconies, their glass vases full of stargazer lilies on two-foot stalks, their tiny town gardens crowded with clematis like starfish crawling over coral, had waves of the poor lapping at the sides.

'I have always tried to live in an ivory tower,' she remembered Ryan saying, quoting Flaubert again, 'but a tide of shit is beating at the walls, threatening to undermine it.'

She smiled when she thought of him. She wondered that there was not more bitterness. The people here had to walk past Ferraris so little used their bonnets were sticky with insect spit, past a boutique full of antique Victorian lights, and here there was a school supported by scaffolding and a corner shop with metal shutters covering every window and most of the door. A notice read 'One child at a time ONLY' and the owner had the skin of an emaciated creature that had lived under a stone for a very long time and had as much use for Mars bars as a millipede.

It was only by walking between tube stations from time to time that you realized the real connections, which station was close to where, and how the jigsaw that was London was built up of pieces with garish pictures, hints of beauty and jagged edges. She got on the Central line and walked to college from Tottenham Court Road, past the murky dark of porn shops and the shark dealers who dealt in megabytes.

Now that she had finished her experiment, Professor Dickinson had asked her to come and discuss the results with him. He was, as usual, ensconced in his room amidst the skulls and his babel of books and papers, half-eaten sandwiches and mugs of cold tea, layers of cracked and faintly iridescent scum floating on the surface. He was analysing data on a computer with a screen that must have been almost three feet square.

'Ah, Sandra,' he said, taking off his glasses, 'won't you take some tea, my dear?'

She declined the offer and went to sit in one of the faded Victorian armchairs in the corner, first removing *Primate Social Systems* and *A Darwinian Perspective on Human Reproductive Behaviour.*

'So I take it the experiment went well? Is it too early to say what the results are?'

'Well, I'd need to go through them and analyse them

properly, but I think it looks as if chimpanzees have got Theory of Mind.'

'Excellent. That'll teach the behaviourists. And, er, what are you doing now?'

'I'm going to start analysing my data.'

He ran his hand through his mane of grey hair and said, 'Do you know there's a conference coming up in a couple of months? Would be right up your street.'

'No, I hadn't heard.'

'I'm giving a paper at it.'

She nodded and smiled. There was a pause.

'Do you know how to analyse the data?' he asked abruptly.

'I've an idea. I did some statistics courses for my undergraduate degree. If I get stuck, I can always ask you.'

'How would it be if I analysed it for you?' he said, leaning forward and putting the end of one arm of his glasses in his mouth.

'That's very kind of you, Steven, but I'm sure I'll be all right. You'll have to check it for me, of course.'

He cleared his throat and leant back. There was silence.

Sandra fidgeted and watched a small cloud pass the tiny window. She was about to get up when he spoke.

'I was thinking that we could present your work at the conference.'

'We?'

'Yes. We could analyse it and then give a talk on it.'

'Both of us together?'

'Obviously I'd be doing the talking - and I have a slot in any case. I can simply shuffle my talk about a bit and accommodate your experiment.'

'It sounds like a good idea,' she said cautiously, 'but . . .'

'Good, that's settled. You send me your data and then we can meet nearer the time to discuss it - in a month, say.'

'But ..

'My dear, there's no point in your trying to do it at such short notice. You are hardly fluent with data analysis - you don't have the experience or a computer as highly powered as mine. It would simply take too long and you're bound to make mistakes. We can't afford to take that risk. But by all means come down and we'll discuss what I've done with it. And please don't worry. I'm not in the business of stealing other people's data.'

'Oh, no, I wasn't suggesting . . . but couldn't I give a talk on my own?'

'Out of the question. Absolutely not. There's no slots left, and you're completely unknown; no-one would listen to you. Whereas I already have a reputation. People are far more likely to take my word for it when I say that all was done in a proper fashion. Now wait one moment.'

He put his glasses on and started rummaging around in a couple of piles of paper on his desk, muttering, 'Where did I put the blasted thing? Aaha. Here's the little blighter.'

He handed her a sheet of paper with a list of talks and the date and location of the conference. He stood leaning over her. She scanned the list, her eye immediately snagged by the words 'Professor Steven Dickinson'.

'I'll look forward to receiving your data.'

She realized that he was waiting for her to go. She stood up reluctantly and had to shrink into herself, he was standing so close. He looked at her with his sharp blue eyes and smiled, the skin on his cheeks so taut that she thought of parchment that had been creased over and over again.

She hurried out, her palms hot, feeling slightly sick and uneasy. She phoned Corin from the nearest call box.

'Corin? Corin, I've just been talking to Steven . . .'

'Who?'

'Steven. You know, my supervisor. He wants my data. He wants me to give it all to him and then he's going to write a paper and present it at a conference and he says "we" but he won't, he'll say "me" . . .'

'Sandra, sugar, this is a really bad time for me. I'm up to my neck with this editing, and I'm in the middle of a meeting. The programme goes out in a couple of weeks.'

'Oh, I'm . . .'

'See you later.'

He hung up. She looked at the purring phone and then slowly replaced the receiver in its cradle. She had a couple more ten-pence pieces in her purse. She dropped another one in and called the zoo. When the secretary answered, she asked to speak to Ryan. She realized sadly as the counter clicked to zero and she fed in her last ten pence that it was completely futile. They'd announce his name over the radio or the tannoy system and he'd have to run from the chimp house at the far end of the zoo over to the office. She didn't have enough change to wait that long. She listened to the hiss of the open phone line at the other end and then her money ran out.

The time passed achingly slowly. In the flat below she could hear the soft hum of people's voices like machinery, the sizzle of something frying, water running: she felt it gurgle in the pipes, the innards of the house protesting. She thought of the house as a person, complete with veins and lymphatic nodes, intestines and a liver; gas and water, heat and oil circulating in its brick body. And where was she, in this attic room at the top? In the cranium, peering through windows in the skull, the eyes of the house blindly gaping into the spring night.

At first she was angry because he wasn't home when he knew she'd been distressed, then she felt upset but she suppressed her feeling. He was busy and it wasn't his fault. She paced up and down his immaculate flat. All the walls were white and there were several pictures placed in strategic points, not too many, never too few, and nothing was out of place. There was a print of what looked like a Turner on one wall, the sea like an oil slick, flames crowding out of a ship, leaping for the safety of the sky and turning it into a blistering burn.

The first couple of times she heard a car drawing up near the house, she rushed to the window and peered out, but the cars, gilded into trash by the orange of the street lamps, were never his.

Eventually there was a rattle at the door and he burst in. 'Hi, I'm home. Where are you?'

'Here,' she said quietly.

He held out his arms and hugged her, then immediately let her go. His hands were full of things.

'I'm sorry I'm so late. Had a really shitty day. Listen, about the Dick character, don't let him do it. What was it he wants to do again?'

'Take my data and present it at a conference.'

'These are for you, by the way.' He held out a bunch of

flowers so she could see them, but he didn't give them to her. He put a wine bottle in the freezer and started unwrapping the flowers whilst at the same time peering in cupboards, looking for a suitable vase. They were stargazer lilies and some were beginning to bloom, white and pink like peeled guavas slit open. They smelt of marmalade.

'Well, don't. It's your work, you did it. Don't let him get all the glory for it.'

'It's not as simple as that. He's my supervisor. He spent time helping me. It's only fair that—'

Corin snorted. 'Don't talk bollocks, darling. Have some alcohol instead.'

He opened the bottle and put it in an ice bucket, poured them out a drink and lit the candles in the candelabra she'd made for him.

'I'm starving.'

'Drink. There's plenty of calories in drink.'

He clinked his glass against hers and downed most of his in one, poured some more and leant against the table, looking at her with half-closed eyes.

'Come here,' he said, and she went.

He started to take her clothes off. She had the impression that he had been moving since he'd got in and undoing the buttons on her shirt was simply another movement, something to do with his hands while he was perched on the table. It was a wonder he didn't smoke, she thought, and slowly, slowly, she felt her body start to respond to his efficient touch.

When all her clothes had been reduced to piles on the floor, he lifted her onto the table and made her lie down. He eased himself into her. The scent of the lilies was heavy in the air and the candles spluttered and guttered softly in a ring above her. His shadow, huge and gangly, cast around the room, searching for a space to call its own.

He started to take his shirt off, unbuttoning it and looking down at her with a half-smile on his face, his one wild eye staring to the side of her lips. He undid the cuffs and started to pull the shirt over his head. She had a feeling of foreboding, but the words choked in her mouth, and then she cried out as hot molten wax rained down upon her naked breasts and stomach.

'What? What is it?' he asked. 'You're shaking, sweetheart.' His words were muffled through his shirt. He yanked it off and caught the candelabra again. More wax tipped down on her, burning her, and she cried out again, but she couldn't move, pinned down as she was, her arms thrown across her eyes to protect them.

'Oh, darling, I'm sorry,' he said. 'Did I knock it?' He reached up and caught the steel cluster of candles and stilled its swinging. Then he began to slide in and out of her again.

She cautiously removed her arms and looked at him aghast.

'It's OK,' he said soothingly, 'it's only wax. It won't have hurt you.'

He gripped her hips and bent his head over her and she could feel the soft tips of his hair sliding like sea anemone fingers over her belly, and the hard plates of wax splintering and pulling her skin taut, pleating it into fine red lines between the cracks. He moved harder now, faster, his fingers buried themselves in her flesh and she felt she was choking again. He pressed himself against her once, twice, and breathed like a drowning man sucking in air after water. He slid out of her and kissed her. He pulled her upright as if she were a marionette and clucked his tongue. She felt she might break.

'Come here,' he said and started to peel away the wax. She winced. It was like someone pulling off the tentacles of an octopus, one by one.

'Nearly finished, sweetheart,' he said, and the word sounded strange in his mouth; a green and red word: heart red, sweet green, brilliant green as glass, as grasshoppers, bitter as crushed ivy, ground down and spat out from between his lips.

Chapter Sixteen

The otter wriggled in his hands. It was only a baby and it wanted to play. Its rolls of fat slid beneath Paul's hands and it bit his fingers gently and scraped him with soft claws as it rolled around on its back.

Paul held it down with one hand, digging his fingers into the otter's fur and tickling him. The baby squirmed in response. Paul got out the chloroform. The wriggling became more frantic as he held the cotton wool over the otter's muzzle. The animal twisted frantically to avoid it and then became still.

Paul took out his scalpel, some nails and his hammer, and smoothed open his notebook at the page where he'd made a neat list of the time it took a heart to die. He wrote 'Otter' and then picked up the first nail.

It had been hard to get a live animal that was so high up the evolutionary tree. He'd looked at puppies in the pet shop when he'd gone into town with his mother.

'I don't think we can really afford to have a dog,' she'd said, sounding worried. 'Their food costs a lot,' she added for her literal-minded son.

He continued to stare at the puppies with their fat, pink tummies who were tumbling about in the straw together.

'I don't want one, I only want to know how much they cost.'

His words condensed on the window pane. He'd have to save up his pocket money for five weeks and six point three days to buy one and he didn't have time. It was coming up to the third day of the month again.

He couldn't think of a way round it because all the cages at the zoo had alarms that were turned on at night and his mother only had the keys to the gibbon cage. He needed to do a mammal that wasn't quite as advanced as a primate, and in any case he wasn't sure he knew how to catch a monkey. In the end he'd talked to Jeff about it. It hadn't occurred to him to ask Jeff at first, not until the day when he'd been looking for Claire.

It was half past six and she was normally in the road outside the flats or in the playground, but today he couldn't find her. He wandered around for a bit and played on the swings. He walked back home to see if she was with her family in their flat. Fat Gerry, her podgy four-year-old brother, was playing with mud and stones at the edge of a puddle.

'Where's Claire?' Paul asked him. It was better than having to ask Claire and Gerry's parents.

'Playing in the playground.'

'No, she's not.'

Gerry got up and held out a muddy hand to Paul. 'I'll show you,' he said when Paul wouldn't take his hand.

Reluctantly Paul took hold of his dirty, chubby paw and allowed himself to be led back to the playground.

'There,' said Gerry triumphantly and pointed to the caravan.

Claire was chatting away to Jeff. He must be sitting down, thought Paul, because their heads are level and so close together. And that was when he thought of asking Jeff. He walked across the playground and opened the caravan door. Jeff jumped.

'I have to go now,' said Claire, slithering off his knee. She adjusted her skirt and ran out, wrinkling her nose up at Paul. Paul explained very carefully to Jeff what he needed.

'It must be a mammal, because they're exothermic and their basal metabolic rate is much higher than a reptile's or an amphibian's - at all times, no matter how cold it is. A shrew's heartbeat, for instance, is faster than an elephant's, but it is said that both animals, and in fact this may be true of all animals, have the same number of heartbeats throughout their life.'

'The light that burns so bright burns half as long,' said Jeff.

Paul blinked and then continued, 'Indeed, shrews have to eat all the time or else they die. Of course, I don't want an animal the size of a shrew. Much larger than a rat.'

Jeff stroked his chin and then said slowly, 'Well, I'll see what I can do. Yes, I think it could be done.'

He didn't ask why Paul needed a mammal with a high

basal metabolic rate that had to be larger than a rat but not as advanced as a monkey.

'You have to do something for me in return,' said Jeff craftily.

'What is it?'

'I can't tell you.'

'If you can't tell me, then I can't do it.'

'I'll show you.'

There was a pause. Jeff said, 'I promise I'll give you your animal.'

Still Paul didn't say anything.

'Of course, if you don't want me to try . . .'

'Yes, I need it.'

'Then it's settled,' said Jeff.

He leaned over Paul and shut the door behind him. He picked up one of the pillows from his narrow bed and plumped it up. He laid it down on the edge of the bed. Then he took out an old and sticky jar of Vaseline from his cupboard. Paul watched, mildly puzzled. But when Jeff started to take off his trousers, his fingers shaking so much he could hardly undo the zip, and bent Paul over the pillow, he knew exactly what was going to happen. He also knew that the best thing to do was relax and let all his muscles go limp. Even so, when he got up stiffly later on, there was a round patch of blood and saliva on the sheet where his mouth had been.

Chapter Seventeen

The letter was lying on the mat when she came down in the morning. The postman hadn't been, and indeed, when she picked it up, there was no stamp or address on it, simply the word 'Sandra' written in beautiful flowing calligraphy in purple ink. The envelope was thick and smooth.

She made herself a cup of coffee and opened it. Inside were two pieces of A4 paper covered with the same painstaking script, as if each letter had been agonized over. It said:

To Sandra from your friend Paul.

Once upon a time, many years ago when I was young, a wicked wizard with a long grey beard came to   me when I was sleeping. He touched me and swore me to secrecy for all absolute endless eternity. He told me he had planted a bomb in my heart and when I listened to my pulse, that was the ticking of the bomb. If ever I told anyone about him then the bomb would blow up and I and all the people around me would be killed. He said to me that there was a good witch who was the only person who could remove the bomb, but I would never find her.

One day I saw her from my window. She was nine feet tall and black. She had long, black hair right down to her elbows and she was wearing a bright yellow dress. Every day I followed the good witch and I loved her with all my heart. When she picked me up in her arms I was so high from the ground that no evil could reach me and the wicked wizard could never find me.

But one day I looked out of my bedroom window and she was not there. I ran out into the street and I asked everybody I met, 'Where is that woman who is nine feet tall with long black hair down to her elbows and a bright yellow dress because I love her with all my heart and she looks so fine to me that she makes me feel great?'

I never found her and I miss her with all my heart. When I lie awake at night I can hear the ticking of the bomb and it echoes in my chest.

Sandra read and reread the letter. She carefully folded it up and went and stood by the window cradling her hot mug in her hands. His letter touched her to the quick. It gave her a sick feeling in the pit of her stomach. What was it that had been done to him and by whom? She had a horrible feeling it was his father, or one of his fathers. She wondered how she could help him. She could carry on lending him books and she could look after him sometimes to give Meg a bit of a rest, but she wouldn't be living in the Midlands for much longer. In any case, he needed much more specialized help than she or Meg could provide. Meg had to accept that her son had an incurable disorder, but that he could be treated, he could learn how to cope with his disability. She sighed. She would have to go and speak to her again but she doubted she would have any better luck this time. Even Ryan hadn't managed to convince her, and he certainly had the gift of the gab. She smiled to herself and then suddenly had a thought. She could try to find the name and address of a clinician who specialized in Asperger's syndrome and give her Meg's address, or even get the clinician to contact Paul's school. That, at least, would look official and not as if some student were meddling in Meg's affairs.

Outside the sky was grey and uncompromising. The line of poplars by the drive thrashed in the wind and their catkins littered the ground like bright beads of blood. Stiffly the leaves of the sycamore crawled in hermit crab fashion from scaled and flushed buds and opened their claws, trawling the sky for sunlight. She sighed and turned back to her work. She'd decided to try to speak at the conference on her own. It was her work, she thought grimly, and she was damned if she'd let anyone else take the credit for it. When she had asked the conference organizers if there were any slots left, they had said no, but told her she might be able to present her work as a poster. You had to write up your paper very briefly and stick the pages on the wall. The best posters were ones with few words and lots of brightly coloured graphs. She sent in a summary of her experiment and, surprisingly, the organizers wrote back and said she would be allowed to speak. They were going to cut down the amount of time allowed for all the talks in one afternoon session and make the tea breaks shorter. In retrospect, she thought, it was obvious that Steven had wanted her to think that the conference organizers were totally inflexible.

But writing the paper was tough going. It was not easy to get up every day with no structure to her life other than the one she dictated. At least before there had been hours to be clocked up on her observational work. She found she missed the chimps and would sometimes sneak back into the zoo in the early morning to say hello to them. To begin with, Jessica and Ferguson still held out their hands, calloused palms uppermost, in a begging gesture and she wished she had a few jelly babies secreted on her person.

God, I'm going to turn into a little old lady craftily slipping peanuts to the monkeys when she thinks no-one is looking, she thought.

Most of the time she spent sitting in front of her computer and poring over data sheets, logging numbers onto the spreadsheet and trying to make sense of the statistical tests she had to do. The flat was old and badly maintained. At least now it was spring it wasn't quite as cold, but the electricity surged unpredictably and her computer whispered in protest like an electronic thrust. She was worried the whole thing might crash and she'd lose all her results.

The Parade of the Dwarfs, Corin's programme, had been broadcast a couple of weeks ago and there had been quite a lot of publicity. People wrote in to the BBC, to chat shows and newspapers saying how disgusting it was that the poor should be portrayed in that light, and that once you had sunk so low it was very difficult to better yourself no matter how hard you tried. There were accusations of misogyny in the way Anjou, a single mother, had been dealt with, and the implication that even if Frank beat up his wife and child it was all right since he now had a job. There were also accusations of racism. The programme review board and the bigwigs loved it. Corin, for his part, said all publicity was good publicity and what, the fuck did the public know anyway? Most of the watchers were probably a bunch of uneducated yobbo *Sun* readers who'd just heard that PC no longer meant something that was IBM compatible.

There had been a viewing of the film at the BBC when it was broadcast and the production team had gone out for a meal afterwards. Sandra went too but had felt left out. There was no denying that his film looked good, but it made her feel uncomfortable because people would watch it and think it were true, not realizing that it was merely his interpretation of events. His interpretation was not even what he really thought, but what he thought would make a good film. The final section had made her feel particularly uneasy. There were lingering shots in Anjou's house of curry-smeared plates and empty bottles of alcohol, a drop of port falling stickily onto the baby's hand as she crawled past.

Anjou and Sita (daughter number one, as Corin called her) were having a row. You could hear them in the background but the camera was low down following baby Shereen as she crawled around. It was something about boys, but the two women were simultaneously screeching so loudly that it was very difficult to make out what was going on. Shereen was oblivious. She picked up a piece of silver foil that was lying on the floor and stared intently at it. She sat up and swayed slightly, her balance not quite right. There was the sound of a crash. She jumped but continued to turn the foil over in her fat little hands. She drooled slightly. Then, as if that gave her an idea, she crawled purposefully across the floor. When she got to one of the blue Jesuses, his feet caked in sweetmeats, she started laboriously to haul herself up. The row was still going on but suddenly you could hear the words quite clearly. Anjou was shouting, 'You dare to go behind my back with this no-good boy, come here and I'll give you two tight slaps.' There was the sound of running footsteps and another crash as something shattered. Cut to close-up of candle guttering and blowing out. Cut to big close-up of Shereen crying. Cut to even larger close-up of the blue Jesus, now smashed so that very little was recognizable apart from his feet. The camera panned slightly to show the fragments of cheap ceramic, yoghurt white inside. And then one final shot of Our Saviour's head, severed at the neck. A blob of wax dripped onto his blank upturned face and rolled like a tear down his cheek.

Highly emotive stuff, but what had actually happened? Thinking back to the conversation she had overheard between Corin and Lisa, she had every suspicion that no drunken debauchery had ever taken place in Anjou's house. Corin had probably ordered a huge take-away for the whole crew and filmed the mess afterwards. As the credits rolled and everyone started to clap, she felt a dreadful and hollow emptiness.

Corin had let his hair down - literally. He no longer wore it in a ponytail and he'd taken two weeks off to eat, sleep, drink and rediscover his flat. He visited friends he hadn't seen for months and was invariably happily drunk whenever she spoke to him on the phone. He seemed to be his old self, on the surface at least, high on adrenalin and alcohol, rushing round on a gruelling self-imposed social schedule, his head crammed full of directors' names and shot lists for every television programme anyone might recently have seen and might or might not have been interested in. When he'd been making his programme he wouldn't stop working for a minute; now that he was back at work, he frequently set up breakfast meetings that went on through lunch until he remembered he had arranged to see a friend on the other side of town and would dash off again.

She couldn't help feeling that he was at a dangerous stage. She imagined him as a sparkler, zipping along the Central line and fizzing unstably in Soho dinners. She hoped nothing would happen that might cause him to ignite before he could channel his energies into the next programme.

'Sandra, sugar, I'm here. Aren't you pleased to see me?' He bounded up the stairs two at a time and crashed into her room.

His more relaxed attitude to work had not improved his timekeeping, she thought. She got up and hugged him for the few brief seconds allowed before he was off rummaging through her fridge for beers and talking without breathing about some guy he'd been at college with and hadn't seen for ten years whom he'd bumped into in a bar when he was meeting some girl from college whom he hadn't seen for three.

She put on her coat. She'd given up cooking anything for the two of them. They always drove into town to get food when he arrived.

'Corin . . .'

He cracked open a can, turned the TV on and slumped on the sofa.

'Mmm? Hey, have you seen this? It's an animal series, you ought to watch it, it's about some, well, it's some creature, but I heard from Mick Rheinman that he'd been told by Lucinda Patel that the producer took two and a half years to make it. Two and a half years! In the most *appalling* conditions and the budget was gastronomical, but he said . . . hey, look at this, that's outrageous, it's a studio setting, look, have you seen, it's all set up, God, imagine feeding some poor little bug to this big-fanged critter, they probably put the bug in the freezer to slow it down, and if you spend two and a half fucking years in the forest you don't really expect to do major shoots in the studio . . .'

'Corin, shall we go?'

'Huh? Oh, I've eaten already. Aw Jesus, a crane shot in the jungle, that must have taken a fucking decade to set up and see that frog, I bet they were dangling mealie worms in front of its mouth to get it to move at that exact time. Or else prodding it up the bum with something . . .' He looked at her face and said, 'Oh, sorry, Sandy, didn't think. Ring for a take-out.'

She sighed. 'It's not bloody London, you know. No

idiot on a bike is going to drive for ten miles to deliver a cold pizza.'

She started to make herself some toast, stifling her anger at his thoughtlessness.

'Corin, something odd's happened. I was going to swap round some of my sculptures - I'm getting bored with the ones in here - and I was looking through all my junk in the garage and I couldn't find the one I made that day, you know that day,' she blushed, 'when you, you know . . .'

He was grinning at her, 'When I what?'

'When you asked me . . .'

'When I asked you what?' He suddenly laughed at her embarrassment, jumped up and pulled her onto the sofa with him. 'Yeah, sure I remember that day. What about it? You haven't changed your mind, have you?'

'No, I wasn't talking about that. I was talking about the sculpture I made that day. I can't find it anywhere.' He was still grinning at her.

She looked at him in surprise. 'Do you know anything about it?'

'Yes. I know where it is.'

'Well, where?'

'I sold it.'

'You did what?'

'Yeah, I forgot all about it. Here.' He rummaged in his jacket and pulled out a crumpled cheque. 'Sorry, I should've given it you ages ago.'

She was speechless.

'It's good money, isn't it? I told you to try selling them, help supplement your grant.'

'Who did you sell it to?' She tried to keep her voice

even but it suddenly got high-pitched at the end of the sentence.

'I don't know. Friend of a friend. Can't remember his name now. It's on the cheque.' He looked at her properly. 'You're not mad, are you?'

'You bet I am.' She struggled to keep the tears out of her eyes. 'It was my *best* sculpture.'

'Well, of course. I'm not going to try to palm your worst onto someone. Oh, come on, you ought to be grateful. It *is* good money, it wasn't any hassle for you, and who knows, you might get some commissions from it. Where are you going?'

'The bathroom.'

Sandra walked down the stairs as if they were a hazard to be overcome with great care. She opened the door into the garage and shut it behind her, leant against it and allowed her eyes to adjust to the dark. A thin strip of light slid into the garage from beneath the door, and gradually she could make out rusting hulks of scrap metal, twisted steel, and the smooth, interlocking curves of her sculptures. She breathed in the bloody smell of metal and the dense smoothness of oil. It reminded her of the wild open sea: every time she smelt steel she thought of salt. Here and there the floor was beaded with drops of spilt solder like solidified mercury. She walked slowly through the dark to the bathroom at the end. The light filtering through the thick frosted glass was milky. She wiped her eyes and peered into the rust-flecked mirror. There was a slight distortion, and her hair, so carefully spiked and rumpled with Dax for Corin's coming, veered off at an angle. She pressed her forehead against the cold of the mirror; her head was starting to throb with a dull ache.

Almost as if she had no control over her body, she found herself retracing her footsteps back into the flat, but instead of going upstairs she opened the front door and started walking down the edge of the drive on the grass so her feet would make no sound, the lower twigs of the poplars scraping her skull and twisting her hair, turning right at the end of the drive and continuing along the road where there were no street lamps and it was so dark she could barely see her feet on the tarmac, leaves of cow parsley grabbing her jeans, the sharp scent of pineapple emanating from crushed camomile when she stepped onto the verge out of the way of the occasional cars that raced through the night far too fast on roads with unexpected curves. She found herself skirting ruts in the track down to the flats and once she stepped into a puddle. She knocked on Ryan's door.

His smile faded almost immediately when he saw the expression on her face.

'Come in.' He motioned her towards the sofa. He looked at her wet trainers and muddy jeans but didn't say anything.

'Cup of tea, duck?' he said, trying to sound cheerful.

'Yes please.' She pulled a twig out of her hair and some grass that had got twisted in with the laces of her trainers.

'So what has he done?'

'How do you know Corin did anything?'

He sighed. 'Let's not go into that now. Two sugars for you. You look like you could do with it.'

She told him about her sculpture. His face hardened, but he said nothing.

'He was trying to do me a favour. And I do need money.'

'Money is not a problem. I can give you some. But that's not the point - the money, I mean. He didn't ask you, that's the point. My hunch is he's jealous.'

'What? Of me? No way.'

'Your sculptures are good and he doesn't do anything like that. Anyway, what do I know, I'm no psychologist.'

'Are you going to quote Flaubert again?'

'Can't think of anything appropriate, but I'm sure he could've done.'

'I should go. Thanks for the tea,' she hesitated, 'and thanks for being here.'

He smiled up at her and she felt like taking him in her arms. She turned away abruptly. He walked with her up the muddy driveway and back onto the road. He steadied her when she tripped in the potholes and walked so close that she could feel the heat from his body. He didn't say a word all the way home, but she felt comfortable in the silence.

They reached the driveway to her house and she stopped. The lights were still on in her flat. The drive seemed immensely long. She felt nauseous and cold.

'I can't go in,' she whispered.

'There's no need,' he said softly.

They turned and retraced their footsteps.

'I'll sleep on the sofa,' he said when they got back. 'You can have the bed.'

'It's OK, I don't mind, really. You take the bed. It's your flat.'

'No, I'll be fine out here.'

She was too tired to protest. She felt as if all her energy had been drained. She could hardly talk and keeping her eyes open was difficult. She allowed herself to be led into the bedroom. Ryan's bed smelt of him, warm and masculine, slightly bitter, a trace of his aftershave on the pillow. She fell asleep almost instantly, but woke up later in the night, troubled by strange dreams. She thought of her sculpture, gone forever. She couldn't bear to think about Corin.

Just as the early morning light started to filter through the curtains, there was a rustle and Ryan slipped into bed beside her. She had her back to him and she was so leaden with lack of sleep that she did not move. He curled himself around her and held her tight in his arms. She held on to his muscular forearms and lay still, willing sleep to come. The first birds began to sing and she thought of Corin and how horrible it all was for him. He had no idea where she was, and here she was, in bed with another man. She shifted uncomfortably. She felt claustrophobic. Ryan's arms were heavy round her and the sheets were hot and itchy.

She pushed him away and slid out of bed.

'I've got to go,' she mumbled and grabbed her clothes. She dressed in the bathroom, then came back into the bedroom. He was lying on his back, staring at the ceiling. The room was awash with grey light and his bedside clock said five a.m. She kissed him briefly and turned to go.

'Sandra.'

She looked back at him. He took her in his arms and hugged her one more time before she left.

Her stomach felt as if it were filled with stones. She

pushed open the door of her flat and tiptoed into the room. She could hardly breathe.

She stopped short. Corin was sitting on the sofa. He was supernaturally still. He moved like a statue turning its head. He was completely white and there were purple rings under his eyes.

'I thought you were dead. I looked for you. I didn't know whether to call the police.'

She immediately pitied him and went over to him. He stood up and wrapped his arms round her. 'I'm sorry. I should've asked before I sold it.' He held her at arm's length. 'Where were you?'

'I went to Ryan's,' she said, but she couldn't meet his eyes.

'Ryan's,' he said with a sneer, but he didn't say anything else.

A change had been wrought on the land. There were no bare fields with crops of seagull's grey as stones and the hedgerows were no longer lines of winter wood strung with dead birds' nests like woven skulls. There was a luxuriance to the verges and embankments chaotically crowded with groundsel, ivy, bramble, policeman's helmet and butterbur, the leaves as tough as hide and large as shields. The elderberry bushes were stacked high with flowers that cast shadows as intricate as bunches of bridal lace; the hawthorn pricked with ballet buds that would soon form a spume of red and white.

Her paper for the conference was finished and she'd had slides made of Jessica, Ferguson and Jo-Lee, her wooden box and some graphs and tables to illustrate her talk. She spent ages agonizing over what to wear. Academics were not known for being snappy dressers. Anything vaguely provocative would be out. Equally obviously she couldn't just turn up in jeans or leggings. She was acutely aware that she was going to be the youngest speaker and the only one who wasn't a doctor. In the end she settled for the shoes she'd bought to wear to the celebration after Corin's programme was broadcast, and a Monsoon floral print dress with a woollen cardigan. It was a two-day conference and Ryan had managed to wangle time off work to go with her. She desperately needed some moral support, and he was so laid back she thought some of it might rub off on her.

As they were driving to Manchester, she reflected that this was a crunch point in many ways. Her talk was the first chapter of her thesis. She still had an awful lot more to do, but depending on how it was received, and the comments people made, she might have to rewrite, or rethink the way she would write the other chapters. It was the first time she'd struck out on her own independently from her supervisor. And perhaps she would decide whether she wanted to carry on in academia, and, if so, in what field. Working with Kim was out of the question. But more important than that, here was a chance to convince the people who mattered, who could often lead the way in influencing people's opinions, that these animals did have Theory of Mind.

It was odd, she reflected, that with Ryan in the car she didn't feel worried and wasn't troubled by her usual macabre visions of crashes. In the corner of her eye, tides of daisies rose and fell, looking as muddied as melting snow. The teasels fringing the motorway were black with tar, their desiccated seed- heads like cruciform hedgehogs strung up on branched gallow trees.

It was also a social turning point, this conference. She needed to move back down to London to do her writing up at university. In a way she was looking forward to the change, but moving was always an upheaval. Then there was Corin . . . and Ryan. She'd miss Ryan. He wasn't going to stay at the zoo, but she wondered how much she'd see of him if he went back to Birmingham. And as for Corin, well, surely everything would be all right when she moved to the city and could see him regularly? But somehow, actually going out and buying a white dress seemed such a remote prospect. It was better not to think about it, better to see how it would all turn out, she thought.

'Penny for them?'

'I was thinking I'd miss you when I go back to London.'

'You're only saying that to get me to pay half the petrol. Don't think I don't know. Flattery is the best way to a man's heart.'

'I thought it was with a bread knife through his shirt pocket.'

'Careful. Fiscal aid can be withdrawn as quickly as it is proffered.'

Dr Ross was speaking on memory, learning strategies and cognition in white rats. After he'd finished talking, Sandra put her hand up to ask a question. It was like being back at school. People glanced at her curiously. Her arm ached, but the chair consistently by-passed her and gave the floor to prominent academics. Each of them gave a mini-speech.

'I thought this was question time,' she hissed at Ryan.

Finally, everyone except her had had their turn. The chair glanced at his watch, cleared his throat and said, 'I think it's about . . .'

'Excuse me,' said Sandra as loudly as she could. She flushed and her heart started beating hard.

'Ah, well, time for a quick one, then.'

'Are you saying that because rats seem to do well at these intelligence tasks they could be as smart as people think chimps are?'

Dr Ross didn't even bother to look at her. 'I made no comparisons between species.' He glanced pointedly at the chair who swiftly wrapped up the meeting.

She felt outraged and humiliated and was reminded of a friend who, when she'd first started her Ph.D., had asked a guest speaker a question. He'd told her to go away and look it up. Three years later after she had submitted her thesis, he'd turned into the very epitome of friendliness. In the canteen, she and Ryan tried to slide past Steven who was talking to Dr Ross, but he saw her and loudly called her over.

'This,' he said, draping one arm round her shoulder, 'is the delightful Sandra Roberts, one of my students, who is speaking tomorrow.'

'Delighted,' said Dr Ross, reaching out to shake her hand, his face now wreathed in smiles. 'I didn't realize you were in this field.'

And that, she thought, was as close as you could get to an apology.

She looked around the bar. The academics were huddled in little clots over their pint glasses. There was a respectful gap and then knots of postgraduates and the occasional keen undergrad hanging on the periphery. A TV flickered at the far end of the room and there was the sweet metallic smell of cider. Her stomach coiled in on itself.

'I'm scared,' she whispered to Ryan.

'Don't worry, kid, you'll be fine. Everyone's nervous, even the guys who've been doing it for years. When they were asking questions . . .'

'Giving speeches, more like.'

'Yeah. They were shaking like leaves.'

'Mm, well, I ought to get an early night. I'm going to head off for bed.'

He ruffled her hair. 'I'll just finish my pint. Catch you at breakfast.'

She didn't sleep. She kept rehearsing her talk and then jolting fully awake, her heart thumping, thinking she'd forgotten a crucial slide. When she got up she ran over her notes. She couldn't eat a thing. Her hands shook and she felt nauseous. She was the second speaker after lunch; all morning her throat was dry and she couldn't concentrate on the talks.

The worst bit was sitting at the front while the first person spoke, feeling people's eyes drift over to her, surreptitiously wiping her cold and clammy hands on her skirt. Ryan winked at her once and she gave him a tight-lipped smile.

The applause died down. 'Our next speaker is Miss Sandra Roberts from UCL whose talk is on the understanding of false beliefs in chimpanzees.'

There was a smattering of clapping and she stood up, her knees trembling. Her voice came out in a quaver. She took a deep breath and asked for the slide projector to be turned on. To her intense relief the machine didn't jam, drop her slides or wobble out of focus, and once she started speaking it was all right. Her nerves steadied and her voice seemed to iron itself out.

'. . . So, in conclusion, all three of the chimpanzees I tested showed evidence that they had an understanding of false beliefs; to be precise, they could comprehend that other animals have thoughts and feelings.' She sat down with relief, but the ordeal wasn't over yet.

The audience clapped briefly and a forest of hands shot up. The chair picked one at random.

'Perhaps, Miss Roberts, you are being overly anthropomorphic. After all, you showed us slides of your experimental subjects and gave them names instead of numbers. When you spoke you referred to them as "he" and "she". Don't you think that your over-identification with these animals may have prejudiced your interpretation of the results?'

'I think I'd find it hard to "over-identify" with a chimp. They were zoo animals with names and personalities,' (there was a muted sucking in of breath at this) 'but to say that calling a chimp Jessica instead of Fl could influence my work is less than charitable. The chimps were picking drawers labelled one, two, three or four. I am not going to confuse a chimp who chooses drawer one with one who chooses drawer three just because I call him or her by their name.'

'You haven't videoed any of the proceedings. Don't you think this calls into question the validity of your work?'

'No. I haven't faked or altered my results. Dr Ross has not recorded any of his experiments on tape. Are you saying that working with chimps requires special procedures?'

'Yes, when it is likely that the scientist, particularly if she is a young woman, is liable to become unduly attached to her subjects.'

The questions didn't get any better. She was accused at worst of deliberately falsifying her data and at best of being so involved with the chimps that she 'accidentally' altered her results. At last the chair brought the session to a close as they had over-run into the tea break. But there was no respite. A cloud of academics hovered round her, stridently voicing their opinions on the validity of her work. Steven Dickinson stood in the background, uncharacteristically silent, and said not a word to defend her. She was close to tears. As soon as two eminent doctors shifted the focus of their attention away from her and started to argue with each other, she slipped away.

Ryan was holding a cup of tea for her. She took it in shaking hands.

Putting on his Irish accent, he said, 'You did really well. Just ignore them. They're a bunch of wankers, so they are,' and she had to smile at the way he dismissed the whole gamut of cognitive ethology researchers as intellectual masturbators.

'I want to go,' she said. She felt she'd lost the battle in a big way.

Ryan took her teacup from her and put his arms round her. 'We will. Go and get your slides right now and I'll drive you back.'

He was holding her when Corin walked in. She saw him out of the corner of her eye, started, and pulled back. She wasn't the only person looking at him. He stood out a mile with his long ginger-brown hair, his natural bearing and, above all, the fact that he was wearing a cream-coloured Armani suit and a hand- painted silk tie. He was looking furious.

She walked slowly over to him and felt, rather than saw, Ryan's presence behind her.

'Well?'

'If you've come for my talk, you're too late. I've just given it.'

'Looks like I'm too late for everything.'

'We were just about to go.'

'I'll take you home.'

'Ryan . . .'

'Frankly I don't give a flying fuck what happens to Ryan. Get your things now.'

'I'll take your car,' said Ryan.

She'd never seen him look so angry; his normally placid face was a mask of hatred. She hesitated but he said, 'Go on, give me the keys.'

She handed them to him and went to retrieve her slides. Corin was waiting in his car for her. She put her bag in the boot and climbed in. She hadn't even shut the door before he jerked the car into reverse. He kept up a constant stream of swear-words as they negotiated the traffic, one-way streets and roadworks in the city centre, then lapsed into a terrifying silence as they hit the motorway.

'I didn't think you'd be able to come,' she murmured.

'Clearly.'

'It wasn't like that. I wanted someone there for moral support.'

'You got a bargain, then. All sorts of other support thrown in too.'

'It wasn't like that,' she repeated, but he said, 'Don't tell me, I don't want to know.'

She sat quietly, her knuckles white, feeling sick, not just because of his reaction, but because they were driving faster than she'd ever driven in her life. It got darker. The night pressed in on them. She felt as if they were driving through a funnel, one that stretched on interminably with no end in sight.

It wasn't until they were back inside her flat that he turned to her and said grimly, 'How long has this been going on?'

'What?'

'You heard me,' he shouted. 'How long has this been going on?'

'There is nothing going on,' she said quietly.

'Let's try again, you dumb bitch. How many times have you slept with him?'

'I haven't.'

'Did he make you come?' he sneered. His voice rose in anger again. 'Did he?'

She turned away from him but he swung her back round to face him. 'Do you like it better with him, then? Do you? We were going to be married and you're off fucking someone else before we've even got to the church. Well, better to find out now than afterwards. Better now than when it's too late.'

'But I haven't. We didn't.'

'You lying bitch.'

Think calmly, think rationally. It must be hard for him, she thought, he feels insecure, he's seen us together at the conference, arms round each other, think how it must have looked, how he must have felt, and you can't deny, you do feel something for him, don't you, and you do spend a lot of time with him and you do keep talking about him, Corin's never with you during the week, how must he *feel?*

She took a deep breath. 'Look, I can understand what you must have felt . . .'

'No you bloody don't, you've no idea what I felt, what I feel, no fucking idea at all, and for once in your life why don't you stop trying to be so fucking sympathetic? Because it doesn't bloody work.'

There was no hope, then, she thought dully. The only way was to get out, out of here, away from him, away altogether. She ducked under his arm and ran down the stairs and out of the door. At first she ran blindly, as fast as she could, her breath hoarse, her limbs oddly angled and ungainly, through the new barley at the back and the fields beyond. Gradually, as she ran out of breath, she slowed down and settled into a rhythm, a slower lolloping run, her breath bloody in her throat. She concentrated on synchronizing her breathing with her footfalls, the night-wet grass wrapping itself in swathes round her ankles, her dress catching on thistles.

Finally, she halted, gasping, and then walked. She didn't have any idea where she was. She had a vision of herself huddling in a ditch until day broke and then crawling like a fugitive with pneumonia into a dawn that had leached the dark from the sky. The night was shades of black except for the pure blue velvet that bruised to plum where Birmingham lay. She became aware of a hulking lowering shape in front of her, its outline like a cardboard cut-out. A wood. The Templar forest. Immediately she felt better. A sense almost of normality descended upon her. She would walk through the wood, walk her hurt and anger away.

She made for the edge of the field and followed the hedge along to a gate, tripping on the tussocky grass, her feet unused to blind exploration. When she found the gate, she climbed over it, the metal cold and flaky beneath her palms. It didn't take too long to find the path that led through the heart of the wood, and to begin with the going was easier. The surface was even and had been thickly spread with woodchips.

She stepped out smartly, confidently. She tried not to think but scattered phrases and words kept coming back. She felt her love for Corin was like something new and shiny, made of aluminium, that had been beaten and scuffed until it had lost its shape and shine. She wondered if it would ever be possible to smooth out the dents, rub away the scratches. A light rain began to fall, the water clinging to her face like a second skin.

The woodchips ended and the path abruptly started to twist and curve so that sometimes she ended up walking off the edge and tripping in the long grass, brambles and bracken that bordered it. The path became rutted and potholed. She slipped and fell with a little cry, pulled herself upright and stepped in a puddle. The water rushed into her shoes, freezing, curdling between her toes. She was walking slower and slower now, feeling her way with her feet, but even so she was constantly sliding on mud, slithering into puddles, stumbling over stones. She became acutely aware of the noise she was making whilst on either side of her the wood stretched dark and silent and full of hidden menace. She stopped and whirled round, thinking she could hear someone else, but she couldn't see anything save blackness and she could only hear the soft incessant fall of the rain on the leaves and the faint moan of the wind in the branches.

She didn't know how long she'd been gone; how long she'd been walking. It felt like hours. There was a crack and she jumped and froze. A second crack made her start and then came a long-drawn-out moaning. She bit her lip and remained motionless. The moan came again.

A tree, she thought, a branch breaking, shifting in the wind. That's all, that's all it is.

She made herself keep moving. She wished that Ryan were with her, or even Corin, that she was anywhere except this wood in the middle of the night. Anyone could come here - might already be waiting here - a mugger, a murderer, a rapist. No-one would know. No-one would hear.

She walked faster and stumbled and tripped. She crashed into a tree and twisted her ankle painfully when she staggered off the path into a ditch. Her clothes were completely soaked. She shivered with cold and fear. Twigs poked her face and ensnared themselves in her hair and ahead of her she could see nothing, behind her she could see nothing, and she could see nothing to either side except the dense black mass of trees.

A chill wind suddenly hit her left side and a fresh bout of trembling shook her. She became gradually aware that there were no more trees on that side, only a ploughed field full of small white stones that glimmered preternaturally. On the far side was the silhouette of rows of pine trees, twisted and bent, with a dark shape in the middle she thought might be a house, a house with a pointed gable and collapsed walls. The rafters looked like charred ribs left over from an incomplete cremation.

And then the howling began. The hairs at the back of her neck rose. One creature began and then another and another joined in, an eerie keening that matched the moaning of the wind. She broke out in a cold sweat and started to run. Her sodden dress kept catching and sticking to her legs. She fell again. There was a sharp pain and she felt blood trickle down the inside of her palm. She smelt of earth and rain. The howling was growing louder. Trees and bushes screened the field. The noise was so loud now she felt that whatever it was must be right next to her. It had turned into a baying. Tears started to course down her face. She couldn't stop shaking.

Abruptly there was silence. She stopped. The rain dripped. The wind softly twisted the fingers of the twigs, and there was the faint cry of trees grating their branches raw against one another.

She saw them then, two pairs of yellow eyes, two black shapes launching themselves out of the darkness straight towards her, maws open, teeth bared. She screamed and staggered back and the animals hit something in front of her face that gave a little and they dropped to the ground.

One continued to stare at her with baleful mineral eyes, the other tipped its muzzle to the sky and howled and a third joined in from somewhere nearby. Wolves. She could see the faint outline of the wire mesh that penned them in and she stood trembling, mesmerized by the night-gold gaze of the animal, so close she could smell its wild canine odour. She remembered something that Pat had said about wolves and Rhum, a breeding programme. She wiped her forehead with the back of her hand and started to walk onwards, trying to ignore the smooth, silent gait of the two creatures that easily kept pace with her as long as the limits of their cage allowed.

She felt bone tired, and she could hardly keep her eyes open. She needed to get home straight away. She couldn't even remember what she and Corin had been arguing about. It seemed so remote.

The wood ended very shortly and as she stood on the road she wondered how to get back. There was no way she was going to return through the wood. She thought she could cut across the field to the rear of the zoo and walk round the edge of it. She stopped for a short while to get her bearings and then set off again.

The field up to the zoo was steep. In the middle was an old dead elm like a rotted tooth, fissured with caries, its remaining enamel a dull glister in the harsh stellar light. At the top corner of the field were some sycamore trees, their leaves whispering roughly, and behind them was the hedge, the boundary of the zoo. She followed the fence up to the top, running her hand across the highest bar for support. She had to force herself to keep her eyes open.

Nearly there, nearly there, she whispered to herself as she reached the first of the trees. Something which was protruding slightly from the top of the fence scratched her palm. She immediately took her hand away and looked down. It was hard to see what it was. It was long and thin and it was pinned to the wood. She touched it. It was tough and grisly and at the top was something flat and hard. A nail. It was a human finger.

Chapter Eighteen

The first week in May was abnormally hot. Corin arrived in the afternoon. He'd driven up with the roof down and his hair was ruffled. They hadn't spoken all week and the air was heavy with the weight of unsaid words. He spilled the Saturday papers onto the floor, turned on the TV and opened a can of beer. She flicked aimlessly through the papers, glancing at him out of the corner of her eyes. He seemed to be totally absorbed and, unusually for Corin, was exceptionally quiet and grave. Before he'd even half finished his beer, he suddenly jumped up, said 'Back in a minute', and raced out. She could hear the gravel tearing as he pulled the car round in a vicious half-circle and shot out of the drive and down the road.

She gave up all pretence of reading the paper and watched the space in the sky that last week had been marred by clouds. It was a perfect summer evening. She wouldn't have minded walking along the canal on a day like this, but a strange lethargy came over her. She felt as if she could do nothing. It was partly the heat. They were all unused to it. She wondered if they ought to say something to each other, and if so what, and who should begin. Maybe it would all blow over.

Paul lay down in the dandelions and held a cockroach between his finger and his thumb. He carefully wrote the letter G on its back with his Tippex pen. He wrote C on the other one. Their legs waved futilely in the air as they struggled with a soft chitinous rasping. He dropped them both in the killing jar and put his head in the flowers. Between the multi-petaled golden globes, he watched the insects trying not to die. There were no crows today, just a starling in the nearest sycamore, and a tree creeper scuttling round the trunk. Some magpies settled in a line on the fence. One dropped into the grass and the others regarded it with their heads tilted on one side. One, two . . . four. Four for a boy. It might be an omen. He looked back at his jar. G was on its back at the bottom while C clawed faintly at glass walls slippery as ice. He opened the stopper and tipped the brown beetle onto the ground. It was certainly not going to live long with a crescent of white scratched on its back; the birds would spot it in no time.

He got up and pushed his way through the hedge. Part of it was hawthorn which scraped at him with its harsh woody claws and dusted him with its pink and white blooms. His grandmother said it brought bad luck. Never bring it into the house, she'd said. She'd died the year after.

Corin torched up the drive, braked the car, spraying pebbles everywhere, and ran up the stairs. As soon as he entered the flat, the unnatural stillness took over. In one hand he held a green paper bag. He filled a couple of glasses full of ice and poured something over them. He put the bottle in the freezer and came and sat next to her. She'd turned the television down so low you could hardly hear it, but he made no move to turn it up and for once had nothing to say about the programme.

'What is it?'

'Lemon vodka,' he said, and went back to reading the papers.

His calmness was making her uneasy. It wasn't a quiet that had arisen from mutual ease in each other's company. It was a quiet sprung from the absence of anything. She swirled the alcohol in her glass and watched the viscous strands wind sinuously round the ice cubes. Outside the birds began to call, faint threads of sound woven into the sky. She felt she might be able to catch hold of an end and the whole fabric would unravel in her lap. Three magpies alighted in the poplar trees and clung to their branches, perched in the crow's nest of a tall mast tossing in a grass-green sea. Three for a girl.

At last he turned to her and almost roughly lifted her face to his. She shrank inside herself. His face was partly in shadow, partly gilded blood orange red by the sinking sun, one eye dark, the other glowing deep and cold as a crocodile's.

'Claire. Would you like to play a game?'

'You never play games. Not proper games,' she said with feminine knowingness.

'We have,' he said, his brow furrowed. Doctors and nurses. That was it. 'Would you like to play doctors and nurses?'

'Oh, all right, I suppose so,' she said wearily, and hopped off the swing. 'You be the doctor and I'll be the nurse.'

'Let's go.'

'Where?'

'My secret place. I'll show you my secret place.'

Her eyes lit up. 'Where is it?' she hissed.

He set off, walking quickly, stiffly and awkwardly. She jogged a little. 'Don't walk so fast,' she whined.

He slowed down but immediately speeded up again.

'I knew it was in the zoo,' she said triumphantly, a little out of breath. 'You always disappear off this way.'

He kissed her and she felt herself trembling. It might be all right, it might be a step towards reconciliation . . . it *would* be OK. He led her over to the bed and they started to take each other's clothes off. He broke away and like a magician pulled a string of silk scarves out of his discarded jeans pocket. They were tissue paper thin so the light shone through: cyan, cobalt, emerald, garnet, lilac and black. She watched curiously as he started to fasten the first one round her wrist. She tried to stop him but he kissed her and stroked her face and she let him continue. She felt that if she struggled it would make no difference. He was so much stronger than her; the muscles in his arms bulged as he held her tight. She felt that if she struggled they might lose everything. This peace as fragile as the scarves. But they were not as delicate as she'd thought. He tied them round her wrists and ankles and secured the ends to the bed. It didn't hurt if she lay still, but as soon as she struggled they twisted into thin cords that bit into her flesh.

The other two scarves he whispered across her skin and she felt their warmth, ultrafine as an animal pelt. He stretched one over her breast and sucked and she writhed and twisted against his muted mouth. There was a moment of cold clear air rushing over her chest and then she felt his thighs either side of her ribs, squeezing her gently. He pressed a scarf over her eyes and one over her mouth.

'Corin, I don't want to do this . . .'

'Don't you like it?'

He ran his finger down her body; she imagined the tip dipped in smooth black fountain pen ink, drawing a line that divided her in two. She struggled to see through the cloth and pulled ineffectually at the bindings. Every fibre in her body strained to see, to feel, to hear what would happen. He turned some music on. Loudly. She thought how sometimes you listened to music and it made you feel incredibly sexy, made you want to have sex right there and then, and how the real thing never gave you that feeling . . . She felt like a butterfly, pinned in place, contorting at his touch, powerless, wanting him inside her, hardly able to bear to wait, arching at the heat of his tongue, a blow torch on her skin . . .

She gasped when something ice cold burnt her hip bone. Water trickled slowly down her side. He moved the ice cube along her ribs, round the underside of her breast, across her nipple, she imagined it beading into liquid, melting at the combined touch of their flesh. The cold was so intense it made her chest constrict.

The lion was right in the corner of his cage watching them with his great, flat, golden eyes, his mane a heavy halo. Sitting, he was easily as tall as them, and he was lying on a rock, staring down at them. To the children he looked enormous. They had to pass very close. He licked his lips and yawned.

Claire giggled. 'Look at his teeth!'

They smelt his breath, putrid with carrion, and his hot, male cat smell. Paul crawled through the hedge and she followed. The lion watched without turning his head. He led her in the direction of the sycamores.

'Now you lie down here and I'll examine you.'

'Doctors don't examine nurses. Nurses make people better.'

He looked at a loss.

'Oh, all right,' she said, 'I'll be a patient, then. What's in that green bag?'

'All my things to examine you with.'

She lay down on the flattened bit of mud, her head resting on the grass amongst the daisies and the dandelions. Paul took some small wooden stakes out of his holdall and started to hammer one in next to each of her limbs.

'What are you doing?'

'I'll show you.'

'Is this where you go when you disappear off on your own?'

'Sometimes. Sometimes I just walk round the zoo.'

'My mum says you're obsessed with animals. She says you'll probably end up a zoo keeper or a zoologist.'

He frowned. He didn't really know what it meant to be 'obsessed with animals'. Was he? Would he become a zoologist? What did they look like? He imagined some kind of metamorphosis. His mother had said that boys changed when they became teenagers. Perhaps he'd change into a zoologist.

'I'm going to be a teacher when I grow up. I'm going to teach primary schoolchildren. Doctor, what are you doing?'

He had torn part of the sheet on his bed into strips and he was now tying her wrists and ankles to the stakes. He'd thought about this for a long time and he knew he couldn't fasten her down the way he'd done with the other animals.

'This is so I can examine you better,' he mumbled.

'Well, all I can say is this is the strangest game of doctors and nurses I've ever played,' she said in a grown-up voice.

He took out the final strip of cloth and started to tie it over her eyes.

'Hey, I don't like this. What are you doing that for?' She struggled. 'Stop that. I'm going to tell my mummy.'

He panicked. She mustn't leave. She mustn't. 'It's so I can examine you better,' he said again desperately. He couldn't think what else to say.

'What are you going to do to me, doctor?' she said in a sudden whisper. 'Is it going to be an operation?'

'Yes.'

'Oh, so I don't want to see. It might make me sick.'

'Yes.'

He tried to still his beating heart. He finished tying the blindfold over her eyes and checked all the knots round the stakes. The lion roared and she twitched.

'He's scary, isn't he?'

'Yes.'

'What are you doing now, doctor?'

'I'm getting out my equipment.'

He laid out everything he would need. He opened his notebook at the place where he had neatly written down the length of time it took a heart to die. He took the top off his little pen and fitted it to the other end. Placing the pen in the centre fold of the notebook, he spread out his dissecting pins, the stem of his scalpel and a brand new scalpel blade. The waxy butcher's paper crackled loudly in the summer stillness.

'You're taking a long time, doctor.'

'Yes,' he said. 'But it won't be much longer now.'

His legs slid across hers and she felt his penis touch her, slide over her. She tried to tilt her pelvis so that he would slip into her. She felt the tendons in her thighs might snap. But he moved away from her and lay down by her side, giving her biting kisses, round her neck, sweet ecstasy of tiny pain. She felt his tongue run up the inside of her thigh and shivered. Then she froze. His teeth were still locked into her neck. She struggled, turning her face towards him, making a muffled sound. The gag was tight and wet round her mouth. She heard someone laugh. Short, deep. Corin fumbled at the scarf round her head and pulled. She opened her eyes.

Kim was standing at the foot of the bed. 'Well, honey chile, you look like you've been enjoying yourself.' She stroked her leg and Sandra struggled and tried to scream. Kim gave that long, low, humourless chuckle again. Sandra looked in horror from her to Corin. But Corin wasn't looking at her. He was looking at Kim. He embraced her and they started to kiss. They were exactly the same height. They faced each other, hips pressed to hips. Arms, thin and muscular, black and white, wrapped round one another. Kim was wearing the silver lycra top that exposed her hard flat midriff and a tight miniskirt. Corin peeled her clothes off. She wasn't wearing anything underneath. Sandra couldn't bear to watch and she couldn't tear her eyes away. Corin's hands circling the small breast, bending his head to take it in his mouth, his thick hair falling, falling against her skin. And then they broke away and Kim turned towards her. The first thing that Sandra thought was that she had an awful lot of pubic hair, heavy and dark. And then she saw. Kim wasn't a woman.

★ ★ ★

He unloosened the screw on the scalpel and slid the new blade in. His hands were sweaty and the blade slipped. Blood ran over his thumb in a bright stream. He put the scalpel down and hunted in his pockets for a tissue. He held the tissue against the cut and the paper dampened and blossomed. The cut was only shallow, but he had to dab it with another tissue. Once the flow had nearly stopped, he wrapped a third scrap around his thumb and secured it with surgical adhesive tape. He carefully wiped the blood and sweat from the scalpel blade and the stem of the knife and this time managed to tighten the screw without cutting himself again.

He started to undo her blouse.

'Are you going to listen to my heart, doctor?'

'Yes.'

He pulled her shorts down too, but not all the way. The scent of hawthorn was sweet and sickly as if the flowers were beginning to rot. The smell made his head swim. He could hear the lion's lethargic footsteps as it paced past the sultry female lying in the shade, her face with its black eye of mutated fur like a bruised plum.

The best thing to do, he thought, was to sit astride her. That way he could hold her still when she struggled. He sat over her pelvic region and rested one hand against her collar bone. He traced an imaginary line down the centre of her body from her throat through her breast bone down to her soft curved stomach, the point of his knife hovering just above her skin. Then he rested the knife gently against the hollow at her throat and started to press. This would be the first shallow cut to remove the skin and thin layer of fat that lay over the breast bone. Blood welled up beneath the knife tip and trickled down her neck.

She/he stretched across the bed towards her and Sandra shrank away as well as she was able. But Kim didn't touch her. She merely arched her back like a cat and stretched out her arms. Corin, behind her, buried one of his hands in her thick, curly mane of hair and gripped her round the waist with the other. The music wasn't loud enough. The bed shook. She closed her eyes and felt the tears slide over her temples, her anger and pain hard as a tumour in her chest. She waited for it all to be over.

The child started to scream. The screaming went on and on. Sweat stood out on his forehead. It was hard to concentrate. His hand began to shake. The noise of it hurt him. His ears rang. The sound was a drill boring into him. He couldn't stand it. He stopped and put the scalpel down. He slid off her body. Sweat dripped into his eyes. The salt stung him. He took another piece of sheet and tried to wind it round Claire's face. But the little girl shook her head so violently that it was impossible for him to get the gag round her mouth, let alone tie it securely.

He was afraid someone might come to see what the noise was. They would not understand, of that he felt sure. He crouched on his heels in the grass and wondered what he should do. He could hardly think. It felt as if the noise was rattling his brain viciously inside his skull. He put out his hands to balance himself and they twitched slightly. He had to make her keep quiet.

Then suddenly it occurred to him: he could cut off her tongue. He wiped his hands on her shorts and picked up the scalpel. When he sat on her chest Claire began to scream with renewed intensity.

When she felt someone undoing the tie round her wrist, she opened her eyes. Kim was nowhere to be seen. Corin was dressed and the room was full of shadows. He didn't look at her. He finished untying the scarf but held her wrist down in the same position. He yanked her engagement ring off and said hoarsely, 'Never be unfaithful again.' He got up and, still without looking at her, picked up his coat. As he went out, he placed the ring on the kitchen table. She lay quite still and listened to the front door slam and the car drive away. It took her a long time to undo her other wrist using her left hand and with her legs still tied down. She realized she was shaking and cold. Her legs and arms ached. The corners of her lips were tight and sore as if someone had put a bit in her mouth. She went and stood in the shower for a very long time.

He put one hand in her mouth. Immediately she bit him hard. He said nothing, but he shook his hand roughly inside her. She loosened her grip and he pulled his hand out of her mouth. She began to scream again. There were crescent-shaped indentations on the middle joints of his fingers. She'd pierced one of them: the skin on his knuckle was torn and a drop of blood was beginning to well up. He tried to put his hand into her mouth again but she clamped her lips shut and twisted her head from side to side. It was impossible. He couldn't prise open her mouth with his left hand and slice her tongue across with his right.

He got up and put the scalpel down on his khaki bag. What he should do, he thought, was get the chloroform. He hadn't brought it because he'd had no intention of using it. After all, unlike his rat and the baby otter, she had not been unwilling when he tied her up. And also, it might be better if he used a razor blade. The blade would be nearly as long as the width of her tongue. The cut would be much neater and it would be quicker. He didn't have any razor blades with him either. It wouldn't take him long to go and get the things he needed, and in the meantime she would probably stop screaming.

He ran back towards the hole in the hedge and squeezed through.

★ ★ ★

The ring glimmered in the last rays of the evening light, the diamond bright as a metal spark. Why had he left it? Surely he didn't think they would get back together again after . . . after he'd taught her a lesson? She felt sick. She picked up the ring and hurled it out of the open window. She felt drained, her very essence had been sucked from her body. She didn't know what to do with herself. She looked round at her little flat, her chemistry apparatus glowing on the window sill, her sandalwood Shiva, her books and tapes, her collection of postcards from Philippe. The flat even still smelt faintly of gingerbread from the night before. But there was another smell too, a woman's cloying perfume, and the bed . . . the bed was a mess, the sheets bunched and twisted, the duvet half on the floor, the pillows askew, a long, curly dark hair on one of them. It was soiled, totally spoilt for her. She felt she could not stand being in the flat for another minute.

She half fell down the stairs in her rush to get outside. In the gravel were marks where Corin's wheels had gouged out part of the driveway, and next to them was a single tyremark from Kim's bike. She did not care where they were or whether they were together, but she did not want to see them. Out here she felt exposed and afraid. There was no way she could go for a walk or stay by herself. She had a fearful dread of being on her own. The numbness of her mind was only temporary; she would start to relive and remember horrific scenes and torture herself with questions if she did not have some kind of distraction.

She knocked on Ryan's door. She was frightened that he would not be there and there would be no-one else she could turn to. There was silence. She banged on the door desperately, bruising her knuckles. He opened the door and she burst into tears.

She would not tell him what was wrong. He sat down with her on the sofa and held her in his arms like a child. She cried in almost complete silence, the tears running down her cheeks as if she had no power to stem their flow. Part of her hated to be touched, and part of her wanted to be held and rocked and reminded that there was someone gentle and kind who cared for her. He put his arms round her and murmured to her, saying that it was all right, it was all going to be all right, over and over again like a lullaby.

When she finally stopped crying, he wiped her face tenderly.

'You're shaking, sweetheart,' he said, and she trembled for she remembered another time and another man who had said that to her and the thought of the hot wax and his callousness made her cry again.

Despite the fact that it was a warm summer evening, she was chilled through to the bone. Ryan fetched a blanket and tucked it round her.

'I'll make you some hot chocolate,' he said. 'It'll warm you up and help you sleep.'

She lay down on the sofa and was distantly aware of

the sound he made as he stirred milk in the pan and the sweet smell of chocolate. He helped her sit up and gave her the mug.

'Thank you,' she whispered, but she could not bear to look at him. She sipped the chocolate. He'd put brandy in it and it made her feel drowsy. She lay down with her head on his lap. He touched her face with long, soft strokes and gradually she started to drift away.

After a while she was aware that he was no longer sitting next to her. The absence of his warmth was tangible. She could hear him humming softly. She wondered vaguely what he was doing, but she was too tired to open her eyes. And then she smelt the fresh scent of orange peel. He was eating an orange.

There was a loud bang at the door and she jumped, her heart racing. She didn't know how long she'd been asleep.

'It's OK,' said Ryan, getting up.

'Don't answer it,' she said frantically.

'It's all right. It won't be Corin. He won't come here.' He opened the door and Paul slipped in like a thin shadow.

He stood in the middle of the floor clutching a bottle that reeked of something vaguely familiar. It reminded her of biology A-levels and hospitals.

He didn't look surprised to see Sandra, but then, she thought, that in itself was hardly surprising. He looked at the far corner of the room. She resisted the temptation to turn and look at whatever nonexistent object he was watching. He carefully placed his bottle on the coffee table. Putting his hands in his pockets, he tried to look at

Ryan. His gaze slid away again.

'I need some razor blades.'

'What for?' asked Ryan.

Paul's hands jiggled in his pockets. 'For something very important. I'm late already.'

'I'm afraid I don't have any, Paul.'

'Darren had some.'

'Yes, but I don't. I've got a pair of clippers to keep my beard trimmed. Have you asked anyone else?' Paul shook his head.

'Why are you late?' asked Sandra. 'And what could you possibly be late for that needs razor blades?'

Paul shifted uncomfortably. The chemical smell emanating from the bottle was pierced by the sharp odour of oranges. It made her feel queasy.

'I'm late because I saw some strange people and I stopped to watch them on my way home to find my razor blades. But I can't find them. Maybe someone has taken them.'

'Strange people?'

'They didn't have keepers' uniforms and anyway it's too late for the keepers to be in the zoo. They've all gone home.'

'There were people in the zoo? At this time of night? What were they doing there? How did they get in?' asked Ryan in alarm.

'They went through the keepers' entrance round the side. I saw them and I followed them.'

'No, that's impossible. It's locked.'

'They had a big bunch of keys.'

'Oh shit,' he cursed softly.

'Go on. What happened then?' asked Sandra.

'Then they had an argument. At least, I think it was an argument, but they were speaking very quietly and not shouting at all, and one of them said her laces had come undone and she stopped to do them up.'

Ryan looked impatient, but Sandra held his arm to stop him from making Paul jittery.

The boy picked up his bottle and turned to go.

'Paul, why don't you go to your mother's?' She tried to speak calmly. Ryan was already grabbing his jacket.

'I must find some razor blades,' he said obstinately. He flapped his hands a couple of times and the liquid in the bottle shook unpleasantly. He pushed past Ryan and ran off towards Jeffs caravan.

He left the door wide open and Sandra shivered despite the heat. 'Who . . .?'

'The AZA,' said Ryan grimly. 'They must have copied my keys.'

Sandra pushed her blanket aside and followed him. 'Look, you stay here.'

'No, I'm coming with you.'

'I don't think . . .'

'I'm coming,' she said again and there was a slight note of hysteria in her voice.

They ran past the flats and down the dirt track towards the keepers' entrance to the zoo.

'How could they have got your keys?' she gasped. She was out of breath already.

'They came round the other week. I should have known.' He swore. 'Got me really drunk. I nearly blurted out what a complete bunch of tossers I thought they all were. I nearly said they were wrong then. They were coming and going all the time - buying more drink, more Rizlas - I was practically comatose – they could have taken the keys any one of those times.' He rattled the keys in the metal gate. 'I should have known.'

'It's not your fault. You weren't to know.'

'They'll let the old chimps out. I'm going to run over there now. I'll catch up with you later.'

Sandra watched him go. She walked slowly to get her breath back, heading for Miss Williams's house. There were a couple of lights on in the top floor. She rang the bell and waited. There was no sound. After a few moments, somewhere deep within the house, a dog barked. She was just about to ring the bell again when an alarm went off. It was the all-purpose emergency alarm which she knew would ring in the police station in town. She wondered whether Ryan had hesitated before turning it on.

Miss Williams would find out soon enough what was happening; Ryan was bound to be on radio talk-back by now, she thought. She ran off in the direction of the big chimp house where Ted, Kevin, Jo-Lee and the others were kept. The alarm was so loud it hurt her ears and it must have sounded even worse to the frightened animals, for a terrible cacophony of distress burst forth: elephants trumpeting, lions and tigers roaring, birds shrieking, monkeys howling and crying. Most of the animals were locked up inside their indoor cages: the alarm calls of the zebra, a strangled honking neigh, were muffled. Silence from the gibbons. In the distance, the panthoot of chimpanzees. Over by the magpie field she saw Ryan. She stopped running, completely out of breath. All her stamina seemed to have deserted her in her relief at seeing him unharmed.

'Did you manage to stop them?'

'Yes. Just got there in time. They'd unlocked the keepers' kitchen and were about to start opening the padlocks to the animals' cages, but when they saw me they ran off. I guess they already knew I wasn't going to help them.'

'What about the chimps?'

'May was still in her cage. Pitiful,' he sighed, 'just cowering there clutching a big wad of hay. I locked her back in. But Pru and Fred have disappeared. Ah, there they are at last.'

Sandra turned to peer in the direction Ryan was looking in. The curator and the vet were careering towards them in a jeep, followed by Miss Williams in her Mini. Away in the distance were two other figures, a couple of keepers running towards them.

'Listen, you must go back. I've no idea where Fred or Pru could be. I don't know how they'll react to freedom, or to us chasing them. You know Fred is unpredictable at the best of times. I've got to stay and find them - the police will have to shoot them if they go off zoo property. Please go home. It would make me very happy if you did that. I'll come round afterwards.'

The jeep skidded to a halt, showering them with mud and pebbles.

'Wait,' she said desperately. 'Let me look too. They

know me. And they don't associate me with being locked up in their cages.'

'It's too dangerous.'

But her stomach heaved at the thought of going back to her empty flat. The vet and the curator jumped out clutching dart guns and tranquillizers.

'You're not even bloody insured if anything should happen to you. Just go home, will you, you stubborn eejit. Here,' he said, handing her the keys to his flat.

She gave in and nodded. 'OK. Take care of yourself. Don't be too brave.' He smiled briefly and then turned to the curator. Miss Williams was already screeching orders as she climbed out of the Mini, both of her big white dogs trying to get out at the same time.

Maybe, Sandra thought, she ought to drink. Very heavily. The lion and lioness were roaring and pounding on the metal door of their indoor cage. She shivered and walked past quickly. And then she stopped. There was a small hole in the hedge. She peered through it and saw a twisted, stunted elm in the middle of a field. That was where she'd been, wasn't it? That horrible nightmarish evening in the Templar forest, and finding the finger, she'd never dared to go back. She remembered the smell of the lions and hearing them pace in their cage as she'd walked on the other side of the hedge. She remembered, too, the howl of the wolves like a lance in her spine, and the thin, sodden folds of her dress clasping her legs. She shuddered and thought of open fields, dipping away from the zoo, falling from her feet. If I were a chimp, I'd go that way, she thought, over the fields and head for the wood. As she walked past their cages, the lion snarled and the cheetah on her left spat.

She pushed through the gap in the hedge. Hawthorn branches snagged at her hair and her clothes. She crouched lower, but their thorn-like twigs, angling for skin, scratched her hand. Wincing, she licked off the blood. She stood up to get her bearings and realized that she was dusted with tiny pink and white flowers. She could hear the stealthy tread of the lion. The big cats must be less than a metre away from her, she thought; if she dug her arms through the froth of May blossoms, she could touch the wire mesh surrounding their cage. She stepped away from the hedge.

It was evening, but the ground retained the day's warmth. The grass was thick and lush and speckled with daisies and dandelions. Further along the hedge were the first splashes of summer's blood: black-eyed poppies with purple veins. The elm tree was there as she remembered, twisted into tortured crenellations, the meridian of the field. The soft swoop of the grass led back down to the wood, the trees a dense mass of shifting green, and she thought of fields of white stones and black holes trapped in forests, extinguishing light, sound and stars. She started to walk towards the dead tree, looking for two black shapes: gambolling in the grass? running for freedom? seeking out the solace of English oak in place of strangler figs and frangipani?

Over to her right was a brace of sycamore trees. Like etiolated shoots that had sprung up deprived of light, they were tall and slender, their leaves in a clump at the very tip of their trunks. Haemorrhaging from the joints in their limbs were clots of raven-black birds. Something white glimmered beneath the trees. A rag fluttering. There was something on the ground. It was hard to see what it was in the dying light. She walked towards it. There were several white rags stirring near what appeared to be small stakes of wood. In between them was some kind of bundle. She walked faster. It was a body. A small body. A child. She nearly burst into tears when she saw her. She was spread-eagled, her arms and legs tied down with strips of white sheet wound round the stakes. There was a blindfold over her eyes. Her thin chest was bare and her shorts were pulled down round her thighs. She immediately thought of Corin and Kim. No, surely they could not, would not, have abused a child.

She didn't know if the girl was alive or not. As she got closer she could see a thin streak of dried blood, the colour of rusted iron, like a ghoulish necklace, and there was a raw slit from her throat extending down her chest bone for a few centimetres. It looked as if it would need stitches.

The child must have heard the faint sound of her feet in the grass. She stirred and moved her head and murmured. Sandra knelt down by her side and touched her. The girl let out a terrible shriek.

'It's all right. I'm not going to hurt you.'

The child continued to scream. Sandra resisted the temptation to put her hand over the child's mouth. Instead she started to untie the strips of cloth from round her wrists. She felt a bitter empathy for the little girl as she did so. The child's hands were so cold. The circulation to her hands and feet must have been severely reduced. And then she saw the khaki bag lying next to the girl. There was an open book with the names of animals and a time in minutes and seconds alongside. Dissection pins were laid out in a neat line by the notebook, and there was a scalpel. The blade was dark with dried blood. She suddenly knew with a cold and complete certainty who had done this to the little girl and she felt all her flesh rise in goosebumps. She took a pair of dissection scissors out of the bag and cut off the blindfold.

'It's only me. You'll be all right,' she whispered to the child who looked up at her, her eyes brimming with tears and filled with horror. She quickly cut the ties that bound the little girl's feet and wrapped her blouse round her chest. The child started to cry and she held her tightly.

'He said we were going to play doctors and nurses,' she sobbed. 'He said it was going to be an operation. I didn't know he meant it.'

She could hardly speak, her mouth was so dry, and she tried to cling to Sandra but her arms were too stiff to hug her properly.

'Well, I won't let him hurt you again. Let me rub your hands. We'll make them better.'

She cradled the child on her lap and softly started to massage the circulation back.

'They're sore,' whimpered Claire. 'I've got pins and needles.'

In the distance they could hear the distress calls of the animals and the howling of alarms. But where they were on the edge of the zoo with the dark countryside falling away all around them, it was as if they were in an enclave of space and peace. She rocked the child, reluctant to move and disturb their small sanctuary. She breathed in her child-like smell; it reminded her of baths in sinks, hot milk, sun-warmed daisies and daisy juice spilt when their stems were threaded together by childish fingers.

There was a faint sound. Sandra barely heard it. It came again. It was a low exhalation, little more than someone blowing out with a faint guttural noise. She had the awful feeling that they were being watched. She looked round very slowly and she felt cold sweat slide down her spine.

Several metres away from her was Fred. He was surrounded by knots of dandelions, and daisies grew between the fingers of his hands. Behind him the thick grass of the fields deepened into blue. He was staring right at her and his coat was standing on end. His lips were formed into a thin pout and he was swaying gently from side to side. His eyes rolled and she saw thin crescents of white glittering in the half-light. Her whole body turned to ice and she felt as if her innards had dissolved.

'I'm scared,' whined Claire. A sob caught in her throat.

'Shussh. Just be quiet for a few minutes,' Sandra whispered back. 'We'll be OK, don't worry.'

There was a movement to Fred's right. She tore her eyes away from the chimp. Paul scuttled from behind the dead, stunted elm and started walking towards them. It didn't look as if he'd seen Fred. But then, thought Sandra, biting her lip, it was so difficult to tell. He was carrying his bottle in one hand and a small cardboard box in the other. A wave of hate for the little boy rose like bile but it was quenched almost immediately by fear.

Fred saw that she was no longer looking at him and he turned to see what she was staring at. He started to sway more violently and a thin reedy sound emerged from his pouted lips. His great head swung from the approaching boy and back to Sandra and the child crouched on the grass. Claire whimpered and clung tightly to her. There was no way they could escape. She would not be able to get to her feet with the child wrapped so tightly round her neck, never mind carry them both to safety. She didn't know how fast a hundred kilos of chimp could run, but she imagined it was pretty fast. Slowly, so that she would not attract his attention, she inched her hand across to Paul's bag, and heard the beginnings of guttural noises in his throat that were a signal he was going to work himself up into a temper tantrum. Please don't let him do that, please God. Her fingertips brushed the bag and sweat beaded her forehead. Dissection pins scattered beneath her hand. She was grasping almost frantically now.

Fred started to make low hoots and she knew it was only a matter of time before he would launch into full battle cry. She touched the blade of the scalpel and relief flooded her. She grasped hold of the stem. Clutching the child to her chest, she held the knife in front of her. But sharp as it was, she realized it would be pitifully ineffectual against a charging chimpanzee.

His cries became louder and stronger. They echoed over the fields, rolling towards the immense stillness of the wood below. Would anyone hear him? she wondered. But with a sick feeling she thought it was unlikely that the calls of one lone chimp could be heard above a whole zooful of fearful animals. And now, one by one, from far away, came the thin howl of the three caged wolves.

Fred's swaying became more violent. He was going to charge, she thought, horrified. Paul was standing a few metres away from them, frozen to the spot, still gripping his box and his bottle for dear life. Who, she thought with dread, was he going to charge at: her and the child, or the boy who stared sightlessly into the dim evening light? I've got to calm him down, I've got to stop him somehow, she thought, but her stomach was tight with the fear that it was already too late.

He took a couple of swaying steps towards her and the child. Claire sobbed and attempted to bury herself in Sandra's neck. She could see his teeth shining as he pulled his lips back in a grimace. She held the knife tighter. The stem was slippery in her palm. She thought she might drop it. Talk to him, talk to him for Christ's sake. 'Fred,' she said shakily. For God's sake, he can tell you're nervous, act confident. 'Fred,' she said again, a little more strongly, tasting blood in the back of her throat. 'Come on, boy, you're going to be a good boy now, aren't you? There's a good boy.'

Fred started to walk towards her making those low hoots. She felt as if her whole body had turned to water. His hooting became louder and louder, became genuine battle cries, and he swayed and contorted and started to stamp his feet. He would charge in a few seconds. Please God, don't let me die. Don't let anything happen to the child. Not after what she's been through.

Nothing she could do at this stage would calm him down. Her throat was dry and she wanted to scream. The child was shaking in her arms.

Fred took a few more steps towards them. His hoots reached a climax. He tensed and crouched. The knife was slipping out of her grasp. She tried to hold it tighter and felt hot tears trickling down her cheeks. She was shivering uncontrollably. At that moment Paul started to walk towards them. What is he doing? she thought. Don't do it, stay still. Fred swung round towards him.

'Paul!' she cried.

Fred twisted back to face her and Claire.

'Paul, stop! Don't move!'

Fred grimaced again and howled at her, his teeth bared. But Paul continued to walk towards them.

'Paul! Get down! Crouch on the ground!' Her voice was drowned by the noise of Fred's screams.

Fred started to run. He covered the ground at an incredible pace. He was heading straight for them. She curled herself and the child closer to the flattened earth. When he was near enough for her to stare right into his mad, rolling eyes, he veered towards Paul. The boy dropped everything he was carrying and began to run. He was no match for the chimpanzee. He managed only a few paces in his strange gait and then Fred bore down upon him. The chimp threw him to the ground and jumped on his back. There was a terrible cracking. He seized him by the shoulder- blades and yanked his upper body towards him. For one dreadful moment she was staring right into Paul's eyes as Fred bit into the back of his skull. His blank look of innocence was slowly extinguished. He made no sound at all. Fred panthooted loudly. She could hardly bear to look. With a sick feeling, she wondered whether his bloodlust was now satisfied, or whether he would turn his attention back to her. The chimp remained crouched on Paul's back and he paused and looked around at the fields and the wood behind as if savouring his freedom, and his kill. His heavy head swung towards her. She looked down, trying not to make eye contact with the animal in case she threatened him. He made a low rumbling sound in his throat, warning her not to move.

Behind her two police officers followed by Ryan burst through the hedge. The policemen crouched down in sniper position.

'Shit, don't shoot, there's a child,' shouted one of them.

Fred, his coat bristling, panthooted again. He stamped his feet on the small body and his long arms swayed, trailing in swathes of dense grass and wild flowers. Blood dribbled from the corner of his mouth, there was a mad glint in his bloodshot eye, and when he opened his mouth his teeth were stained with the young boy's blood.

The hedge started to shake and the vet followed by the curator crawled through and pulled up short. They looked in horror from her and the little girl to the dark shape of the chimpanzee and the young boy beneath him.

'Sandy, it will be all right. You'll be all right. Just hang on,' she heard Ryan say, his voice tight with worry.

She pulled the child closer to her. There was a moment of terrible stillness. The alarms were shut off, the animals had quietened, and the wolves no longer howled. Fred's mouth remained in a pout but no sound came out. He tilted his head, bird-like, from one side to another, and regarded the row of people in front of him with a dull curiosity. In the silence, a crow cawed in the sycamores. Fred half turned his head towards the trees. He gave a low grunt. Then he reached down and ripped Paul's arm from his body.

She thought she would never forget the tearing, splintering sound that filled the silence of that summer's night. As if it were a trigger, as if that action were the last that could possibly be endured, one of the policemen opened fire. A single shot smashed the air and echoed through the valley. The force of the bullet caught Fred full in the chest and hurled him a few metres backwards. For one long moment, he lay still, and then he started to struggle to his feet, heavy and black, rising from the sea of grass.

Both policemen opened fire and the sound splintered through her head. This time Fred did not get up. When the reverberations died down there was complete silence, and then Ryan was running towards her, his face a mask in white.

'Are you OK? Are you hurt?'

She couldn't speak. She was watching Fred. She wanted to make quite certain he was dead and was not suddenly going to charge her, savage with pain. The body in the grass remained motionless. The two policemen cautiously approached and were leaning warily over the chimpanzee. She could hear the siren of an approaching ambulance. It was a little too late, she thought as she hugged the shivering child. She did not want to look at the place where Paul lay.

Ryan dropped to his knees in front of her. He tried to prise the scalpel out of her fingers. Her hand was clenched shut; her limbs felt locked into position.

'It's all right,' he said and she allowed the knife to slip from her grasp. He tossed it to one side.

'Are you hurt? Please answer me.'

She was still shaking. Her cheeks were wet and she could not trust her voice. Ryan's face was blurred, but as she stared at him he wavered into focus. He was so pale she could see faint blue veins throbbing at his temple. She shook her head.

'Thank God,' he said and put his arms round her and the child.

She became acutely aware of tiny things: the ache of her calves, the pattern of grass tattooed into the skin of her legs, the rusting flakes of Claire's blood on her fingers, a chipped button on Ryan's shirt, one mauve forget-me-not-shaped flower growing by the root of a sycamore. Stiffly she freed her arms from around the little girl and pulled Ryan closer to her.

THE END

ND - #0461 - 270225 - C0 - 203/127/25 - PB - 9781861515483 - Matt Lamination